Grilled, Chilled
and **Killed**

OTHER BOOKS BY LESLEY A. DIEHL

Murder is Academic
Book 1 in the Laura Murphy mystery series

Failure is Fatal
Book 2 in the Laura Murphy mystery series

A Secondhand Murder
Book 1 in the Eve Appel mystery series

Dead in the Water
Book 2 in the Eve Appel mystery series

A Sporting Murder
Book 3 in the Eve Appel mystery series

Mud Bog Murder

A Deadly Draught
Book 1 in the microbrewing series

Poisoned Pairings
Book 2 in the microbrewing series

Angel Sleuth

Dumpster Dying
Book 1 in the Big Lake murder mystery series

*The Aunt Nozzie and Grandmothers stories—The
Killer Wore Cranberry: Thanksgiving
Anthologies Vols 1-4*

*Bobbing for Murder novella—Happy
Homicides4: Fall Into Crime*

Grilled, Chilled
and Killed

Book 2 in the Big Lake murder mystery series

Lesley A. Diehl

Disclaimer

This is a work of fiction. The characters,
dialogue and events in this book are wholly
fictional, and any resemblance to companies and
actual persons, living or dead, is coincidental.

* * *

ISBN-10 0-9972349-3-8
ISBN-13 978-0-9972349-3-0

To Jan Day Fehrman,
good friend and great critique partner

ACKNOWLEDGMENTS

As ever, my love, support and inspiration—
Glenn. Thank God you can cook.

CHAPTER I

E mily shook the metal canister filled with ice, liquor and mix until her hand numbed from the cold. *Perfect.* She tapped the edge of the lid to loosen it and tossed the ice cubes she'd placed in the martini glass into the sink. A young man stepped up to the bar and opened the lid of the container, which held cherries and slices of lime and lemon. He reached in to extract a piece of the fruit.

She slapped his knuckles with a mixer spoon. "Yow!" He snatched back his hand.

"I do the bartending around here. Keep your hands out of my stuff." Emily shook the spoon at him, threatening to hit him once more. He spun on the heel of his boot and left.

She poured the icy concoction into a glass and placed it on the bar in front of the man sitting there.

"You're a tough gal." The man's gaze swept over the tiny blonde bartender with admiration. "But I already knew that."

"He just came out of the bathroom. I'll bet he didn't even wash his hands before he pawed through my fruit." She plunged the shaker into the soapy water in the sink and looked around the bar.

"Good drink. Just enough vermouth. Almost as good as mine."

"Don't sass your boss."

"Where'd you learn to use the word 'sass'?" There was almost a chuckle in his voice.

Emily knew Donald Green rarely laughed, never chuckled and chose to dole out his smiles with infrequency. The bass fisherman with the tall, muscular body and long, silver ponytail didn't care if anyone found him pleasant or not. Emily figured he didn't care about most people. Sometimes she worried she might be an exception. She didn't need Donald paying attention to her as a woman, so she tried to aggravate him as much as possible. She thought that might take his mind off romance and put it back on catching bass or mixing drinks.

"You drink that drink, and I'll drive to the festival grounds. It would look bad for the country club if their backup bartender got picked up for DWI."

Donald said nothing, simply slugged down the martini, grabbed his black cowboy hat and strode out of the bar. Emily threw her apron down and yelled back to the relief bartender to "check the cooler." She ran after him. In the parking lot, he tossed her his keys. She caught them and climbed into Donald's huge truck. She stuffed her purse behind her to reach the steering wheel.

He settled into the passenger's side and pulled his hat down over his eyes. "I'll grab a little shut eye. I had a hard night last night."

Emily knew better than to talk to him on the short ride to the Big Lake Bar-B-Que Competition. She was content to consider her own thoughts. She was looking forward to the evening. All she had to do was pull beers all night long. No hard liquor was served at the festival. Better yet, she and Donald would be in different stations at either end of the fairgrounds, and she wouldn't have to deal with his surly mood.

The money tonight wasn't great, but it was money. Her life partner's will, discovered over a month after his death, was finally probated and settled. Emily inherited his estate, which consisted of not much cash, some mortgaged property and a few debts. Emily's small pension didn't cover all her expenses, so she served as head bartender at the Big Lake Country Club and took odd jobs for additional cash. She liked tending bar, talking to all the folks who came in. Barely over five feet tall, she'd developed an ability to cajole drunks out of their pugnacious intentions and send others on their way with a firm "Out." If she had trouble, Donald was usually there to give them a look of cold, hard steel.

Yep, she thought to herself, she was pretty happy of late. Her daughter was joining her tonight at the competition, and they were leaving tomorrow for a short vacation to Jekyll Island, Georgia, to celebrate Naomi finalizing her divorce.

"I can hear you thinking, and it's keeping me awake."

"That's only because I'm having happy thoughts. If they were mean ones, you'd be dozing away, content in a familiar place. You are such a grump." She jerked the wheel abruptly to the left to make the turn into the fairgrounds and onto the bumpy dirt road that led to the back of the booths. The movement sent Donald's hat flying.

He grabbed it from the floor and brushed it off with his forearm. "You ruin my 10X Stetson, you'll be in trouble, little lady."

"It's not nice to point out how size-challenged I am. I'm sure that's some kind of ism or other and may be against the law."

Donald growled something under his breath, and Emily laughed. Donald gave her his version of a smile—one side of his mouth tipped upward—to show her they were good friends, although Donald wanted more, and she knew that. She wondered if he did.

They parted at the gate for the vendors and workers. "I'll drive you home," he offered.

"Naomi's coming. She's a better driver than you and much better company." She loved to kid him. He didn't see the humor in it, and that seemed funny itself. He growled something under his breath again. She waved goodbye, threw her apron with the official competition worker badge pinned to it over her shoulder and took off in the opposite direction looking for her assigned beer station.

She strode past the barbecue tents, sniffing the air filled with smells of meat cooking slow and low on huge cookers, some homemade, others state-of-the-art industrial smokers and grills. Her mouth watered in anticipation of later, after the competition when the contestants would offer their barbecue for tasting to the public.

As she passed by one of the tents, a short man with red hair and a big belly called out to her. "Hey there, I got some ribs here, ma'am, and I need someone to tell me if they're any good." He held out a meaty bone dripping with brown sauce to her. "Here you go. Sink your teeth into that." He shoved a napkin into her hand. "Wha'd ya think?"

"Good."

The meat was tender, juicy and the sauce spicy and sweet.

"Wish you were a judge," the man remarked.

"I'll just bet you do, ya bum." The angry voice came from a skinny fellow with his hair in pigtails. He towered over the red-haired one. "You the guy who took my sauce mop? Someone took my sauce mop, and Barney over there said he thought you had it."

"I wouldn't contaminate my meat with your inferior sauce. I'd have to soak that mop for days just to get out the overpowering taste of that cheap vinegar you use."

Oh, oh, thought Emily. She'd heard the guys at this competition were serious about their barbecue, but these two looked as if they wanted to clobber each other and throw the loser onto a bed of coals.

She wiped the sauce from her mouth and backed away.

A hand stopped her. "Don't worry about them. Dirk and Casey go at it every year, accusing the other of doing something against competition rules. It's a good show."

She turned and looked up into the brown eyes of a man about her age. He held out his hand. "Name's Charlie. Actually it's Charlie Brown. People call me Chuck or Big Chuck." He paused, and the look on his face seemed to suggest he worried the "Big" might be offensive to one of her stature. "I'm the organizer for this affair. I see you've got one of our aprons in your hand. You a competitor?"

"Gosh no. I'm one of your bartenders. Emily Rhodes. Nice to meet you, uh, Chuck." She wiped off the stickiness onto the napkin before she offered her hand to him.

"Don't worry about the sauce. I shake so many barbecue-covered hands in the three days of this shindig, you'd think my paw was a rack of ribs."

"I demand the right to search your booth," said the tall man.

"I guess things are getting a little too hot. I'd better step in before it gets serious." Chuck strode forward and separated the two before they got any closer. By the time Emily had finished her rib and tossed the bone in the trash, all three men were laughing together. She was relieved it was a show as Chuck said and not serious.

At the beer booth, the two men, her fellow bartenders, showed surprise she was a woman and such a tiny one. And of course, they just had to make comments. By the sly smile that crossed the older man's face, she knew they were planning to have a little fun with her.

"Say," he said, "this keg is getting low. I don't suppose you could go get us another one."

"Now, Ralph, don't be silly. This here is just a little bitty gal. She can't be expected to lug a keg out of the cooler truck. I doubt she can even pull a beer without some help."

Emily walked up to the older guy, placing her foot hard on the top of his shoe. She rested it there bearing down with all her hundred pounds. "Why sure, fellas. I know you've been standing here for at least an hour or so, tiring yourselves out with telling tasteless jokes. You sure do need a break. You rest easy. I'll get that keg for you."

Ralph's masculine pride wouldn't let him ask her to move her foot, not in front of his pal. His face began to turn red, and his smile lost its lift like a push-up bra without the foam inserts.

Emily spun on her foot, delivering a final crunch to Ralph's instep and eliciting a muffled moan from his lips.

She was glad to get away from those two. She checked her watch as she walked toward the cooler truck. It was only eight in the evening. *This is going to be a long night.*

Several men wearing badges indicating they were festival officials stood near the truck. Emily pointed to her worker badge. "Gotta get a new keg." They nodded and ignored her. *I could have flashed my AARP card. They wouldn't have noticed.* She wondered who would get the blame if some of the kegs came up missing.

She flipped the heavy plastic curtains aside and entered the cold of the truck. The weather for the barbecue festival held in Florida's Big Lake country in early April was signaling the heat of the summer; today it was in the mid-eighties. The air inside felt good to her. Maybe she should spend the rest of the time in here and forget about pulling beer. She sat on one of the kegs to consider how she would handle her fellow workers when she got back. Was the crushed foot message enough?

She got up and checked the kegs for one that held the light beer she was seeking. When she moved it from between two others, something flopped into the space she'd created by dislodging it. An arm! It scared the hell out of her. She leaned in to get a better look. It was attached to a man who seemed to have fallen between the kegs and was wedged in there.

"Hey, buddy," she said. It had to be a drunk looking for a place to get cool and sleep it off. She tugged at the man's sleeve. "This isn't a hotel. Get up." She grabbed the man's arm and tugged harder. Something cold and slippery came off on her hand. She held up her fingers in the dim light. It looked brown. She took a sniff. It smelled like barbecue sauce. *What a slob,* she thought.

A few more tugs and some jockeying of the kegs allowed her to free him from between them. Now she could see the man was covered with sauce from top to bottom. And with all her efforts at extracting him, so was she. She looked into his saucy face and noticed something truly odd. A red apple was stuck in his mouth. And something even odder. Another substance on the side of his face, red not brown, mixed with the barbecue sauce. *Good God. He's got ketchup all over him too. Maybe I should look for other condiments. This gave a whole new meaning to beer and brats.*

The giggle about to erupt from her throat lost its way, headed off by a sickening smell, an odor not associated with barbecue. Not ketchup. That was blood on the side of his face.

She backed out of the cooler and then hiccupped, her usual response to finding dead bodies.

This was her second body. *Please, God, let it be my last.*

CHAPTER 2

"Well, I see you got yourself in another fix," said Detective Lewis, the head detective for the Big Lake Police Department.

He ignored the angry look she shot him. He expected it. He had pointed out the obvious and, as usual, she took offense.

"Hey," she said. "If you're going to accuse me of creating trouble, you can at least look at me when you do it."

Stanton Lewis liked Emily, and he particularly liked her when she was all riled up, like now. The anger painted her lips a bright red and her cheeks flushed with color. It was, Lewis thought, a wholesome and healthy look. And not, he also acknowledged, the look of a guilty woman. He knew Emily well enough that he was certain she had nothing to do with the death of the man in the cooler.

And just who was the dead man, Lewis asked himself. There was no I.D. on the body, and no one he'd talked to yet seemed to be able to identify him. Or they were lying to him. Someone had to know him; otherwise, how could he have gotten into the festival? The medical examiner told Lewis he thought the body had been on the cooler truck for a while, several hours at least.

"Probably hit on the head sometime this afternoon," Doc Melbourne said. "Died soon after, I'd guess. I'll have more for you tomorrow."

Lewis turned his back on Emily and bent over the victim before the techs zipped him into a body bag. Emily stood close enough to Lewis that he could smell her cologne. Kind of spicy. Like the woman herself.

"I thought you didn't like looking at dead bodies."

"I don't."

"Well, then you should try not finding them so often."

"Is it my fault they turn up when I'm around? I was just doing my job, both times. These guys pop up around here like mildew on the siding of my house. Besides, I was kind of curious what could cause all that blood. There was no weapon I could see."

"Oh, so you had a look around before you called us."

"No, I did not. The cooler held only beer kegs. And the body. I'd notice if there was anything else there, wouldn't I?"

"She's a real stickler for detail," said a voice behind them.

"Donald Green. Another person who always seems to show up when the bodies do. Now the only one we're missing is Clara."

"I'm right here." The woman who spoke was as tall as Emily was short, almost as tall as Stanton and Donald. Her height was accentuated by her long legs and her mop of flaming red hair. "You bothering my friend again, Detective Lewis?"

Lewis threw up his hands as if to ward off Clara's attack "You know better than that, Counselor."

Both Donald and Clara stood behind the yellow crime tape. Lewis walked over to them, pulling Emily with him.

"Have you read her her rights yet?" asked Clara.

Donald stepped as close to Lewis as he could get without trespassing on the crime scene.

"Hey, hey, guys. Stop behaving as if I'm not here. First the detective acts as if I don't exist, then you two rush in here like the Russian mob. I'm just fine." Emily hiccupped and put her hand on her abdomen. "I could use a bathroom though."

Lewis, Clara and Donald were too into their altercation to acknowledge Emily. If Emily's stomach didn't feel so odd, she might have laughed at the picture of the three of them trying to defend her by ignoring her. It was one of the problems of being short, she thought. She tugged on Lewis' sleeve and got no reaction. She screwed up her face and crossed her eyes, but Clara and Donald were too busy getting in Lewis' face to see Emily's.

She shrugged her shoulders and turned her back. And threw up on the crime scene.

Clara held her up with one arm while she wiped Emily's face with a paper towel. They were in the fairgrounds' bathroom. Other women entering and leaving gave them wide berth. Emily heard a mother tell her daughter, "That's what happens when you drink too much. It's not pretty."

"You could have told us you were feeling sick," Clara said.

Emily rolled her eyes.

"You're not going to pass out on me now are you?"

"I did tell you I was sick."

"You need to learn to speak up, Emily. You're such a tiny thing, people tend to overlook you."

"People treat me like I'm an elf."

"Not at all. It's just that you're so short."

"It's just that you're so tall."

Clara stepped back to look at her cleaning job. "Point taken. I'm sorry. The combination of Donald, Lewis and me, well, it's lethal."

"Yet you're all friends of mine. Couldn't you put a hold on the fighting for my sake?"

"Sure, honey. I got carried away seeing you there with Lewis. I thought he was going to arrest you again."

"He knows I had nothing to do with this one. I don't even know the guy. I just found him."

"I suppose Lewis lectured you about doing that, right?"

"Yep." Emily turned on the water faucet and stuck her mouth under it. "I'm so thirsty." She gulped down the liquid for several minutes. "Tastes good." She turned her head and let the cold water splash over her hair and into her eyes. "Feels better."

"Mom, you in here?" a voice called from outside.

"Oh, damn. I forgot Naomi was meeting me here. Don't tell her what happened."

"Mom! What are you doing?" asked Naomi. Blonde like her mother, but taller, the young woman rushed forward to throw her arms around Emily.

"I'm taking a shower?" Emily gave Naomi a goofy grin.

"She did it again." Clara threw the used towels into the trash.

"Offended one of the customers at the club?" asked Naomi.

"She found another dead body."

Naomi looked only mildly put off by the information. "Someone you know, Mom?"

"Someone no one seems to know." Emily turned on the hand dryer and stuck her head under it. When the dryer turned off, she stepped to the mirror. "Yikes! Anyone have a comb?"

"Ladies, I hear you in there. No more hiding. Come out here, Emily. Our conversation isn't over yet."

"It's your detective, Emily." Clara laughed and punched her friend in the arm. Despite his attempts to keep his feelings under control, all of

Emily's friends knew Lewis had a thing for her. Even Donald knew that. And didn't like it.

"I thought Mom was more enamored with the other guy. That tall, skinny, silver-haired one with no sense of humor and the need to fish the lake dry. You mean she and Detective Lewis are an item? Hoowee. I like that," Naomi said.

Emily turned from the mirror and entered one of the stalls, slamming the door and muttering under her breath.

"What's she so worked up about?" asked Naomi.

"I did just find a dead body, you know." Emily spoke from behind the stall door. "And stop talking as if I'm not here."

A tall, well-proportioned Nordic-looking woman entered the bathroom. It was Vicki, Emily's next-door neighbor. "I was sent in here by that hunky detective to roust you, Emily. Emily? Where are you?"

"Good lord, everyone I know in this town is here. It's like a quilting bee. This is not a social occasion, you know. I dragged a dead man out of a cooler. It's not fun work."

"No one was there to help you?" asked Vicki. "Was he a big guy?"

Emily slammed open the stall door. "I'm getting out of here."

"Oh, good. The detective is waiting for you." Vicki accompanied Emily out of the restroom. "I'll catch up with you later. I've got to drop off my pie.

They're having a contest for desserts. I made my Key Lime pie."

Naomi caught up with them followed by Clara. "I love your pie. Is there any more where that came from?"

While her daughter and her friends conferred about the pie supply, Emily, shoulders slumped in fatigue and despair, trudged over to Lewis who had been joined by Donald.

"Got yourself another dead one, huh?" asked Donald.

She shot him a dirty look. "What else do you need, Detective? I'd like to get home and take a bath."

"Why do you smell like barbecue?" asked Donald.

"Everybody smells like barbecue around here. Haven't you noticed?" snapped Emily.

"I kind of like the smell. Sexy, in a condiment-like way. Makes me want to buy you a beer." Donald winked at Lewis.

"That'll have to wait a bit. Right now, I need her to come down to the station and give a statement." Lewis paused. "That a new hairdo, Emily?"

She shook her head. The still damp and mangled curls shivered with the movement.

"I like it. Better than the cologne you're wearing," said Big Chuck, the manager of the event. "I hear you found a body, and we're missing one." Behind him stood a woman, slack jawed with the saddest look on her face that Emily had ever seen. She wore baggy jeans, bleached almost white from numerous washings, and a shirt that once must have been bright red. It had been reduced to a lighter shade by too many meetings with Maytag. At her side stood a boney hound dog, his expression an exact replica of his mistress'. He gave an occasional scratch to his belly with one hind leg, then settled into the dirt with a sigh.

"We just set up this morning," said the woman in a monotone voice. "Our dog was worrying himself with a bout of fleas, so I took him off to the vet. Had to wait a while. When I got back, Everett was gone." The woman gave a sigh too and settled back on her heels, waiting.

"This here is Melanie Pratt. She and her husband Everett are barbecuers. They signed on just last week for this competition," said Chuck. He leaned in close to the detective. "From the description I think the barbecue-covered corpse is Everett."

"I'd like you to come down to the county medical examiner's office, Mrs. Pratt. I'm sorry, but there's a chance the body of the dead man is your husband's," said Lewis.

Melanie Pratt didn't blink. Her expression of extreme fatigue with life softened a bit, but there was no other sign she worried her husband was dead. "What'll I do with Milo?" She nodded toward the dog who stood up at the mention of his name. His tail gave half a wag, then he settled once more into the dirt. "Can I take him with?"

"Leave him at your camper," said Chuck. "I'll have my wife stop by and check on him while you're gone."

"Nice of you, but he'll howl. Hates to be alone. Maybe he could ride along, and I'll tie him up outside."

"Okay." Lewis gestured toward his car and opened the back door.

Milo and Melanie ambled over and settled themselves in the back seat. "Could you move over a bit?" he asked. "I've got another passenger." He put his hand on Emily's back and pushed her toward the car.

Emily shook her head. "I'm not riding with a dog who has fleas. Naomi will drive me."

Lewis nodded his approval, and then took Chuck to one side.

"What can you tell me about this Everett Pratt? He one of the usual competitors?"

"Not until this year. He's only recently been hitting the circuit, and he does damn good barbecue. He's won the last five competitions held in Georgia and Florida. He's a local. He's got the others real riled up. They've spent years perfecting their sauces and techniques and then this nobody appears and puts them all down. If you're looking for suspects, try all the competitors here."

Wasn't it just the way, thought Emily, saddened for the job Lewis had ahead of him. *Too many suspects, too few leads.*

※

He drove Mrs. Pratt to the medical examiner's office, leaving Milo in the backseat of his cruiser. Mrs. Pratt gave a slight nod indicating she recognized the body as that of her husband. Lewis marveled at her containment. Or was it simply fatigue? Depression? Guilt?

True to the word of his mistress, the dog howled the entire half-hour they were inside. Neighbors called the sheriff's office only to learn the dog was being held inside one of the department's cruisers. Because of the complaints, Chief Worley called Lewis to try to hustle things along, then sent another cruiser to take Mrs. Pratt and the dog home.

By the time Lewis appeared in his office, Emily had been sitting there for almost an hour. She wasn't in a good mood, and she was still covered with sauce. He threw open his window to let the smell dissipate. He was beginning to think it would be a long time before he ate ribs again.

As uncomfortable as Emily was in her sauce-encrusted clothes, Lewis was feeling far worse. He squirmed around in his chair, twitching his shoulders and ducked behind his desk to scratch his ankles.

"What is wrong with you? I'm trying to cooperate here and you leave me waiting in this tiny tin can of an office for an hour, and the air conditioning doesn't even work right. Now I'm sweaty as well as saucy. Then you can't even pay attention to what I'm saying. What are you doing?"

"I'm scratching," he said. "I think I've got fleas."

CHAPTER 3

By the time Emily got back to her own little park model in her condominium park, the sun was about to come up. Her daughter tossed her bags on the floor inside the door, then they both flopped down on the sofa. They sighed in unison.

"I guess this feels just like last year when you found that rancher's body in the dumpster, huh, Mom?"

"Yeah, and I really wish everyone would stop reminding me of that. It wasn't a pleasant episode in my life."

Naomi leaned her head on her mother's shoulder. "But look what came out of that. Me. And you met Detective Lewis. And Donald, too, although I sometimes wonder how great that is. He certainly likes you a lot, but he's one strange dude."

"The men in my life. One's a detective with the personality of an alligator hunting down his prey. Donald's got absolutely no sense of humor. And I work with him. Sometimes I really miss Fred."

"I wish I'd met him. He sounds like a great guy."

Emily pulled the pony tail clip out of her hair and shook the curls free. Sometimes days went by without her thinking of Fred. Other times the smell of a man's cologne could set her thinking of her dead partner with a longing so intense she thought she'd die herself.

"He was wonderful in his way. Except he was forgetful as hell. It would have been nice if he'd told me he made out a will."

"You've got your weird men, and I unloaded mine." Naomi's face puckered up in distaste.

"Divorcing Barry was the right thing to do. You know that, don't you?"

Naomi nodded. "But sometimes I wish it could have been different."

"I understand." Emily tried to stifle a yawn. "Sorry, honey. I hope you don't mind, but I'm too dead tired to drive to Georgia today. Can we put it off and get a little sleep?"

Naomi didn't answer Emily. She snored quietly on her mother's shoulder.

Emily got off the couch without disturbing her, looked longingly at the coffee pot, then decided she couldn't risk making a pot without waking her daughter. She tiptoed off to the bedroom. Halfway down the hall, Naomi called to her. "I can't see Detective Lewis as an alligator. More like a charging Brahman bull. Big, handsome. Just needs the right woman to tame him."

Emily harrumphed and continued toward her bed.

❖

Not certain her old faithful car, Stan the Sedan, could make it all the way to Jekyll Island, Emily was happy to have Naomi drive her car, a two-year-old Mustang convertible Naomi had purchased against her now ex-husband's wishes.

"Barry thought I was cruising the town looking for dates. I just loved the feel of wind in my hair. Made me think I was free." Naomi's ex, Barry Montrose, an abusive cop from the West Palm Beach area, left his job with the West Palm Beach Police Department and hadn't been seen for several months. Before he disappeared, he'd willingly signed the divorce papers. Emily smiled to herself. She was certain pressure from Donald and Lewis convinced him to sign.

As they headed up I95 the Monday after Emily stumbled on Everett Pratt's body, Emily tried to put the murder out of her mind. Naomi, sensing her mother's mood, put down the top and tuned the radio to oldies. Emily had given up her daughter for adoption at birth, and the two of them looked forward to this bonding experience. At Melbourne, Emily took over the wheel while Naomi perused the brochures on Jekyll Island she'd obtained through a travel agency.

"Oh, boy. Would you look at this?" She stuck the brochure under Emily's nose.

"Honey, I'm driving. I can't see with that in front of me."

"Sorry. Anyway, it looks as if there's a barbecue festival on Jekyll this weekend. How about that? I can get me some ribs. I never got the chance to sample any because of the murder and all."

Emily shuddered. "If I never taste another rib or brisket or chicken half, it won't be too soon. I smelled barbecue sauce in my sleep last night. I'll let you go by yourself. I'll stay in the campground and read."

"That was kind of insensitive of me. I'm sorry. You had a bad time. I can do without barbecue. Seafood is what we need, right?"

Emily shook her head and smiled. *A lovely shrimp and clam plate.* She licked her lips in anticipation.

It was early in the season, after the long Easter weekend, but not yet May when the tourists rushed in from central Florida and Georgia looking for the sound of the surf and some beach sand between their toes. The campground was only half full, so Emily and Naomi chose the best spot, to the back of the tent sites under one of the live oak trees. No one else had set up near them, and the woman at the registration desk said they had only a handful of reservations for the week.

"You here early for the barbecue festival?" the woman asked when they signed in.

"God no," said Emily.

"Well, it'll be quiet here for the next few days, but we're full up for the coming weekend." The woman swiped Emily's credit card.

"We might as well enjoy the quiet before the hordes of meat-eaters arrive." Emily signed the registration form and scribbled her name on the credit slip.

⚜

The tent popped up with no problem, and Emily drove the last stake into the ground. "Weather looks a little iffy for tomorrow. I want to make sure we've got her staked down well."

Naomi unfolded the chairs and placed them in front of the fire circle. "Sit down and let's take a look at what there's to do around here. The guy whose name I will not speak and I honeymooned here, but we stayed at the Jekyll Club Hotel and didn't do much exploring." She blushed. "I want to tour the historic village where they've restored many of the houses, and I hear they have a great dining room at Crane Cottage. Let's have dinner there tonight."

"When I suggested this as a get-away for us, I had no idea you and the ex had been here. Fred and I usually stopped for an overnight on our way back and forth to Florida. I hope this isn't going to bring back bad memories for you."

"Nope. I was still in love with him then. Besides, I never got to see the island, and I always wanted to." She reached down to get another brochure out of the pile she'd placed beside the chair. "Here's the menu for Crane Cottage." She handed it to her mother.

"Pricey. Let's save this for another time. We can go to the supermarket and pick up supplies. Tonight I'd like to just kick back with a burger on the grill and a bottle of red."

Naomi shook her blonde curls in agreement.

By nine that evening both women were on their second glass of wine, staring into the campfire Emily built.

"This is the life." Emily shifted around in her camp chair and yawned. "I think when I finish this glass, I'm off to bed."

"Me too. All this fresh air and the wine made me sleepy."

Before the women could get out of their chairs, an old Ford pickup drove by the site. Emily couldn't see the driver's face in the dark. There appeared to be no one with him. The truck rattled its way over the ruts of the road and headed toward the very back of the campground.

"I guess he didn't want to camp next to a couple of women," said Emily.

"Fine with me. We don't need someone on top of us anyway."

Along with sunup came the sound of someone yelling and banging on metal.

"Get the hell away from my truck. Go on, shoo." The voice was male and came from the direction Emily and Naomi had seen the late arrival take last night.

Naomi sprung out of bed. "What's that? Sounds like something has invaded the guy's camp site. He might need help."

Emily laughed and turned over in her sleeping bag. "I'll bet it's those dang blackbirds. If he didn't cover his side mirrors, the birds are pecking on them."

"I wondered what you were doing when you slipped the plastic bags over the mirrors last night."

"The birds around here fall in love with their reflections. They can crack the glass if you're not careful."

Emily sat up and stretched. "I'm awake. And nature is calling. I might as well make coffee when I get back from the restrooms. I'll check on our neighbor to see if he's alright."

After using the campground facilities, Emily headed out of the bathrooms, intending to walk by the campsite of the man they'd seen come in last night. As she approached his site, she saw the man get into his truck and drive off. In the morning light she caught the glare of the sun off a broken side mirror and chuckled. The only thing left at the campsite was a pile of beer cans next to the smoldering fire.

I'm glad he's not staying here, she thought. With all the beer he'd gone through last night, he couldn't have been a good camping neighbor.

She shook her head and continued back to the tent. *Huh.* There was no sign of Naomi, and one of the bikes they'd rented yesterday when they arrived was gone. *Why would Naomi leave without me?*

She opened the tent flap and noticed a scrap of paper on her sleeping bag. A note from Naomi:

I'm sure the guy in that truck is Toby Sands. I'm going to follow him to see what he's doing here.

Oh, no, thought Emily. *Naomi could get herself into trouble taking off after Toby.*

Crooked cop Toby from the Big Lake Police Department had lost his job because he'd been involved in some shady business with the rancher Emily found dead in the dumpster several months ago. *What was Toby doing here?* His appearance and theirs couldn't be a coincidence. But Emily thought he was in jail. Her peace of mind was dependent upon his being in jail. *Maybe he got out on good behavior.* She grimaced at the thought. There was nothing good about the man. He took money for doing things against the law and almost got Naomi and Emily killed. *How could the man be out of jail?* Emily extracted her cell phone from her shorts pocket and hit the button to connect to Detective Lewis at police headquarters.

"Sorry, Ms. Rhodes, but the detective is out of town for several days. I can put you through to his voice mail," said the officer answering the phone.

Emily told Lewis where she and Naomi were and that they'd spotted Toby at the campground. "Is he out on bail or what?" Her tone of voice was accusatory as if Toby's presence was somehow Lewis' fault. After she hung up she called back to apologize, then decided she had a perfect right to be offended that a criminal was at large. She called into Lewis' voice mail again.

"Never mind what I just said. Don't you have any responsibility for telling citizens who are victims of a crime, especially if it's been committed by one of your own when the guy is free and running around, able to repeat his victimization? Besides, he's an environmental threat with his tobacco chaw, spitting it all over the ground. This is a beautiful spot here. We don't need the animals coming in contact with noxious chemicals." She hung up. *There.* She felt much better, safer somehow.

She found Naomi had made coffee, so Emily poured herself a cup and slid into her camp chair, the picture of a woman who'd accomplished something, and it wasn't even eight in the morning. By nine o'clock she began to worry about Naomi. *She should be back by now.* At ten, Emily hopped on the other bike and pedaled toward the campground entrance, but stopped when she reached the main road. *Which direction should she go? Toward the shopping area or to the left, the road leading to the historic village?* Before she could decide, she spied Naomi walking her bicycle toward the campground.

"Where have you been? I've been worried sick."

"I was chasing Toby."

"Chasing him? How could you keep up?"

"He didn't go far." Naomi signaled to the road leading toward the beach. "He headed off that way and parked his truck under the trees at the beach's edge."

"He didn't see you, did he?"

"No, but I'm concerned Toby may have spotted me when he drove off this morning. He kind of gave a start as he passed by. Do you think we should leave?"

"I'm not letting that fat troll run me off of one of my favorite vacation spots. I put in a call to Detective Lewis."

"Good. What did he say?" Naomi kicked her tire. "Flat. That's what took me so long to get back here. Plus I had to push the bike off the road when I heard a car coming in case it was Toby. Do you know there are alligators here too?"

"Yeah, but they're only small ones. They can give you a scare though. I had to circle around one taking his afternoon siesta on the bicycle path once."

"Small? This one was at least five feet. So what did Lewis say?"

"He wasn't in. Off somewhere for a few days. Maybe he and Donald went bass fishing together."

"Listen to yourself."

"They respect each other."

"That doesn't mean they would voluntarily be in the same room together unless you were there."

They stopped in front of the campground store.

"I'm going to get another bicycle. This time I inspect the tires."

"Sorry about that, dearie," said the same woman who'd signed them in yesterday. "Take the bike on the far right. It's just been reconditioned."

Naomi grabbed the bike, and they continued back to their campsite.

"Toby's got a new look."

Emily tried to imagine what that could mean. *Maybe he replaced his cowboy boots with dock siders? He had his hair permed? He tried one of those lash growing medications and now had long, luxuriant lashes, which he batted furiously at women?*

"I can hear your brain working, Mom. None of what you're thinking. It's worse. He grew a beard."

"Is he still chewing tobacco?" A disturbing image took shape in Emily's mind.

"Right, and it grew in white, so now he has dark brown stains on the hair around his mouth and down his chin."

Emily and Naomi shuddered together at the picture.

"That kind of takes away my appetite for those pancakes we planned this morning," said Emily.

They parked their bikes in front of the tent. The morning air smelled like the salt marshes, and a breeze blew through the evergreens and live oaks.

"I, for one, am not going to let Toby ruin my vacation." Emily put her arm around her daughter and squeezed. "What do you say? Are the Rhodes women going to retreat just because the troll has arrived?"

A twig snapped behind them. "What troll?" said a familiar voice.

Naomi whirled around. "Detective Lewis. What are you doing here?"

"I might ask you two the same."

"No, you don't." Emily placed her hands on her hips and faced Lewis. The top of her head almost came up to his chin. "You're not going to put me on the defensive as if I have no right to be vacationing in my favorite spot in the world. I came here several times a year with Fred. It's a perfect place. I love it here. We have every right to be here."

Lewis smiled down at her. "Sounds pretty defensive to me. Running from the law, are you?"

"Coffee, Detective?" Naomi smiled and took a cup for herself and stepped back to watch her mother and Lewis square off. As usual.

"Thanks, no. I just stopped by to tell you I got the message you left a while ago. I gotta run. I'm late already for a meeting."

His glance never wavered from hers. Emily held tight to her gaze too. "Who are you meeting?" she asked.

"Toby Sands. You remember him. Your favorite dirty cop."

CHAPTER 4

"Don't you mean you're arresting him? He has to be violating his bail by leaving Florida and coming here." Emily still stood toe to toe with Lewis.

"We sent him here."

"We? Who's we?"

"The district attorney for the county thought we could use Toby's services in the murder investigation. The barbecuers here for the festival on Jekyll are most of the same ones from last week's contest back home."

"You can't mean he's a cop again?"

"No. He's a police informant. He's a good 'ole boy. He can get close to the barbecue folks. They might talk to him."

Emily stepped back and relaxed her shoulders. "He was here last night." She nodded her head toward Toby's abandoned campsite.

Naomi interrupted her mother. "But he's not coming back tonight. He left, and I think he's going to find a hotel room."

"I know about his checking out. We were supposed to meet up here, but the woman at the desk told me he'd gone." Lewis paused and directed his next question to Naomi. "How do you know he's going to stay someplace else?"

She told him about following Toby and eavesdropping on a conversation he had with a man he met on the beach.

"You see who he met?"

"I was hunkered down in the trees on the other side of Toby's truck. It blocked my view, and I was too far from them to hear most of their conversation. I ducked further into the trees when the man drove off. I didn't want to take a chance I'd be seen."

"Nice work, but I don't want you putting yourself in danger. Don't try that again." His tone was firm, his jaw set.

"Fine. It was for our own protection. How did we know you'd hire someone as sleazy as Toby to do your detecting work?" Now Naomi's accusatory tone matched Emily's. Emily smiled. Her daughter was coming to the same opinion of Lewis as she had. Definitely an alligator on the hunt.

Lewis' face took on a look Emily had not seen there before. It was embarrassment. He took off his cowboy hat and slapped it hard against his thigh.

"This whole thing wasn't my idea. In fact, I was against it. I've no interest in working with Toby, and I know he's crooked enough to be setting something up for himself. It'll be a deal to make him money and make us look like fools. I've got a bad feeling about this."

"Well, that shows some good sense." Emily smiled at him. *Time to make nice,* she thought.

"Thanks." It was said sarcastically.

She'd hurt his feelings. *Well, la dee da for him.* She felt Naomi's hand on her arm.

Naomi whispered in her mother's ear, "Look at him. He's dead on his feet. We're being too hard on him."

"Maybe you'd like that coffee now." Naomi gestured to Emily's chair. The big detective strode over to it and let his body fall into the chair as if he were bone tired.

"I haven't had a full night's sleep since the murder. They closed down the barbecue contest, and rescheduled it in three weeks, unless I haven't found the killer by then. Three weeks! To wrap up a homicide where all my suspects have left the county, the state? If that wasn't bad enough, the D.A. told me to find Toby because the man had begged the county he'd do anything to stay out of jail. I finally located him in an old cabin out on the Kissimmee River. What a dump. No electricity or running water. Must have been a hell of a place to settle into awaiting trial."

"Are you saying you feel sorry for the man? After all he did to screw up your investigation into the rancher's murder?" Emily could hardly believe Lewis' sympathetic tone.

"Well, not exactly. But he is human."

"You could have fooled me." She stepped in front of him, and took the coffee cup out of Naomi's hand. "Here's your coffee, and get the hell out of my chair."

He complied, eyeing her warily.

"You can have my chair," said Naomi.

"When did the two of you become best friends?" Emily stretched her legs out in front of her and put her hands behind her head.

Neither answered her. Lewis gulped the coffee and handed the cup back to Naomi. "I'd better get going before I'm thrown out of here."

"How long will you be around?" asked Naomi. "I'm asking because I need someone to take me to the cook-off this weekend. Mom says she's sick of barbecue."

The detective blushed at Naomi's invitation. "Well, I...."

"Maybe Detective Lewis is also tired of roasted and sauced meat," said Emily.

"I have to hang around here until the cook-off begins. Some of the contestants who were at the festival in Big Lake moved on to other venues this week, and won't be here until the weekend. Captain Worley didn't see much sense in my following up leads by traveling all over the country when I could investigate everyone when they rendezvoused here again. Of course, now I have to track down Toby, unless he used this as an excuse to simply skip out."

"Oh, do you really think Toby would do such a thing?" Sarcasm dripped off Emily's voice like ooze out of a mud bog.

"It seems, little gal,..."

"Don't call me that."

Lewis turned to Naomi. "I'd be honored to accompany you to the festival. Shall we say Saturday around seven? I'll pick you up." He nodded to both of them, clapped his hat back on his head and started down the dusty dirt road that led to the camp entrance.

"I hope the birds pecked holes in both your mirrors," yelled Emily to his retreating back. He turned, smiled and tipped his hat.

"I hate that man," said Emily.

Naomi tried to keep her laughter to herself, but she couldn't help letting out a chuckle. "Oh, you do not. You're dealing with sexual attraction thwarted by his being right most of the time."

"What? He's almost never right."

Naomi shook her head and grabbed the dirty cups. "I'll wash these up."

As she started toward the shower house, Emily called after her, "I absolutely forbid you to go out with that man."

—◈—

Where would Toby go on an island with only one campground and where the motels were fancy, not flop houses, wondered Lewis. Back to the mainland? Not likely, unless he decided to leave permanently and not come back. The island authority charged a fee to get onto the island, and Lewis knew Toby had little money. He could have found someone to bunk with, perhaps the man he'd met up with this morning, but Lewis figured no one wanted to be Toby's roomie. That meeting told Lewis Toby had some kind of deal going, and he would hang here until he scored.

Lewis decided to try the parking area where Naomi had found him earlier.

He was in luck. Near the restrooms sat a rusted truck with Florida plates. From the snoring that came from the open window, Lewis knew he wouldn't be heard until he was on top of his prey.

He walked quietly over to the driver's side window and looked in. Toby slept slumped sideways, his head lying on the passenger's side of the bench seat. Brown drool trickled out of the side of his open mouth. He seemed undisturbed by the flies that buzzed around his head.

"Toby! Get the hell up."

The man bolted to an upright position. Still groggy, he swiped at a fly and looked up to see who was disturbing his morning nap. When he recognized Lewis, his bloodshot eyes filled with fear.

"You think I couldn't find you, Toby?"

"I knew you could. I just needed a little snooze before I meandered back to the campground for our get-together."

"The woman at the desk said you'd checked out."

"Right. Yeah, I did. I decided it was too noisy there for me. I need my rest."

"The place is less than half full. How noisy can that be? Oh right, I forgot about your drinking situation. Alcohol does make things a lot louder and has a tendency to multiply the number of people you think are around." Lewis opened the driver's side door. Toby, followed by a half-dozen or so beer cans, toppled out, managing to land on his feet by grabbing the side of the truck for support.

"Litterbug," said Lewis. "Pick those up."

Toby tried to bend over to do as Lewis commanded, but he lost his balance and fell face first into the sand. Lewis grabbed him by the collar and set him on his feet. As he did so, the smell of stale beer, sweat and fear mixed with chewing tobacco assaulted his nostrils.

Toby grabbed the beer cans off the ground and threw them into the trash.

"Let's go for a walk," said Lewis. *The wind off the water might blow away the smell of the man.*

"I got some information for you, so it ain't like I been doin' nothin'. I got a line on a guy from the festival, and I only been here since last night." Toby seemed eager to please now that he was fully awake, but Lewis wasn't fooled.

"Oh, I'm sure you've been real busy, Toby, but I told you to wait for my instructions. If you go off and do what you want, the deal is off for a reduced sentence."

Toby ran ahead and stepped in front of Lewis, dancing around like a delighted child. "I know, I know. I wouldn't do anything like that. I've learned my lesson, and I want to do the right thing."

"That might be helped by your sobering up."

Toby eyes darkened. "I have a nip or two. It never affected my work. You know that."

A laugh erupted from Lewis. "I know you spent a lot of time sleeping it off so that you were sober enough to pick up your paychecks."

"You're a hard man, Lewis. Always were. You treated me like dog dodo. Someday you'll get yours."

"Payback, Toby? I don't think you're in any position to be contemplating that." Lewis held out an envelope, which Toby grabbed for with a grimy hand. Lewis snatched it back.

"This is your letter of introduction to the festival organizers. They're expecting it...unopened. Present it, and they'll find you a job at the cook-off, something where you'll be able to blend in and keep an eye on things, meet some of the folks, get to know them."

"What kind of job? I won't do just anything."

"Oh, yes you will. You'll shovel horse manure if that's what they want. That's the deal."

Toby nodded, and Lewis turned to walk back to his car, but Toby grabbed his arm.

"Where can I stay? I got no camping equipment and no money for a room."

Lewis wanted to tell him it wasn't his problem. But, of course, it was. Toby was his informant.

※

As soon as he laid out Toby's duties and warned him again about playing loose with the men associated with the barbecue, Lewis left him on the beach and headed back to the parking area. The tide was coming in, and Lewis knew it would soon sweep the beach clear of all debris, but not Toby, unfortunately. Lewis needed information, but not information tainted by any deal Toby might make with persons of interest or the killer. *A line on some guy with the festival? More likely some guy selling illegal booze.* Lewis was so certain it was a lie, he didn't bother to pursue it with Toby. *Why do I put up with this?* Lewis kicked at the wet sand.

If Toby hadn't been thrown off the force, Lewis had contemplated quitting. Working with the man was like being surrounded by poisonous snakes. One was bound to bite you. He knew that, so why was he so pissed today? It was probably because he had to give Toby motel money so he wouldn't be rousted off the beach by the authorities. Now he had to find an ATM and replenish his cash. *Damn Toby. Toby probably wouldn't be able to find a room, probably wouldn't even look for one. He'd just take the money and buy booze.* Lewis looked across the expanse of water toward Brunswick, Georgia, where he'd once lived. The thought of those days didn't improve his mood any. He kicked the nearby trash receptacle and heard the rattle of Toby's beer cans, which only underscored the impossibility of this investigation and made him wish for a stiff drink himself.

His next stop was at the island authority office to present his credentials and let them know of his business here. He was only gathering information and not talking with island residents, only visitors, the barbecue folks. Still he needed to tread carefully so as not to upset anyone. Jekyll Island was a manicured, carefully managed paradise. Having cops running all over the place questioning suspects gave the place a less than genteel feeling. He'd have to soft pedal Toby's presence. If he was lucky, they'd never have to see the man.

When he got to the office of the Jekyll Island Authority, it was closed for lunch. The sign said they'd return at one o'clock. Lewis suddenly realized he was hungry as well as tired. He'd arranged his week's stay at the Villas by the Sea. He'd check in now and grab a quick sandwich at the restaurant down the road on the beach, then return to the authority office.

The condominium he'd been assigned was spacious; one bath, one bedroom and a small kitchen. He could buy food and cook in. He sat down on the bed and stared out the window at his car in the lot. The bed was inviting, but he knew if he lay back for even a short nap, the afternoon would be gone. He got up and washed his face in the bathroom sink and rethought grabbing lunch. He decided to treat himself to something better and headed out of the parking lot toward the historic village.

—※—

The dining room at the Jekyll Island Club Hotel was full with a half-hour wait for a table. They directed him to Crane Cottage, only a short walk away. A table had opened up in the courtyard. He checked the menu and chose a shrimp dish and an iced tea, then looked around at the setting. He sat under the second floor balcony overhang, which surrounded a center courtyard housing a fountain bubbling gleefully on this sunny day. The doors behind him led to an inside dining area. While he waited for his food, he told the waiter he wanted to walk around a bit. He entered the cottage, more of a small mansion, and walked through the room to the doors beyond. They led into a small garden and patio. Beyond, the lawn with its giant live oaks stretched down to the water. Across the expanse of blue lay Brunswick, Georgia. *Another world, one he wanted to avoid.* He shook free of his thoughts and returned to his table. The waiter set his plate in front of him, but before he could take a bite of the food, he heard a familiar voice.

"I thought this was a classy place." Emily hovered over his table, her blonde hair blowing free in the afternoon breeze. He froze mid-bite and looked up expecting to see those blue eyes looking at him with disgust. To his surprise, there was a twinkle in them.

"You got the last table, but I told the waiter we knew you, and you wouldn't mind if we shared."

The waiter laid another two place settings and pulled out the chairs for the women. Lewis still held his fork mid-air, piled high with sweet Georgia white shrimp.

"Don't mind us. Go ahead and eat." Emily waved her hand dismissively at him. "Oh, and we'd like to see a wine list." The waiter scurried off.

Emily smiled. "I know you're on duty and won't be able to have the wine, but this is our vacation."

"I'm being used, aren't I? You're only being nice because you want my table. Right?"

"Of course." She continued to smile while Naomi looked embarrassed.

"Oh, tell him the news, would you?" said Naomi.

"He might not be interested. After all, he has other informants who work for him. And we were told not to butt in."

Lewis put down his fork very carefully as if he were controlling an anger which if let go might result in his throwing the food across the room.

Emily seemed to read his mood and shook her finger at him. "I wouldn't do that, not if you want to stay on this island. They are very picky about manners here."

"Okay. I'll bite. What news?"

"If our victim hadn't been stabbed and sauced, he would have died anyway. Someone was poisoning him."

CHAPTER 5

Lewis' expression on hearing the news was not a happy one. Hmm, thought Emily. He should be delighted with the information. It might make solving the case a lot easier.

"What's the problem?" she asked.

"Where did you hear this?"

"I've got my sources." Emily looked up from the wine list and gave him smug smile.

"That's the problem. You have sources you shouldn't have." He tossed his fork onto the plate and signaled the waiter.

"You're sore because I know something you don't."

The waiter hurried over to the table. Naomi slid down in her chair. "Sit up, honey. If not because you have nothing to be ashamed of, then at least because this is a classy joint. It wouldn't look good to have you lying on the floor."

"Check," Lewis said, his voice crisp.

"Don't you want to know what I know?"

"I can call in and find out."

"But I'm here and so eager to be of help." Emily batted her blue eyes at him.

Lewis looked around for the waiter again, but he was taking an order at another table. "How do you get people to move around here?"

"Relax, and let me fill you in." Emily could hardly contain herself.

For once it appeared she knew more about a case than he did.

"I told you. I'll simply call in and get the story." He stood, scanning the room for the waiter.

"Oh, come on, Detective Lewis. Let my mom tell you what she knows. Don't be a spoilsport and ruin her entire day."

Lewis slipped into his chair again. "Fine. I give up."

Triumph radiated from Emily's face. It felt so good to get her way just once with this guy. This really sexy guy. This really handsome, smart, desirable...

"So get on with the story if you must. These fancy chairs are hard on my butt."

"Okay then. Clara called me and told me."

"How the hell would Clara know anything?"

"If you keep interrupting me, I'll simply stop talking."

Lewis grabbed his spoon and began tapping it on the tablecloth. Emily shot him one of her teacher's looks. He stopped and placed the spoon very carefully back to the right of his dinner plate.

"Clara plays poker with the medical examiner and some other prominent citizens on Tuesday nights. She told me the medical examiner thought the victim was yellowish looking because of all the sauce on him, that it kind of dyed him an orange-yellow color, but after they washed him down good, the color remained and his eyes were yellow too. So guess what? It was..."

"Something he ate? Too much to drink?" Lewis eyes twinkled with a note of triumph.

Emily looked mollified for a moment, then shook her head and raced on. "Right. Rat poison. How appropriate. His liver was affected."

"He could have had liver disease or been an alcoholic. Why jump to poison?" asked Lewis.

The waiter arrived with his check, but Lewis waved him away. "I'd like a coffee."

"Oh, I thought you were asking for the check, sir."

"I changed my mind. The lady's got me captivated with her story."

Emily's eyes danced at the word "captivated."

"Really? You want me to continue?"

"Sure. This will save me a lot of time."

"Clara heard that he ran around on his wife, so it's pretty clear to me what with the apple in his mouth and the sauce, you should take a look at her. You know, as in he was a 'pig'?"

"So do you like her for the bop on the head that killed him or the poison that would have?"

"Both. She got tired of waiting, so she hit him and ended it then."

Lewis shoved his chair back and glanced across the room. By the contemplative look on his face, she hoped he was seriously considering her theory.

"Be back in a jiffy. I've got to talk to someone." He threw his napkin on the table and once again strode into the dining room and through the doors opening into the garden.

"How rude," she said to Naomi. "And don't you tell me I was being rude too."

"Yes, ma'am," said Naomi.

The waiter served Lewis' coffee and took Naomi and Emily's wine and entree orders. Several minutes passed, and no sign of Lewis. The waiter returned with the wine and their salads. They talked about plans for the next day. When the waiter stopped by the table to say their entrees were on the way, Emily got out of her chair.

"I'm going to find out what he's up to."

She entered the dining room and started toward the open door to the garden beyond. She could see two men engaged in conversation in the shade of one of the palms. The sun in her eyes blinded her. She approached, careful to hide herself behind the statue at the garden's edge. She recognized Lewis as one of the men. The other was short and fat. The breeze off the water blew the smell of chewing tobacco her way, and she retreated back into the dining room.

"Find him?" asked Naomi.

"Yep," said Emily. "Do you believe that man? He left our table to talk with that scumbag, Toby."

"What were they meeting about?"

"I have no idea. I didn't want to get close enough for Toby to see me. I hope Lewis is smart enough not to tell him we're here."

"Oh, Mom, of course he would keep our being here a secret. He knows Toby holds you and me responsible for his getting caught."

The waiter placed a dish of succulent white Georgia shrimp in garlic cream sauce in front of Emily, and she immediately forgot about Toby as she lifted a forkful to her mouth. She moaned with pure pleasure at the taste of the sea and the pungent aroma of garlic and herbs.

"Is that a sigh of welcome that I'm back?"

Emily looked up at Lewis who leaned down to catch a whiff of her shrimp. Their noses bumped, and both pulled back.

"Drink your coffee," Emily said. "For a while there I thought we were going to have to pay your bill."

"So you came looking for me."

"Did not." She spoke through the mouthful of shrimp and pasta, hoping the food would help obviate her lie.

"I saw you out of the corner of my eye. I hope Toby didn't. Emily, why do you have to take chances all the time? It's as if you're trying to make up for your earlier safe life as a preschool teacher. Why can't you let me do my job? Or do you think I'm not up to it?"

"Of course you are." Naomi reached out and patted his arm.

Lewis sat again and took a sip of his coffee. "See there. Your daughter has confidence in me."

"Of course, we did help you out on your last case," Naomi said. "A lot."

"Yes, you did." Lewis seemed to have gotten control of his irritation at Emily. "Your theory about the wife killing her husband is absurd, however."

"Why is that?" Emily ran a piece of bread around the sauce left on her plate.

"You forget. She was in the vet's office having her dog treated for fleas." Lewis grimaced and reached down to scratch at his ankle.

Emily swallowed her food. "I guess the cure didn't work. So how're you doing with that, Detective? Are you flea free now?"

⚜

Toby slid back onto the seat of the bicycle he'd rented and pedaled out of the historic village district and down the road past the old tabby ruin of what was once a fine plantation home. He barely gave it a glance. He wasn't here to sightsee. He had a job to do; well, he had some work he thought others might be able to do for him if he played the system right. As he always did. He smiled to himself thinking back on all his schemes. And then his smile slid off his face when he thought about how Detective Lewis and that little northern gal and her daughter got in his way. The big lake country would still be Toby Sands' domain if it hadn't been for them, Toby told himself. Well, this time he'd fix them.

He thought about what Detective Lewis had to offer him if he did as Lewis suggested and insinuated his way into acceptance among the barbecuers— a reduced sentence when he came to trial, a deal with the state, maybe only probation. Toby moved his tongue over the chaw of tobacco between his lips and teeth. *Well, it damn well wasn't enough.*

The wind blew out of the south toward Toby as he struggled with the bicycle. It saved on gas and was a dandy way to get around the island, but it required work, especially in a head wind. He continued to pedal toward the far southern end of the island where the fishing boats docked. Money beckoned him. The thought of it made him pedal faster.

A pleasure sailer, a sloop of about thirty-five feet sat at the end of the docks. Even Toby could see she was a beauty with polished teak decking, her hull painted a Mediterranean blue. Everything about her spoke of places of romance and intrigue. Toby took a second look at her when he approached the man standing on the dock at her berth.

"I see you're impressed with my boat," the man said.

"Oh, right. She's great. I guess. Now about this deal..."

"A man of business, I see. Get right to it. Come below."

The man, dressed in khaki shorts and a silk knit shirt let his glance travel over Toby. A scowl found its way onto his face. Toby noticed the man's expression and his words did not match. He was distracted by the thought of money to the exclusion of almost all else until a note of warning popped into the part of Toby's brain he used most, the reptilian old brain, the part that gave fight, flight and feed signals. The other "F" signal rarely presented itself any longer. What might appear to be simply a rich European playboy sailing the world to others didn't fool Toby. The man's eyes gave him away. Toby had seen eyes like that before, on drug dealers, murderers and extortionists. This man was all of those and more. For a moment Toby had second thoughts about dealing with him. *Not that he was out of the stranger's league, but he'd have to be extra cautious when it came to getting his share of the pot. Extra careful.*

"I'm not real crazy about being on boats. I get seasick."

The man laughed. "I'm not offering you a pleasure cruise, just a meeting place."

"I get sick even when tied up to the dock."

The man scrutinized Toby for a few minutes, seemed to come to some conclusion in Toby's favor, and shrugged. "I'm not taping this conversation, you know. I'm not a cop. Like you were."

The words put Toby on notice. The guy knew too much about him. Toby was right to ask for a place to talk where they could be seen by others. A crawling sensation worked its way up Toby's back and around his neck. *Extra careful.*

The man gestured to some seats located in a shady area near the restaurant and bar. At this time of day, few strolled the shady area, and the noise of people dining at the restaurant drowned out their conversation to curious passersby.

"I'm Toby. I guess you figured that out. What do I call you?"

The man laughed, but although it sounded like a laugh to Toby, when he looked at the man, nothing about his face said he found humor in the situation.

"Mr. Smith."

"Now it's my turn to laugh." Toby did, but he stopped short when he saw the man's eyes go dark and cold. "Fine then. Mr. Smith it is."

"I'm in touch with your friend, a man for whom you worked a job in the past. He'd like you and me to do some work for him."

Toby nodded. He understood. The friend, Barry Montrose, also an ex-cop had contacted Toby and let him know some of the details of the job. Toby wanted to know more.

"And how do you figure into this?" asked Toby. As quickly as he asked it, he knew it was a mistake.

Smith reached out and grabbed Toby's arm with the powerful grip of a bull alligator. The sensation was so painful, Toby was convinced his arm would be permanently paralyzed. He felt lucky he hadn't been death rolled and left at the bottom of the bay.

"Don't ask questions. You're being paid, aren't you?" Smith let go.

Toby rubbed his arm, and the feeling slowly returned, but when he looked at it, the impression of finger marks remained. That's gonna hurt for a while and turn ugly colors, thought Toby.

"Last time I didn't get all my money from my friend, so I'd like a gesture of good will on this one. Up front." He knew he was taking a foolish chance demanding anything of this character. The continuous throbbing in his arm reminded him of that, but Toby had to be smart about how he spent his time. He had too many deals all interconnected to let any one of them go south. *Yep*, thought Toby. *He was a real criminal multitasker.*

Smith said nothing at first, merely looked at Toby like he was lower than a nematode.

"I'll see what I can do for you."

"You've got that nice boat there." Toby nodded in the direction of the sloop. "I understand Barry wants you to take some people for a ride."

Smith smiled. This time his eyes twinkled as if he'd found something terribly amusing in Toby's words. "That's not all, is it?"

"These people will find their way into the hands of some traders in North Africa." Toby emphasized his seriousness by spitting onto the gravel at their feet. Some of the juice splattered onto Smith's expensive dock shoes, leaving a brown spot on the left one. Smith looked down and said nothing. He left the bench and headed back down to the dock area. Before he stepped onto his boat, he glanced back at Toby.

"You'll pay for the shoe," he said.

Toby knew he would. He just wasn't sure how.

Toby didn't feel comfortable dealing with Mr. Smith. His brain ached with the questions and concerns he had with this job. He liked things simple, and this was shaping up to be anything but simple. Why couldn't he have direct contact with Barry, face to face? When he and Barry had worked together before in an unsuccessful scheme to kidnap Barry's wife, Toby had kept his mouth shut about it. Why say anything bad about the guy to the authorities especially if it implicated Toby? Toby knew Barry was lying low, and he also suspected Barry was nursing a grudge against the now ex-wife and her mother, a grudge as big as Toby's against Lewis. Smith was another matter. A shudder worked its way up his spine. Smith wasn't someone to play around with.

As Toby pedaled down the dirt road leading away from the docks, he could feel Smith's eyes on his back. Only when he turned onto the bike path leading along the shoreline and northward toward the convention center did Toby shake himself free of the sensation of having been trapped like a mouse by a deadly snake. The reptile had let him go, but only for a while. *Smith was playing with him. It was what he did. He did it well.*

The wind increased in velocity and had shifted direction. Instead of picking up a tail wind as he had hoped, he was again heading into the blow. This time he didn't spit his tobacco. Despite the size of the chaw, his mouth felt dry. A dust devil touched down on the path just as his front wheel crossed through it. The bike wobbled for a moment and toppled, throwing Toby onto the graveled surface. He hit head first and was unable to pick himself up because his foot had become entangled in the front spokes. He flailed around on the ground, but his arms were too short to reach down over his large belly and free his ankle. He lay there for a minute, like an upended turtle, then began thrashing around once more. This time foul words accompanied his gyrations. They did not help, so again he flopped back onto his side and began to cry softly. *Life was hell,* he thought to himself.

"Need a hand, buddy?" asked a voice that was familiar to him.

CHAPTER 6

By noon the day after their lunch in Crane Cottage, Emily and Naomi had become fans of the history of the island. That meal was only the beginning of their exploration of the historic district. They had left Detective Lewis in the courtyard sipping his second cup of coffee while they arranged to go on the tour of the cottages. Naomi asked him to join them, but he declined.

"Work," he said.

Murder, Emily thought, and was glad she was out of it. She had few fears she and her daughter would run into Toby while on tour. Learning about the Jekyll Island Club and its members, the Vanderbilt, Field and DuPont families who came to the island for a simpler life didn't seem to Emily to be the kind of activity Toby would enjoy. But eating piggy was. Besides, making friends with the barbecuers was the assignment Lewis had given him, so she warned Naomi to stay away on the weekend.

"Look, Mom, I'll be with Lewis, and so what if Toby knows then we're here? We'll be leaving Sunday morning. By then the competitors will move on, and Toby will be back in his shack on the Kissimmee. Lewis will see to that."

Emily had no doubt Lewis was smarter than Toby and was a good detective, but she also knew how slippery Toby could be. And she didn't trust he might not have some scheme cooked up for getting back at them.

"I'm keeping a close eye on him," Lewis had assured them.

Neither Naomi nor Emily had seen the detective since their lunch together. Emily envisioned him getting reports from Toby about the barbecue contestants and discovering which one of them killed Everett Pratt. Yet, the rumor the victim was a womanizer kept coming back to Emily, and it convinced her that his death was not related to barbecue but to zipper problems. Maybe not the wife, thought Emily, but perhaps a girlfriend who resented his other honeys?

Toward the end of the week the two of them were picnicking on the beach near the new convention center. The barbecue contest and festival had set up in the center's parking lot, but Emily and Naomi avoided it, using a beach access stairway closer to the campground.

"Boy, this is a bigger contest than the one back home." Emily eyed the large number of tents and trailers housing the festival contestants as they lugged their beach gear around the side of the parking area and out onto the beach.

"It's a regional cook-off." Naomi spread a blanket and set their cooler on one end of it. She stabbed the end of the beach umbrella into the sand and flopped down.

Emily shaded her eyes and looked up at the sky. "No sign yet of that storm predicted to roll in."

"I'm glad we decided to spend the afternoon here. I think I've had enough history for a while. I just want to relax and take in a few rays. Here, Mom, would you put some of this sunscreen on my back?"

The two women took turns slathering each other with lotion, then settled into their beach chairs.

Later in the afternoon, the wind blew more strongly, yet the sky remained bright blue with no sign of storm clouds.

"I love this beach, but I've got to say, the water is brown and muddy looking. Not my preference for a swim." Naomi rolled over onto her side and scanned the waves coming in.

"I only swim in pools," said her mother.

Naomi sighed, and Emily could tell her daughter was bored with simply sitting and watching the choppy water.

Emily sipped the last drop of her soda and dropped the can into her beach bag. "The wind is whipping the sand into my face and hair. I'm getting a wind burn and a sand blasting. My face is going to look like I've had a chemical peel."

"Back to the village to look around some more?" Naomi's tone said she wasn't excited at that prospect.

"I think we've heard enough about the wealth of the members of the club at the turn of the last century. It's made me feel very poor." Emily glanced at her watch. "Maybe we can get nine in before the sun sets."

"Golf. Now that was an exclusive club. Still is in some places. No women, no minorities. You had to be from the right family—the Vanderbilts or the Morgans. Don't you think it's interesting that the Jekyll Island Club membership allowed women? Pretty progressive for the late eighteen hundreds," Naomi said.

"There must have been a very good reason for that, and I'll bet it had to do with money and not equality."

"Mom, you are so suspicious."

"I am usually so right."

Naomi smiled. "You and Lewis. Never wrong about anything, or at least you never admit to it."

Emily shaded her eyes from the sun and looked over at her daughter. *I'm glad we finally found each other after all these years, and happier yet we've had this time together.* If Naomi's abusive ex-husband crossed her mind these last few days, she hadn't said anything to Emily. She looks so content, thought Emily.

"Okay. Golf it is." Emily grabbed her cell and connected to the course. After she clicked off, she stood and began packing up their blanket, chairs and cooler. "If we hurry, there's a spot open in half an hour. Let's go."

⚜

As Naomi pulled into the golf club's parking lot, a large cherry red Cadillac entering from the opposite direction cut them off. Naomi honked at the driver who rolled down the Caddie's window.

"Sorry, honey," said the woman in a honeyed southern drawl. Naomi nodded and proceeded into the lot. The Caddie stopped to let them into a parking place, then moved ahead nearer the clubhouse into a handicapped slot. As Naomi and Emily extracted their clubs from the trunk, Emily noticed the driver of the Cadillac was struggling to remove a wheelchair from the back of the car.

"Here, let me help you with that." Emily ran ahead and reached into the back seat to move the chair to the pavement.

"That is so nice of you, and after I almost plowed right through y'all." The woman was tall, and had auburn hair. Kind of reminds me of Clara, thought Emily. The woman set up the wheelchair, opened the front passenger's door, and held out her hand to someone inside. A frail-looking older man with wispy white hair emerged, and with her hand to support him, dropped into the chair. She tossed the Caddie's keys to the cart attendant who smiled and opened the car's trunk.

Another attendant appeared and strapped Emily and Naomi's clubs into a cart.

Naomi handed the attendant two dollars and jumped into the cart.

"I'll meet you out back." She drove off in the direction pointed out by the attendant while Emily entered to pay and get a course card.

Through the back windows overlooking the course, Emily could see the attendant pull up with the elderly gentleman in the cart. He parked it next to the one in which Naomi waited, took the tip offered him by the man and nodded his thanks.

Emily stepped up to the desk as the woman from the Cadillac finished paying. "That's wonderful."

The woman turned to look toward Emily with curiosity. "I mean, taking him out on the course with you."

"Oh, he plays. He loves to play, doesn't he, Dan?" she said addressing the pro.

The tanned and muscled pro shook his head and grinned. "That he does."

The woman headed out the door to join her companion.

Now that must be something to behold, thought Emily. It had to take them four hours to play the front nine. *Spare me being hooked up with them in a foursome. We'd be playing with flashlights.*

"Well, you'll get to see him play up close. I paired you and your daughter with them. You're a foursome. Hope you don't mind, but we're jammed up today." Dan continued to produce his hundred watt, Rembrandt white smile as he spoke, and his eyes told Emily he knew just what she was thinking. The joke's on me, thought Emily.

As Emily approached the carts, the woman stepped up to her.

"Well, I declare. It's you two. I guess we'd better introduce ourselves. I'm Daisy DuBignon St. Simonton, and this here is my hubby Rodney."

Emily introduced them and tossed her arm around her daughter. "Wonderful. This will be great." She felt her daughter give an inward groan.

"Great," said Naomi.

"Oh, don't you worry, sugar," said Daisy. "We won't hold you up." Naomi continued to smile but her eyes said she doubted that. "Promise." Daisy crossed her fingers and her heart, then giggled.

"Want to wager on the holes?" asked Rodney.

"Don't you do it," warned Daisy. "He's a ringer." She laughed.

Emily and Naomi laughed. Rodney looked hurt.

"It's no fun if there's not some money at stake," said Rodney.

Emily hesitated giving an answer as Daisy stepped into the tee box. Rodney leaned on his driver and looked as if he might keel over onto the fairway before he could step up to take a swing.

"Sure. Why not? How about Bingo, Bango, Bongo?" Emily was about to say a dollar a point, but Rodney interrupted her.

"Five bucks a point."

The Cadillac told her they probably had money, and they were known here, so that told her they played often, but she felt guilty taking advantage of a guy in a wheelchair and his wife whose swing looked like she'd just bought her clubs at Wal-Mart.

"You're on," she said.

Naomi grabbed her mother's shoulder and steered her away from the tee box. "What are you doing? These people are old, and crippled to boot."

"He said he likes to play for money. We'll buy them drinks afterward with the money we win. That'll kind of even things up."

On the first hole, Daisy hit first, a nice straight shot that went a good two hundred yards, stopping just short of a small stream that cut across the fairway.

"Nice lie," said Naomi. "A hybrid should put you right on."

Rodney still leaned on his driver, his face expressionless. Emily thought there was a chance he'd fallen asleep and would topple over before he could take his shot, but when his wife called to him, he sprang forward with surprising bounce in his thin legs. Daisy teed up his shot for him. Rodney stepped forward, addressed the ball and hit. The ball arced high into the air, sailed straight over the stream and landed about thirty yards short of the green.

"Astounding," chorused Emily and Naomi.

"What was that? Two hundred seventy yards maybe." Emily looked at the small white ball nestled in the middle of the fairway then back at the specter of a man who hit it there.

"Lucky shot," whispered Naomi to Emily.

"Yeah, he's still fresh. We'll see how he does after he's taken a couple of swings." Emily was certain the man had expended more energy in that swing than he had the past five years of his life. Well, almost certain.

Both Emily and Naomi hit their shots directly into the stream. The remainder of the hole went the same. Bingo—Rodney was first onto the green. Bango—Daisy's third shot put her only five feet away from the pin. Bongo—Rodney put in an amazing twenty-foot putt. Flubbo—Emily and Naomi took drops on the other side of the water then both lost their balls in the woods. When they found them, Emily's lie was so bad she hit the side of a large oak two times. When she finally hit out of the rough, she landed in the sand trap. Naomi fared better, hitting the green on her third shot and three-putting it. Daisy and Rodney patiently waited for them to finish the hole. The foursome behind them asked to play through.

"Not bad, honey. That's two points for you and one for me. Sorry, girls. Bad luck. You'll do better on the next hole." Daisy said all this without a note of condescension in her voice. Emily felt the woman was actually rooting for her, and the confidence she expressed in Emily, although knowing her for only several minutes, made Emily feel she would do better.

They hopped into their carts and headed for the second hole. On this one Rodney needed help from his wife to make it out of the cart and onto the tee box. Emily and Naomi gave one another knowing looks. Another straight hit, over two hundred and fifty yards.

And so it continued. To her credit Emily did do better than on the first hole. She didn't lose a ball, and she managed to get out of the sand trap on five in two strokes.

By the sixth hole, neither Emily nor Naomi had earned a single point. Emily was entertaining all kinds of unkind thoughts and feeling guilty about them—a strong wind to blow Rodney over when he teed off, an alligator on the fairway to grab Daisy's ball and chase her away, or, at the least, a thunderstorm with ground lightening. None of these materialized, and Emily was thankful the golf gods were not as petty as she was.

Yet by the second hole the foursome spent as little time focusing on their play as they could get by with and still contend they were playing a round of golf. They told golf jokes, talked about southern cooking, exchanged preferences for cocktails and discussed family.

At the end of nine holes with the sun only a smidgen above the horizon, they walked off the course laughing at how they had scored. Emily and Naomi owed Daisy and Rodney one hundred thirty dollars. Emily had made five bucks on the eighth hole with a lucky one putt.

Emily gulped when she totaled up their loss. "I don't suppose you'll take a credit card?"

Rodney laughed. "Not on your life, but I will take both of you to dinner."

"We can't do that, Mr. St. Simonton. We made the bet and owe you."

"Listen, I had the best time today I've had in months. Everyone around here knows me, and no one will take my wager. You did."

Emily blushed. "You know why we did. We underestimated you because of your..."

"Disability? Because of this wheelchair?"

"No, not that. We figured you had to be a bad player if you used thirty-year-old Ping clubs with brass heads." Emily pointed toward the ancient irons in his bag. "I should have had at least fifty yards on you with my Big Bertha." It was a lie, but only a little one. Emily did think his equipment was dated.

Rodney threw back his head and laughed loudly enough to catch the attention of the other players coming off the course.

Pro Dan heard the laughter too. "You ladies must have given Rodney a run for his money. How much did you win off him?"

Emily walked toward the door of the club house and held her five-dollar winnings over her head.

"Sassy little thing, ain't she?" Rodney asked his wife who nodded her agreement. He continued to laugh as Daisy pushed him across the parking lot. Emily and Naomi stashed their clubs in the Mustang and followed the couple to their car.

Daisy settled her husband into the passenger's seat. Rodney continued to grin.

"He's not kidding about dinner and neither am I. Meet us at the Jekyll Island Hotel in an hour."

"Didn't you think my Big Bertha would do it for me?" asked Emily of Naomi.

"Not after I saw him hit one off the tee with that ratty old driver of his. I knew then we were sunk."

"If we were playing eighteen," Emily said to Rodney, "I could have won a lot more off you."

The couple laughed so loud, Rodney almost fell out of his seat. Daisy shoved him upright and got into the car. As they drove off, Emily and Naomi could see their heads bobbing merrily through the back window.

"I guess we made their day," said Naomi.

"I appreciate the invitation to dinner, but I've still got to cough up the money to pay him. A bet's a bet, especially in golf."

"There's something more serious to consider, Mom."

"What's that?"

"What can we pull out of our duffle bags presentable enough to wear in the Jekyll Island Hotel's dining room?"

Now that was serious. Dressing for dinner trumped debt every time.

CHAPTER 7

Emily hated to spend the money, but swimsuits and shorts would not do for dinner that night. She and Naomi stopped off at the Jekyll Island mall located across from the convention center. It held several gift shops, a bicycle rental store and a small grocery. They rushed into the gift store, which sold island clothing, and purchased two beach cover-ups that could be belted to make them presentable as dresses. Emily hoped she wouldn't see the identical outfits on others tonight, but reasoned no one but some gals from rural Florida would have the bad taste to wear beach togs into the fancy dining room. Gold belts and black flip flops completed the ensembles. They were as presentable as two women camping in a tent could be.

At the hotel, the maître d' gave them a haughty look that seemed to suggest they had lost their way to the hotel coffee shop. Before he could speak, Emily indicated they were joining Mr. and Mrs. St. Simonton for dinner. He replaced his unwelcoming look with a syrupy one. Emily thought the sour demeanor was a better fit for him. Daisy and Rodney waved as he led them across the large dining room, which was filled to capacity. Everyone stared.

"Must be the haute couture we're wearing that's catching everyone's eye," whispered Naomi to her mother. The toe guard of Emily's flip flop pulled free of her sole, and she stumbled as they reached the middle of the room. She reached down and pulled the sandal off her foot.

"I'm sorry, Madam, but you can't go barefoot in here," said the maître d'.

If he thought a mere sandal malfunction could put them out of the dining room, he was mistaken.

"Here hold this." Emily shoved the beach bag she was using as a purse into his arms and poked the toe guard back into the sole. "There. So hard to get quality Ferragamos today. I think I'll have to go with Jimmy Choos from now on." She looked around the dining room and smiled a dazzling Hollywood star smile.

The maître d' continued forward, the large purse hanging off his arm, nose in the air. At the table, he held out her chair and handed her the bag. "Madam's, uh, bag, I believe."

"Madam is so pleased you could hold it." Emily tried the same high wattage smile on him. His expression changed in warmth not quite two or three degrees.

"Thanks so much, Mr. Lemon. Please send our waiter." Rodney could almost not get the sentence out of his mouth for the chuckle Emily could hear working its way up his throat. Daisy hid her smile behind her menu.

"His name is Lemon?" asked Naomi. "Perfect."

"Well, to his credit," said Daisy "his job can't be an easy one. We've seen him chase young men and women in wet bathing suits and towels out of here."

Daisy lowered her menu and stared at the two women. "The beach shop," said Emily.

"Really? It's a divine look, but I'd send the shoes back. No sense paying good money for shoddy workmanship." Daisy's eyes twinkled. "Now, how about a martini?"

The remainder of the evening was as much fun as their golf course adventure. What Rodney lacked in mobility he made up for in great stories and a wonderful sense of humor. Daisy wasn't far behind him in the laughter department.

"We've been learning about the island," said Naomi, "and your maiden name is the same as that of the earliest settler, DuBignon."

"Well, don't be misled by that. I'm from the wrong side of the DuBignon blanket. No money on that branch of the family tree, and we get no respect either." Daisy said this without regret or envy. "I come from the poor, but fun-loving DuBignons."

Rodney fastened his gaze on Emily and Naomi. "I know what you're thinking. That she married me for my money, but my folks were poorer than hers."

Maybe we misjudged them, and they aren't as wealthy as they appear, Emily thought.

As if reading her mind, Daisy poured the remainder of the champagne into Emily's glass and beckoned to the waiter for another. "My mama was yearning for some land so she bought some of that bottom land just south of Brunswick. Everyone figured it was pretty worthless, and it was at the time. Mama waited and finally sold to some developers. They paid my mama a lot for that land, then they went belly up. Smart or lucky? You decide."

"Good timing," said Emily. She looked up from her dinner and ran her gaze over the people seated in the dining room. Nearer to the windows, sat Detective Lewis with a tall woman with dark eyes. She was wearing a sleek red dress that clung to her like a wet tee-shirt in Panama City during spring break.

Emily nudged Naomi who nodded. "I saw them. So who's the woman?" Before she could stop her daughter, Naomi waved to them. Lewis looked uncomfortable but he gave a terse nod of recognition.

Daisy turned her attention to the pair. "Oh, so you know the Lewises? A handsome couple, wouldn't you say?"

⸰⸰⸰

"I know why you're so mad," said Naomi. She and Emily were heading back to the campground in her Mustang. Although the night was windy, the air was still warm, and Naomi had put down the top. The sweet smell of the marshes rushed to them on the strong breeze.

"I don't know what you mean." Emily stretched her arms over her head and looked up at the night sky. "Clouds are moving in fast. We might be spending a wild, wet night in the tent. We'd better make certain we've staked it down well before we go to bed."

"Don't avoid the topic. You know exactly what I mean, and you have no reason to be furious with him. You never gave him a nod, but now you're acting like he betrayed you somehow."

Emily thought about that. "Well, he did. He acted like he was interested in me. Didn't you get that feeling too?"

Naomi turned into the campground and slowed for the 10 mph posted limit. "You're right. He did act all flirty, I mean flirty for him, I guess. Maybe you'd be better off with Donald."

"Those are my choices? A married cop and a weird bass fisherman turned part-time bartender? I'll pass."

"Maybe you should try online dating." Naomi pulled up in front of their camping site and got out of the car. "Oh, damn. You're right. Several tent pegs need to be driven farther into the ground. We did a pretty sloppy job when we pounded them in."

"We didn't know it was going to blow." Emily looked around the area. There were no other tents there. Lights from an approaching car illuminated their site.

It was the camp host.

"Thought I'd better tell you ladies that we're in for some heavy rains and high winds, maybe a tornado. I came by earlier, but you weren't here. You might want to find another place to stay tonight."

"Where would that be? With the barbecue festival here, all the hotel rooms are taken." Emily grabbed Naomi and put her arm around her.

"Maybe we should just pack up and head for home."

"I think we've both had too much champagne. I shouldn't have driven this far tonight."

The camp host looked sympathetic. "Tell you what. If the storm gets too furious, you can run for the bathhouses. They're made of cinderblock. They should hold off a heavy blow."

"Where we're from, they set up shelters when there's a hurricane and evacuate everybody." Emily was scared, but the fear came out sounding like irritation.

"You can't predict a tornado like a hurricane." The host looked chagrinned at the situation. "Maybe you should just head on over to the bathhouse now and spend the night there. You'll feel a lot safer."

After he left, Naomi and Emily discussed their best option. The wind was whipping around the branches of the pines and the live oaks. What had looked like the sheltering arms of the big trees on a sunny, calm day now appeared more like dangerous battering rams coming at them from unpredictable directions. Raindrops began to fall as Naomi put up the top on the car.

"I say we grab our sleeping bags and head for the bathroom," said Emily.

⸙

Mr. Smith ordered his man to prepare to leave, then walked to the stern of the boat and flipped open his cell. "There's a big blow coming in. I'm getting out of here before she gets too bad."

He listened to the reply for only a moment, then, interrupted. "I'm not risking this boat for any amount of money." The only sign of his increasing irritation was the change in his eyes. The pupils took on the color of steel ball bearings, grey and ice cold. Impatient with his contact's continuing attempts to sweeten the pot followed by intimidation, he broke in once more. "Do not threaten me. You'll get your cargo. In time. Have patience." He disconnected.

The crew member threw the lines onto the deck and the big schooner slipped the dock. Smith motored toward open water and a safer harbor.

Toby stood in the protected alcove of the harbor's breezeway, watching the boat glide silently away through the gathering storm. There went his chance at big money and sweet revenge, he thought. He was on his own.

❦

The wind picked up in intensity as Naomi and Emily jumped into the car with their sleeping bags.

Naomi pulled up in front of the bathhouse door so they wouldn't get wet. "This isn't good." She shoved her sleeping bag at her mother and slid back into the car before Emily could object. "I need to move the car out from under all these trees. I'm going to park it in the lot in front of the campground office. I'll be right back."

"You'll get soaking wet," Emily yelled, but her words were cut off by the howling of the wind. She watched the car's taillights disappear down the road. "Naomi!"

Minutes passed. Emily paced back and forth between the window and the doorway. She could see little outside through the rain-streaked glass, and the strength of the wind made it impossible for her to open the door and look out into the night without taking a soaking from the rain gusts. *Where was she? Maybe she decided to take shelter in the camp office instead of chancing the run back here. But there's no one at the office to let her in.* The sound of the wind and the rain hitting the window grew louder. Emily covered her ears and shut her eyes. *Would this never end?* With a tremendous roar and the sound of shattering glass, a window blew in. The shards exploded around her. She felt them prick and slice her hands and bare arms as she fell to the cement floor and covered herself with her sleeping bag.

Tree limbs were thrown against the tiny bathhouse until finally the giant oak overhanging the building gave up one of its large branches and sent it hurtling down onto the building. It hit with a crash, caving in the section of roof over the shower area. Rain poured in after it.

Emily moved farther into the far corner of the building near the door, which now began to shudder and shake as if an enemy army's catapults were flinging giant boulders at it. The shaking stopped for a moment, then the door slammed inward.

A man stood in the doorway, his large frame backlit by the campground street lights. Emily raised her head from the protection of her sleeping bag cocoon to look death in the face. The figure hesitated only a moment before he strode across the floor and grabbed her, lifting her into his arms and carrying her back out into the howling storm. *Was she being rescued or transported into hell?* A car with lights on waited outside. He opened the door, shoved her in and slid into the driver's seat. She was afraid to look at his face. Whoever he was he was a lunatic to drive in this weather and to carry her out into this storm.

"You're soaked through," the voice said, barely audible above the sound outside.

"Lewis. What are you doing here?"

"Saving you, it would seem."

"I don't need to be saved. I was fine."

The penetrating sound of a crack from behind them drew their attention. Lewis slowed the car, and they both turned to see the oak by the bathhouse pulled up by its roots and dumped onto the building.

"Right," said Lewis. "You were snug as a bug."

"Naomi."

"I saw her pull up to the office when I drove in. She's so damned attached to that Mustang she refused to get out of it to come with me to find you. She told me you were at the bathhouse, but I took a wrong turn and tried the other bathhouse. That's what took me so long. I almost didn't make it."

Suddenly a gust of wind rocked the vehicle sending Emily across the seat into Lewis. His mouth turned up at the contact. Emily noticed and scooted back to her side.

"I'm fine. Let's see abut Naomi."

"Can you persuade her to leave the convertible and come with us, do you think?"

"No. She loves that car."

But something or someone persuaded Naomi to leave the car because it was empty when they got back to it.

"We've got to find her." Emily was more frantic over Naomi's disappearance than she was with her own experience at the bathhouse.

"Where? We'd be endangering all of us. We need to find shelter. This storm is only going to get worse. We should be inside a building."

Emily's cell rang. She pulled it out of her jeans pocket. The connection was poor, but she could hear her daughter's voice.

"Mom, where are you?"

"Where are you?"

"I'm with Daisy and Rodney. They came by right after Lewis did and convinced me to go with them to find you. I'm in their car. We looked for Lewis, but there's a tree down. We can't get to you. We'll have to use the back way out of the campground and rendezvous somewhere."

"Where?" asked Emily, but the connection was lost.

"Naomi's with Daisy and Rodney. They're heading for the other exit. We can swing around on the main road and meet them."

"It's not such a good idea to be riding around in this blow looking for them."

Emily shot him a look filled with contempt. "Don't be a wimp. It's a little wind and rain. I think it's letting up." A piece of the metal roofing on the office peeled free and came racing at them. Lewis snapped the wheel to the left to avoid it.

She wasn't about to leave her daughter the way she had to when the fire came through her condominium campground earlier in the year. If necessary, she'd get out of the car and start walking down the road looking for Naomi.

Lewis glanced at her determined face and gave in. He pulled out of the campground onto the main road.

Less than half a mile later, Emily spied the lights of a car turn onto the road ahead. "That's them. Hurry." Emily watched the car continue up the road toward the historic village. "I'll bet Daisy and Rodney couldn't get across the bridge so they took a room at the Jekyll Island Inn for the night."

"How could they do that? They're full up." Lewis gritted his teeth and maneuvered around small limbs blowing into the roadway.

"Oh, I think Daisy has pull everywhere. For all I know, they maintain lodging there full-time just in case."

"You're probably right."

"Daisy seems to know you and your wife well." She knew now wasn't the time to take up Lewis' personal life. It was like picking a scab that wasn't ready to come off. She should leave it alone, but she couldn't.

Before he could answer, a huge limb fell onto the slick road in front of the car. Lewis stood on the brakes, but it was too late. They smashed into it with an impact powerful enough to deploy the air bags.

"Well, now you've done it," said Emily, her voice muffled by the airbag pressing on her chest.

"Me? I wasn't the one who wanted to chase around in this storm. I was willing to take you back to my lodging, get you dry and..."

"And do what?" Emily began to wiggle in her seat. "How do we get out of these things?"

"They'll deflate on their own."

"I guess now we'll have to walk." Emily's cell rang. This time the signal was stronger. As if satisfied it had thrown all it could at the two of them, the storm seemed to let up. The winds died and the rain lessened. Emily could almost make out the lights of Brunswick across the river.

"Hey, Mom. You okay? I thought that was you and Lewis right behind us, but then you disappeared."

"We're fine. How about you?"

"Daisy and Rodney took me to the Jekyll Island Inn to their suite there. You can come stay here they said. Once the storm lets up a bit more, they'll drive me back so I can check on my car."

"You can't get through on the beach road. There's a tree down. With all the wind, there are probably lines down and other roadways blocked. It might not get cleared until morning."

"Where are you exactly?"

"We're not far from the cut-off to the other side of the island and to Cottages by the Sea where Lewis has rooms. I guess I'll stay with him until morning. I think you should stay put also. The car can wait. It's not such a good idea to go driving around in this even though it is letting up."

As if to assert the storm was still present, a gust of wind threw another tree limb across the hood of the car.

"Yipes."

"You okay, Mom?"

"Oh, I'm just a little wet and cold."

"Well, tell Lewis to turn up the heater and head for his digs."

"Sure. I'll do that. See you in the morning."

Emily looked over at Lewis. "So I guess we walk."

"You didn't tell her we couldn't drive the car."

"I didn't want her to worry."

"We walk. Think you can make it?"

"Of course." She shoved open her door and stepped out onto the roadway into several feet of water.

Lewis extracted himself from the driver's side of the car and started down the road. When he realized Emily was not by his side, he stopped and looked back. "What are you doing back there?"

"Swimming," she said.

CHAPTER 8

It took them over two hours to make it to his condo. The water drained off the road's surface quickly, but they had to climb over tree limbs or detour around them. Other storm debris including road signs, sections of roofing and house siding made the going treacherous also.

Emily knew Lewis would have been more than happy to carry her, but she wasn't willing to get that close to the handsome detective. She didn't trust herself. She didn't trust him even though he was married. Matrimony might not be an institution she'd tried, but she respected it and wasn't about to cross the line with someone who had taken vows that included a promise of lifelong fidelity.

"Here we are." Lewis unlocked the door and gestured for her to precede him into the condo.

"Nice. It's very nice. And dry."

They looked at one another. Two wet, exhausted, shivering people, each wary of the other.

"The bathroom's in there. You can hit the shower first."

"Oh, no, I couldn't. It's your place. You go first."

"No. I insist. You first."

"Okay."

"You don't want to argue about it anymore?"

"No, we argue too much. Besides, I never asked you to come riding in like a white knight. That was your idea. It's really your own fault you're in this mess."

"I guess you're right."

"Of course I am. Besides, while I'm in the shower you can make coffee. And do some hard thinking."

"About what?"

"If you've got a wife, why do you flirt with me all the time?"

"I don't flirt with you."

She gave him the eye. "Do so."

"Do not. You flirt with me."

"Do not. I don't even like you." That was true sometimes, but then there were others when she thought he was kind of funny and interesting. And he was oh so cute in a really big man way.

"You do like me." He crossed his arms and leaned back against the counter dividing the living area from the kitchen.

"Maybe a little. And you like me."

"Not really."

"Why not?"

"Do you want me to like you?"

"Of course not. You're married."

"Am not."

"Are."

"Nope."

"You aren't?" Emily walked back toward him. He approached her.

"I'm divorced."

"Prove it."

He reached into his soggy coat pocket and extracted a bulky set of papers, soaked through from the rain.

"We just signed these tonight." He handed them to her.

Emily opened the papers to read them. "Uh, they're soppy. I can't read this mess."

Lewis approached even closer. "Here let me help you." They stood toe to toe, he towering over her. She looked up at him.

"I don't need your help. Anyway, I trust you. If you say you're divorced, then you're divorced. Why would you lie to me? Unless you thought you could take advantage of a little gal who's been tossed and scrambled by a storm and is about to get naked in your bathroom."

"I'd never do that."

"Wouldn't you?"

He shook his head and closed the gap between them so that her forehead was inches from his chest.

"Good, because I want to feel safe here."

Lewis took her chin in his hands and leaned down. His lips were only a silly millimeter away from hers. Her head told her to run away, back out into the storm, but her hormones were playing Mantovani, and the string section was drowning out the warnings. This was what she feared, that she wouldn't be able to resist this irritating, sexy man.

"Emily," he said. He brought his lips closer to her.

"Can I ask you something before we proceed?"

"Sure. Anything."

"What kind of soap do you use?"

His head snapped up. "Huh?"

"If it's that guy stuff, maybe you could call room service and see if they can rustle up something more generic and not so testosterone-laden, something that won't exfoliate off several layers of my skin."

"What?"

"Or isn't the condo office open all night? If it isn't I could just rinse off."

"I'll check." Lewis made a sound in his throat like a growling animal, backed out the door and slammed it behind him. It shook the building with a force not dissimilar to that of the storm.

Like I'd believe him about the divorce, Emily thought. She picked up the papers he'd dropped on the table and carefully peeled off the cover sheet. Well, I'll be damned, she said to herself.

"I'm back with your soap. I had to wake the night manager." He didn't sound happy, and it was her fault. *Ah well, perhaps she could remedy that. Or was he so angry with her that he wouldn't co-operate?*

"I'm in the shower. Bring it in here."

Lewis groaned, but opened the door to a roomful of steam. He walked over to the tub and moved aside the curtain only enough to hand her the soap. She grabbed him and pulled him into the shower with her. Now this is what I call cooperation, she thought.

"What the hell are you doing? You're getting me all wet."

"You're already all wet. Here, soap me up."

All he could see of her was her tanned back. "I can't see a thing in here."

"Pity." She laughed.

He dropped the soap, and the two of them got down on their hands and knees searching the bottom of the tub for it.

The sound of someone banging on the condo door cut short her giggles.

"Who the hell is that?" he snarled.

"Mom! Are you in there?"

⁂

Emily and Lewis sat on the couch looking like teenagers caught necking in the car. Emily grasped a terry robe tight to her neck. As for Lewis, he had donned sweat pants and shirt. They clung to his still damp body.

"What were you two doing?" Naomi sounded like a scolding parent.

"Showering." Emily's voice was filled with contrition.

"Obviously. There was so much steam in the bathroom and the rest of this condo it's a wonder the paper isn't peeling off the walls."

"Your mother was cold. I worried about hypothermia." Lewis' voice carried conviction and authority, but not with total success.

"When did the cure for hypothermia become a shower for two?" Naomi's lips twitched around the edges.

"Body heat," they both replied in unison.

Naomi doubled up with laughter. "I really couldn't care less what you were up to, but you both looked so guilty, I had to play along."

"Nothing happened." Emily pulled the robe tighter to her neck.

"Absolutely nothing. Unfortunately." There was a note of regret in his voice.

Emily shot him an indignant look, then turned her eyes to Naomi. "What are you doing here if not to check up on me? I thought you were staying with Daisy and Rodney?"

"I am. They're waiting for me in the car. I insisted we drop by to see how you two were doing. Rodney's got a short-wave radio, and we heard about a limb down on a car on the Beach Road. It sounded like your police cruiser, so we came looking. You must have walked all the way back here."

"We did," said Lewis.

"Actually I take back what I said before, Detective. You're a married man, so you really should keep your hands off other women, don't you think?" Naomi's face took on that stern look again.

Lewis moaned and rolled his eyes. "This again."

"Show her," said Emily.

Lewis pointed to the divorce papers on the table. Naomi got up and grabbed them, then read the first page.

"Fine then, but let me caution both of you against getting into something on the rebound."

"If either one of you had read further, you would have noted that my ex-wife and I have been separated for several years. Tonight was the first night I've seen her in over five years. She's been living with someone else."

"You could have told me, you know." Emily's eyes snapped in anger.

"I never got the chance."

"Oh, but you took plenty of chances to flirt like crazy."

"Children, children," said Naomi. "We'll sort this out some other time. Right now, you're coming back to the hotel to stay with the St. Simontons in their suite. They've got a spare bedroom." Naomi looked around the condo. "One bedroom, I assume?"

"I could take the couch," offered Lewis.

"Yeah, he could."

"Your choice, Mom, but what you need is a good night's sleep, and I have a feeling you wouldn't get it here, couch or no couch."

⚜

"Nice timing," said Emily. She and Naomi were in the back seat of the Cadillac heading toward the Jekyll Island Hotel. "We had gotten beyond all the fighting."

"That's because you were too busy soaping each other."

Daisy looked in the rearview mirror but said nothing. Rodney chuckled.

"There's the rebound thing I warned you about, and I was serious," cautioned Naomi.

"If he's been separated for several years, there is no rebound."

"I meant you, Mom."

"Oh." Emily sighed. "You're right. I was just so thrilled when I read he was divorced. All the guys I run into at the club are married or older than dirt. I jumped at the first available man I guess." That wasn't quite true, Emily thought. He wasn't only available. He was desirable. She sighed again and looked out the window. The sun was coming up, and the rain had stopped. "You've got to admit. He's one hunk of a guy."

"Ánd not as weird as Donald. Is that what you're thinking?"

"Donald's his own person."

"Donald likes fish. And gators. And maybe you, Mom, but not much else."

"Uhmm. Looks like it'll be a great day for the barbecue festival. You still going to it with Lewis?"

"Wait a minute," said Daisy. "I thought since you discovered Lewis is divorced, you were interested in him and he in you, but he's dating your daughter?"

By the time Naomi and Emily straightened out their hosts, they were pulling up to the hotel.

The St. Simontons' suite of rooms was spacious; two bedrooms, two baths and a small living room area.

"This is nice," said Emily, "but we can't stay here indefinitely. Once Naomi and I grab naps, we'll need to get back to the campground to see if there's anything left of our tent. And your car, Naomi."

"The car's fine. Rodney sent someone from the hotel to check on it. But you're right." Naomi turned to the St. Simontons. "We can't put you out."

"Oh, pish," said Daisy. "We keep these rooms year-round for family and friends. They came in handy last night, but we're back to our digs in Brunswick today. You're not putting us out."

Emily tried to argue, but Daisy held up her hand and shook her head.

By late morning, the clouds had all disappeared, and the sky was sunny and clear, the weather a bit cooler, but it was as if the storm never happened. The roads had been cleared, all signs of the night's blow erased.

"The authorities certainly take pride in this place. I didn't expect the clean-up to be so fast." Emily rode in the back of the St. Simontons' Cadillac, windows open to the smell of newly laundered air.

Naomi's car sat in the parking lot of the campground, unharmed. She rushed over, and for a moment, Emily thought her daughter might put her arms around the grill and kiss it.

The scene at their campsite was not so welcoming. They found the tent blown up into one of the large trees and had to call on Lewis who showed up shortly after they did to get it down for them.

"I was certain you told me you were a tomboy as a kid." He grimaced down at Emily as he climbed into the leafy branches. "You never climbed trees?"

"You never tried doing a favor for a friend?" She said it in a warm tone of voice and then laughed aloud.

"Favor? If I fall from here, you can pay back the favor by taking care of my hospital bills." He grabbed the tent and pulled. It came free in three pieces.

"It looks as if we won't be doing anymore camping. We might as well go home. Damn. I wanted to at least get a rack of ribs." Naomi tossed the tattered tent away in disgust.

"You can do all of that. Rodney and I are going back to Brunswick to our house. You two can have our suite of rooms at the hotel."

"Or you could stay with me. Like I said before, I can sleep on the couch." Lewis jumped down from the tree and landed inches from Emily. He looked down at her. "What do you think?"

"I think we went through this earlier today. I'd have to chain you to the couch."

"I'd have to Velcro you to the bed."

The two of them looked at each other with a mixture of anger and laughter playing across their faces.

Naomi interrupted the standoff. "I'm for the suite. You can go with Lewis and finish up what I interrupted last night."

Emily blushed. Lewis only made the situation worse by repeating his feeble excuse of showering together to get warm.

⁂

Having run into Toby on the bicycle path midweek, his cousin Bill had offered to let Toby stay in his trailer.

"I've got lots of room. I'm seeing a little gal from Backyard Barbecue, so lately I've been staying at her place. She and her brother have a huge fifth wheel, two bedrooms."

Relieved he'd have someplace to bunk for free, Toby agreed and moved in his small duffle of belongings. The little trailer rocked and rolled when the storm hit, but it remained upright, and Toby was grateful he'd run into his cousin when he did. Of course, Toby knew before their encounter that Bill was at the cook-off. He'd planned to get in touch with him. Their "chance" meeting was perfect. Bill's hospitality played right into Toby's hands.

"What're you doing here anyhow?" Bill was slapping together some pulled-pork sandwiches for the two of them.

"I had to get away from the Kissimmee River. It's too damn depressing there." Toby had kept his troubles with the law from his cousin who thought he'd taken an early retirement. "I got a letter of recommendation from some contacts who told me to take it to the Island Authority and they'd get me a temporary job. Just plain luck I ran into you here. I didn't even know about the cook-off."

"We ought to stay in touch more." Bill handed him the sandwich. "We're family, you know."

Toby nodded and bit into the pork. Sauce oozed out of the side and ran down his chin onto his beard, joining the other stains there. Bill handed him a napkin.

Toby was about to wipe the sauce on his sleeve, but, after a moment's hesitation, he took the napkin. "Thanks."

A trailer all to himself and the best barbecue in the southeast.

Toby thought he was one lucky guy.

—◈—

Toby's luck ran out. The day of the storm, Toby had presented his letter to the Island Authority Office, expecting, given his background, they'd place him in some position of authority, perhaps a security supervisor for the festival. To his surprise, they handed him a tee- shirt with the word "Staff" printed on it and a broom and dust pan with a long handle. Toby kicked himself for not finding a way to take a look at what was in that letter. Someone must have ratted him out as a felon awaiting trial. All lies, of course.

He worked his way through the festival grounds, sweeping up half-eaten food and napkins, paper plates and beverage cups. People were such slobs, thought Toby. Why couldn't they put their trash in the receptacles provided? He wiped his runny nose on his tee-shirt sleeve.

He was so resentful at the low-level job he'd been given that he'd spent most of his shift plotting revenge on the Island Authority, Lewis and the Florida authorities who put him in this position. The night after he watched Mr. Smith depart and while the storm howled around the trailer, Toby drank.

The day after the storm, as Toby was stepping out of the bathroom on the festival grounds, buttoning up his pants, he bumped into Lewis.

"I've been looking for you."

Lewis was about the last person he wanted to see. "What the hell do you want?"

Lewis dragged him back into the bathroom. "We don't want to blow your cover. I hear you've been assigned the job of sanitation engineer."

Toby noticed the smile on Lewis' face. "I suppose you think that's funny."

"Given your personal hygiene and how you live, it is kind of amusing. I've seen your place on the Kissimmee, you know."

"It's comfortable." Toby resented the detective's tone of voice. Toby lived alone and had the place fixed up the way he liked it. Maybe others thought it was a shack... *Well, it was,* thought Toby. But it was home.

"You're supposed to be doing an undercover job for us. I haven't heard squat from you. This won't earn you a day off your sentence if you don't produce something."

"It takes time to get to know folks. You can't just start asking them questions. They get suspicious."

"You don't work but eight hours a day. Take your spare time and hang out with some of them. They're pretty friendly folks."

"I gotta git working."

Lewis' visit shook him up. Toby needed to stay on his good side, at least until something else materialized. He didn't check into work until noon, but all the barbecuers had been up since day break, repairing damage from the storm, then stoking up their smoke ovens and preparing the meat for the evening. No one would be at their trailers. Toby could take a good look around, and who knows, he might get lucky again.

By the time he reported for work, Toby knew the insides of all the trailers intimately. There wasn't a nook he hadn't explored, but nothing of interest showed itself. Until he happened by a battered pickup. Among the junk lying on the floor of the truck bed Toby spied a fire poker, the kind barbecuers used to move their coals around. Toby climbed into the bed, and with his handkerchief picked up the poker to examine it. He spied some rusty substance on the end of it. Might be something, might be nothing, thought Toby, but he had to get word to Lewis. He flipped open the cell phone Lewis had given him. Chain of evidence. Toby couldn't move the poker. Or could he?

CHAPTER 9

When Lewis presented himself at the door of the St. Simonton suite on Saturday night, he looked like a changed man. Emily opened the door and confronted a smiling Lewis, his eyes twinkling with good humor and perhaps a little mischief.

She turned in the doorway and yelled at her daughter. "Wow. Hey, Naomi, it's the proverbial cat who swallowed the canary." Emily gestured for him to enter.

She posed with her hands on her hips, willing him to notice her. Her hair was pulled back in a mass of curls on top of her head and ringlets framed her face. She wore a saucy little sundress that she'd purchased at one of the shops in Brunswick. She had on make-up, and her nails were polished. Earrings dangled from her lobes and sparkled in the light from the chandelier in the room. She felt like queen of the prom. Perhaps if he'd been just a little more friendly, concerned or sensitive, she might have chosen her words differently.

Instead, whatever he had on his mind that moved him from depression to top of the world, seemed to render him blind. Oh, she was happy he was happy. She didn't expect him to put his arms around her and plant a passionate kiss on her lips, but she would have forgiven him if he had uttered one complimentary word about how she had fancied herself up for him. And just to answer the door.

He wasn't stepping out with her for barbecue. He was taking her daughter, yet Emily had devoted time to transform herself from an efficient little apron-clad bartender into a desirable, tempting, door-opening dish. Couldn't he see this?

His glance hardly took her in. He strode into the room with his old confidence, and Emily decided, his old arrogant attitude. *What had she ever seen in this guy to make her drag him into the shower that night?*

Naomi entered from one of the bedrooms and stopped short. "Here you both are. Now I can tell you my news. You'll never guess what happened!" He was about to share his victory with them, but Emily interrupted before he got another word out.

"You found the murder weapon and have arrested the guy who killed Everett Pratt."

Emily and Naomi watched Lewis deflate like a New Year's balloon on Jan 2.

Just one compliment. One word and I'd have been nice to you and let you believe we didn't know your news. But oh no, you're so full of yourself, you couldn't acknowledge someone else.

Naomi shot her mother a dark look. Lewis sank into the couch. "You know?"

"No, it was just a wild guess." She willed him to get her sarcasm, or would he miss that too?

"Mom, you don't have to be nasty."

Lewis dropped his head into his hands for a moment. "Clara must have called you with the news," he said to his feet.

"Yep." Emily couldn't help putting a note of triumph in her voice. "But," she said, feeling a twinge of guilt about how she was treating him, "I'm sure we're all glad the guy is behind bars. What a horrible way to die."

When he looked up, he seemed to see Emily for the first time this evening. "You look different."

"Oh, crap," she said, then stalked out of the room.

"I missed something, right?" said Lewis.

"Let's just go eat barbecue, and you can give me all the details about the arrest."

"You don't think Emily wants to go with us? She looks like she's dressed for a date."

"She's got a date. Kind of."

⬥

"I never thought Toby would come through for us, but he did." Lewis fairly bubbled over with details of the case as he and Naomi walked the festival grounds. "Right after Everett's murder we took barbecue samples from each of the contestants from the festival to compare against the sauce covering our victim. No match. I thought we'd hit a dead end, but now we've got the murder weapon. I know you find Toby repugnant, but this time he came through for us."

"Well, I hope his cooperation doesn't make you forget what a bottom feeder he is."

He looked at Naomi and saw disgust and fear there. Better to change the subject, he thought.

"Tonight is the big competition and the last night of the festival. This should be fun."

Naomi gave him a thin smile. "Thanks for bringing me. And don't worry about Mom. She'll get over her mad at you."

He hoped Naomi was right.

People crowded the grounds, stopping at the competitors' tents to taste the food. The judges had decided on winners in each category. Now it was time for the attendees to vote.

Lewis and Naomi paid their entry fees and were handed an envelope in which they found tickets. Each had the name and number of a barbecue contestant on it along with a label indicating the kind of barbecue.

"Okay, now what do we do with these?" asked Naomi.

"Let's ask this guy." Lewis approached one of the festival's officials.

"Take one half of your ticket and present it to the barbecuers in the booth and they'll give you a sample of their barbecue. When you finish tasting all you want to, take the other half of your tickets and go down there to vote for your favorites." The man pointed to the far end of the row of booths.

"So all we have to do is eat and enjoy, I guess." Naomi approached the first booth.

The sign over the tent read "Sam's Sauce: A Taste of Louisiana." Naomi gave the woman in front of the grill a Sam's Sauce ticket labeled "chicken." She was handed a small Styrofoam cup with a piece of chicken in it.

She popped it into her mouth and chewed. "Oh, that is heaven. So moist, and the sauce is just tangy enough."

"If you think so, don't forget to vote for us by putting the other half of that ticket in the box." The woman smiled at Naomi and pointed toward the ballot boxes. Naomi nodded her head in enthusiasm.

They worked their way down the line of booths, trying all the meats at each booth. They had sampled food at half the contestants when Naomi grabbed Lewis' arm and stopped him.

"I'm so full of barbecue, I don't think I can eat another bite. How can I make a decision which one I like best?"

"Why don't we take a break? I'll buy you a beer, and we can sit over there." Lewis pointed out an area where chairs had been put up and a tent erected. "Looks like there's going to be music."

A band was setting up under the tent, and people seemed to have the same idea as Lewis and Naomi. The seats began to fill up.

They grabbed their beers and sat. After several minutes listening to the music, which was so loud

Naomi thought her eardrums would burst, Lewis leaned over and spoke.

"What?"

Lewis leaned closer. "I said, let's walk off the food and the beer. I'm not crazy about the music."

They continued strolling along the booths, sipping their beers. On occasion, they'd stop and sample the barbecue again.

Near the end of the line they encountered a booth with a basset hound tied up at the side of it.

"The Pratts are here. I heard the family needed the money." Lewis gave the dog wide berth. The hound opened one eye and examined the tall detective stepping near his food dish. The canine gave a short, but unenthusiastic woof as if to warn the human away from his vittles.

"Howdy, Mrs. Pratt." Lewis tipped his hat to Melanie Pratt who greeted him with as much enthusiasm as had her basset hound. "I guess you're relieved we found your husband's killer."

Melanie Pratt served up a helping of barbecue to a customer, then looked at Lewis with skepticism. "I suppose. If you got the right man. It's hard to believe Bill would murder someone. He seemed like a good guy."

A tall man, skinny, but with a large belly, stepped in front of Mrs. Pratt. His apron was covered with reddish-brown sauce, making it look as if he had been in back butchering the meat they were cooking. "Trouble, Mama?" He held onto the large barbecue fork as if he was prepared to skewer anyone who gave his mother lip.

"You remember Detective, uh, the detective who's working your daddy's murder." This was said with a monotone Lewis was growing to expect from the woman. It seemed as if she could find nothing in her life to be interested in, not even knowing who killed her husband.

"What're you doing here? I thought you got daddy's killer." His tone was both suspicious and challenging.

"We got him. I'm just here to taste some barbecue."

The son turned without a word and headed back to the smoker, muttering under his breath.

Mrs. Pratt's gaze followed her son then shifted to Lewis. She paused a moment as if she saw something in Lewis that made an explanation for her son's behavior necessary. "He's aggrieved cuz of his daddy's death."

"And taking it out on the world," said Naomi low enough that Mrs. Pratt wouldn't hear her.

"I suppose you want a taste of this here barbecue." Before either Naomi or Lewis could answer, Mrs. Pratt slopped a spoonful of meat and sauce into two cups and handed the samples to them.

"Go on. Give it a taste." They did.

Naomi groaned in pleasure. "This has to be the best barbecue here."

"Told ya." Again there was no joy or pride in her voice, just that flat tone as if she was describing doing her laundry, but suddenly she flashed a smile. "It's my daddy's recipe." As quickly as the smile appeared, it was gone.

The dog raised his head and gave his stomach a scratch, then moaned and plopped his head on his paws. His gave Lewis a final look and closed his eyes.

"Let's go." Lewis tipped his hat to Mrs. Pratt and steered Naomi to the next booth.

"What's with you and the Pratt dog? He acted like he knew you."

"All too well. We've shared the same close friends." Lewis bent over to give a scratch at his ankle.

"There must be twenty or more contestants here. More than back in Florida." Naomi's eye wandered over to the ice cream booth. She was full of barbecue, but not of ice cream.

"This is bigger, but with this murder wrapped up, some of them will return to Florida, and we can do the Big Lake cook-off there now." Lewis let out his breath and sighed in relief.

Naomi stopped, grabbed Lewis' hand, and squeezed it. "I'm glad this case is over. I'm not glad Toby played a role in it, but I'm happy for you."

"Toby found the murder weapon. I've got to admit he surprised me. What also surprised me was its appearing like that. I know we searched everyone's trucks and trailers thoroughly. Why would it suddenly turn up and so out in the open too?"

"Maybe the murderer planted it there thinking somehow it would throw suspicion off himself."

"Some odd form of reverse psychology? Maybe." *Did Toby have something up his sleeve?* It was a thought Lewis didn't want to entertain, but, he had to admit, it had occurred to him. He shoved it to the back of his head as he'd done earlier, then admitted it was something he'd have to consider more carefully.

"How do you know it was the murder weapon?"

"It matches the victim's wounds, and we're waiting for the analysis, but it's a good bet the blood on it will match our victim's." Lewis watched Naomi's face blanch at his words.

"I think I've had about all the chicken, rib and stuff I can eat." She tossed out her sample of pulled pork, and the man in the booth who gave it to her looked as if she had slapped him in the face.

"That bad?" the man asked.

"Oh, no. My stomach is a little off tonight, that's all," she lied.

They continued down the line of booths heading toward the ballot boxes.

"They should be ending the voting soon. Do you want to stay to see who the people's choice in each category is?" Lewis thought perhaps he'd ruined her evening by talking about the murder.

"Sure. Why not."

The booth just before the balloting area was closed. "What's that all about?" asked Naomi.

"That's the guy who's our murder suspect. Name's Bill Harper. Toby found the fire poker in the bed of his truck."

❖

Toby watched the big detective and the young woman seat themselves and await the announcement of the winners. Toby didn't care who won the barbecue contest. Tonight Toby was the big winner. He ducked behind his cousin Bill's closed booth and waited in the shadows for the man he had arranged to meet at nine. *Too bad that fire rod had been found in Cousin Bill's truck, but it fit so perfectly.* He told Lewis that too. Everett Pratt had come in first in the last five contests beating out Toby's cousin who took second place. Bill was furious, and that kind of anger could erupt into a killing rage. Toby had seen it many times as a cop.

Toby spit chaw juice onto the ground and patted his pocket as he waited. Lewis had given him fifty bucks for his good work and made him promise to return to Florida the next day. He said he would. *What choice did he have with only fifty bucks that soon would be spent on a bottle of whiskey and gas money for his truck?*

He'd taken a cash advance on his credit card, maxed it out and given ten of it to one of the kids on the cleaning crew and had him buy some jars of barbecue sauce, specific containers from one of the contestants. They weren't for Toby's use, but, if he was right about police procedure in this case, the bottles were insurance. He carried the bag with them in it as if he was transporting gold. It was, thought Toby.

"Toby Sands?" The voice came from behind him and to the right, but the blow to his head came from the other direction.

Toby awoke a few minutes later and fifty dollars poorer. Not only did he lose Lewis' money, but he failed to finalize his deal. To others it might look like simple robbery. It wasn't. That Toby knew. A whack on the head wouldn't scare away ole Toby. He prided himself on what others thought was his stubborn nature. He thought himself dedicated. To making money. He chuckled a bit.

And he was smart too. Because the man called his name, he knew he had the right fish on the line. Toby just needed to take great care to reel this big one in. He looked around on the ground near him. The bag was still there, but were the jars intact? Toby rummaged in the sack. Yes. They had been carefully wrapped in paper, and not one was broken.

"Help," he called. "I've been robbed."

Detective Lewis seated only yards away, came running, and with him came the chance of additional funds to get Toby back to Florida, back to home ground where he could finish up on several of his schemes. Toby smiled to himself as people came to his aid.

―⚜―

Lewis sent Naomi back to the hotel in a taxi while he talked with Toby as they waited for the festival paramedics to arrive.

"I ain't going to no hospital." Toby allowed them to examine his head and bandage the abrasion, but he refused further medical aid.

"You might have a concussion," insisted one of the paramedics. Tony remained adamant. *No hospital.*

"Well, at least get him home. He needs to rest," the paramedic said.

"Where are you staying? I never did ask." Lewis really didn't want to know now, but since no one else seemed willing to help out, it was up to Lewis to take Toby somewhere, and it wasn't going to be back to Lewis' condo.

Toby gave Lewis a slidey-eyed look. "Uh, I'm staying with a friend."

"You have no friends."

"A guy from the festival let me have his trailer. He was spending all his time at his girlfriend's so it was empty."

Everything in Lewis' head got very still and his body froze. "You don't mean you were living in Bill Harper's trailer, the guy who owned the truck where you found the fire rod?"

"Yeah. Now isn't that a dirty shame? Guy seems like a real dude, gives you a place to stay, and it turns out he's a killer."

Lewis grabbed the back of Toby's shirt and pulled him onto his feet. "I should have known better than to let the captain talk me into using you to help find the murderer."

He shoved Toby in the direction of the trailers and fifth wheels. "I thought there was something fishy when we searched his trailer. He was so well groomed and clean yet the trailer was a pig sty."

At the door of the trailer, Lewis groaned and slapped his forehead. "How could I be so blind? There's your spit can. I shouldn't have missed that."

"So what? I didn't know the guy was a murderer until I found that rod. And I called you right off, didn't I?"

Lewis shoved Toby into the trailer. "Go to bed. And be back in Florida by tomorrow night. If you're not dead by then."

Lewis knew his case was about to suffer severe damage. He didn't know what Toby did, but he did something. If ever a concussion killed anyone, Lewis prayed it would be Toby. He could have killed Toby himself.

⚜

"Mom? Are you here?" Naomi was breathless as she rushed through the door of the suite. The room was dark with only the small lamp on the desk left burning.

Emily stuck her head out of one of the bedrooms. "What are you doing back so early?"

Naomi explained about Toby being robbed. "Good. It's what the slime ball deserves."

"Well, I agree, but it was cash Lewis had given him."

"Lewis is an idiot giving that man money. And for believing him about that fire poker, too."

"You don't think he found it where he said?"

"Oh, I think Toby found it, but who knows where. And finding it in someone's truck doesn't mean that person is guilty. It would be just like Toby to have planted it there."

"Why?" Naomi plopped down on the couch.

"Who knows what goes through that cretin's addled mind, if he has one."

Naomi looked at her mother in surprise. "You weren't going to tell Lewis that, were you? Earlier tonight, I mean? You would have ruined his entire evening."

Emily smirked. "Nah. Good thing I held off. I'll let Toby ruin it instead."

Emily continued to look pleased with herself.

"What's up?" Naomi could see she was dying to divulge some tasty morsel of information.

"Well, you know how Lewis got fleas from that dog, the one Mrs. Pratt claimed she took to the vet the morning her husband was killed?"

"So?"

"When the authorities called the vets to confirm her alibi, the person on the desk looked at that day's schedule and told them she had scheduled a flea bath."

"So? That confirms her alibi."

"But if the hospital gave him a flea bath, why was he still scratching so much? He still had fleas, and they jumped off onto Lewis."

"And you've figured out why."

"The hospital had an emergency that morning. Mrs. Pratt waited for half an hour or more, but the staff was tied up. She was given shampoo and flea treatment, and she left."

"How do you know all this?"

"I had the evening to think. And I called Clara to do some sleuthing for me. If Lewis had talked to the personnel on duty that morning, he would have found out another story. Of course, it would have taken a bit of digging to find out what happened because things were in such a state that morning at the animal hospital."

Naomi was about to interrupt, but Emily took a quick breath and held up her finger to signal there was more.

"Lewis was so certain I was wrong about the motive for Pratt's death. He thought it had to do with the barbecue competition, and, of course, I knew it was more personal than that. Lewis isn't such a smarty detective as he thinks. Ha."

"So Mrs. Pratt had plenty of time to get back home with her flea-infested dog, bump off her husband, plant him in the cooler and then sic the dog on Lewis."

"Right." Emily had a smug and triumphant look on her face. "Do you think he's back at his condo by now?" She walked over to the phone.

"You're not going to call him, are you? Hasn't the poor guy had enough trouble for one night?"

"He hasn't had trouble from me yet tonight."

"This is all about your embarrassment over the other night when you jumped into the shower with him. Then tonight you got all gussied up, thinking he'd notice, and he ignored you because he was preoccupied. You're punishing him for your flirtatiousness." Naomi looked disappointed in her mother.

"No, I'm pointing out his shortcomings, that's all."

She grabbed the phone and punched in the numbers. It rang and rang and rang.

"He must be in the shower." She was angry with him, certainly, but she hoped he was soaping up alone.

⁂

The next morning, they said goodbye to Daisy and Rodney, thanking them for their hospitality and extending an invitation to come visit the Big Lake Country.

"Of course, aside from the country club, fishing on the lake and kick-up-your-heels music at cowboy bars, there's not much to do around there."

"Sounds like where I grew up in rural Georgia. The only excitement we had was chasing an occasional gator out of the chicken coop. I'd be right at home." Daisy smiled and pinched both their cheeks.

With hugs and kisses all around, Emily and Naomi hit the interstate. Before they took the bypass around Jacksonville, Emily spotted Lewis' police cruiser in front of them. "Pass him."

"I'm already going five miles over the speed limit. I don't need a ticket."

Emily slumped down in her seat and pouted.

Lewis slowed and took the next exit. As Emily and Naomi sailed past, Emily stuck out her tongue at him. Lewis looked at her in surprise, and almost ran off the road.

Oh God, thought Naomi, it's difficult trying to raise a mother with hormones so unruly they hurled themselves in adolescent rebellion at a cop and a bass fisherman turned bartender. Emily had taken on Lewis in this murder case, and Naomi was certain her mother and Donald would find something to spar about. They always did. Both men had personalities like two Brahman bulls in the same pasture. There wasn't enough room in the entire county for both those men's egos when it came to her mother. She gripped the wheel and drove, happy to be going home, but knowing the level of testosterone was about to become dangerously high across the Big Lake.

CHAPTER 10

"It's good to have you back on the job." Clara checked the shelves and coolers behind the bar and the back room taking inventory of their booze supplies in preparation for the coming week.

"Did Donald give you trouble while I was gone?" Emily toted in cases of beer and put the bottles on ice.

"No more than usual. He belly ached daily about not getting in enough fishing because he had to work. And, of course, he blamed you for eating into his time on the lake."

"Of course." Emily looked up and spotted a familiar truck through the window. "He just pulled in."

"Good. I'm glad I finished up here. I'm not in the mood for another Donald day." Clara scooted through the door into the kitchen.

"I had a wonderful vacation. Thanks for asking." Emily lugged a case of beer toward the cooler and turned toward the storage room.

"Yeah. I heard. Wonderful if you like windstorms and tornados." He paused. "And detectives."

"I hardly saw Detective Lewis. He did take my daughter to the barbecue cook-off. I stayed in. I can't seem to get rid of the connection between the victim's body and barbecue sauce. The smell of smoke grilling makes me ill."

Donald followed her through the back door into the storage area.

She grabbed another case of beer. Donald was right behind her.

"So I guess you aren't interested in bartending for the festival. I hear they rescheduled it for two weeks from today. Maybe this time the competitors won't murder one another."

Emily tore open the case and inserted the bottles into the ice, tossed the empty case into the corner and started for another one.

"Are you working this morning, Donald?"

"You know I am."

"Well, I know you're on the schedule, but I don't see any work happening."

"You seem to be handling this just fine."

"I'm still your boss, you know. You get the beer. I'll handle the prep work."

Donald mumbled something under his breath, but grabbed two cases, stacking one on top of the other and headed back into the bar.

"See there. You're twice as efficient as I am."

He muttered again.

Nothing ever changes around here, smiled Emily to herself.

"So are you gonna tend bar at the festival or not? Money's good, better than here."

"Nope. I'd prefer working here where the only thing I can smell from the kitchen are fries and burgers."

After her shift, Emily tossed her apron into the laundry bin inside the kitchen door and headed for her car. Sparring with Donald all night left her feeling as wrung out as a tub of laundry at the end of the spin cycle. It would be nice to get back to her little home and sit in front of the TV with her daughter, eat popcorn and fall asleep halfway through the program.

She stuck the key in the ignition and turned it. Nothing happened. She tried it again. Again nothing. Someone banged on her window. She looked up and saw Lewis standing there. He signaled to her to roll down the window. She shook her head. First Donald all day at work sniping away at her. She didn't want to face the other man in her life who made her feel like aluminum foil on a tooth filling.

On the third try with no success, she rolled down the window and looked up into Lewis' face.

"Go ahead say it." She leaned her chin on the steering wheel waiting for his words.

"Need a lift?"

"No, say it."

"No, you don't need a lift?"

"Not that." Here we go, thought Emily. Round two of the day, this one with Detective Lewis pointing out her obvious shortcomings, rather the shortcomings of Stan the Sedan.

He said it. "You need a new battery or a new starter motor."

"No, you're only partially right. I need a second job to pay for whatever Stan needs." She dragged herself out of the car and walked toward Lewis' cruiser, knowing she'd have to bartend at the festival whether she spent the whole time nauseated by the smell of barbecue or not. *Life just wasn't fair.*

She turned toward the bar and saw Donald watching them through the open window. He was drying a bar glass.

"Shit!" she heard him yell. He held up the cracked glass, and she watched blood run down his arm as the broken pieces cut into his hand.

He tossed the glass into the trash. "Damn woman." This time he hollered even louder and shook his fist.

"Did you hear something?" Emily asked. "Coyotes, maybe?"

"We need to talk," said Lewis as he steered out of the country club and turned onto the highway.

"I'm bone tired. Make it some other time." Emily laid her head on the headrest and closed her eyes.

"Not about us, if that's what you're thinking. I need some information and your opinion."

"My opinion?" Emily was shocked. *When did smarty detective need her view on anything?*

"Seems your sources are better at getting information out of people than I am."

"I've got the touch."

"Or somebody you know has the touch." His words came out through clenched teeth.

That wasn't true, thought Emily. The reason she knew what had gone on with Mrs. Pratt's dog was because she asked Clara who dated one of the vet techs at the animal hospital who was friendly with the person working the front desk the morning of Everett Pratt's death. And so on. But there was no point in telling Lewis this if he thought she or those close to her had special sleuthing sensitivities he did not possess. *Let him think he needed her.*

"What else did you learn about Mrs. Pratt? I mean, other than she didn't give her dog his flea bath and neither did the vet's office." Lewis reached down and scratched at his ankle. Emily thought the itching should have subsided by now, but she noted there were still bumps and redness there.

What she care who killed Everett Pratt? Why get involved in this murder at all? Unless it was to show did up Lewis. Maybe Naomi was right. She was acting like a spoiled adolescent girl who had given away too much to a boy who didn't really care for her. She was trying to obliterate her embarrassment by making him look inadequate. She thought this over for a moment. *Okay, Naomi was right. So what?* Or maybe, said a tiny voice of her own, maybe it was so she could spend more time with the handsome detective?

"I know nothing about Mrs. Pratt," said Emily. And, if I'm smart, we should remain strangers, she added to herself.

"What are you keeping from me?" asked Lewis. He slowed for her community's security gate. "Got your card with you?"

"No. It's in my car back at the country club."

"How am I supposed to get in? Run through the gate? There's no one on duty at the office at his hour."

"I'll just walk the rest of the way." She put her hand on the door handle just as another car pulled up behind them.

"Hi there, Emily. Detective Lewis." It was Vicki, her next-door neighbor shouting out of the window of the car that had just pulled up. "You two been out on a date?"

"No!" they both shouted at once.

Vicki jumped out of her car, ran up and inserted her card in the card reader. The gate's arm swung up.

When Lewis pulled into her drive, Vicki again hopped out of her car and rushed over. "I've got Key Lime pie. I just made it today. I'll bring it right over."

Emily shook her head. "I'm a little beat after my shift, so maybe another..."

"I love Key Lime pie," said Lewis. He turned off the engine and followed Emily up the steps into her house.

"Naomi's here, so don't get any funny ideas about using my shower."

Lewis shrugged and gave her his best innocent look.

⁂

The next day Emily awoke early, just in time to see the sun make the pasture across the canal rosy with early morning warmth. To her surprise Naomi was already up and had made coffee. Even more surprising was spotting Naomi's bags sitting next to the porch door.

"Now, before you get all crazy on me, you know I need to get back to West Palm. I've got an apartment there, and I need to find a permanent job. I can't hang around here working on and off at the bar."

"I thought you liked being here. You seem to be getting over your fear of your ex. You haven't talked about him lately."

"He's always in the back of my mind, but there's been so sign of him since I signed the divorce papers. I think he's gone somewhere to mope or lick his wounds. I don't care where or why. I'm just glad he left. The little talk Lewis and Donald had with him after we found who killed the rancher you found in the dumpster helped convince him to make scarce, I think."

Emily reached out and enveloped her daughter in her arms. "It seems like I just found you and now you're leaving."

"I have to go. I need a life, my own life, not one where I'm hiding out terrified he'll show up again and hurt me."

"So you are still frightened."

"Sure, but it's less and less each day. Besides, I'll be only an hour away. I can call on you or Lewis or Clara or Donald if I need someone. And I'll be back for the barbecue festival. I wouldn't miss it. Maybe I'll bring Mom and Dad along." Naomi was referring to her adopted parents.

Emily walked her out to the car and helped tuck her luggage into the trunk. Naomi slid into the driver's seat and put down the top.

"It'll be a great drive to West Palm." She pulled her sunglasses off her head and slid them over her eyes. "I don't have to worry about you getting into trouble snooping around that murder case, do I? You are going to let Lewis work on this one alone, right?" Naomi removed her sunglasses and stared into her mother's eyes. Emily nodded her head.

"Is that 'yes I'll interfere with the case or no, I'll back off'?"

Emily shrugged, gave her daughter a final hug and waved her out of the drive.

"I won't help him if he doesn't need it," she said to the taillights of the car as it stopped at the corner, turned and pulled down the street.

Emily was delighted she'd be seeing Naomi in two weeks' time at the festival, yet when she went back into the house, her ebullient mood left. She threw herself down on the couch and stared at the living room wall. Naomi was on to a new life, which Emily knew was the right thing for her to do. Sure, Naomi had lots of friends here, but she needed a circle of friends younger than fifty and not all involved in law enforcement or snooping. She needed normal buddies her own age to hang out with.

Emily had her own life. Or did she? The living room's beige walls stared back at her with accusing dullness. She had her job, a good start on paying off the mortgage on this park model trailer, close friends here, a steady, but lousy paying job and a car badly in need of some part, probably expensive. The men in her life were simply trouble unless she counted Hap, Clara's father and Emily's lawyer. If she were twenty years older, she'd marry the guy, if she could pry him loose from all those blue-haired ladies at the retirement home, the ones who hovered around him and also managed to find their way into his bed. Men were always a problem, one she thought she'd avoid until she sorted out her feelings for Lewis. Or Donald. So that left what in her life? Nothing. Unless she got involved in solving this murder. That might be fun, engaging, challenging, but what could she do?

Hmm. Thinking about the murder and Hap's consorts brought back an image of a slim, eighty-year-old she'd seen Hap with at the movies right before she and Naomi had gone to Jekyll Island. He'd introduced her, and Emily had promptly forgotten her name. Sylvia or Sophie, but her last name was Pratt. Or was it? Maybe it was Taft. She'd call Hap and ask.

Someone pounded on her front door before she could complete her call. She dropped the phone back into the cradle.

"Hey, Emily. You up?" It was Donald Green.

"What do you want?"

"Now that's not very neighborly. I stopped by to see if you needed a ride to the club today. I know you're not working and neither am I so I thought we could go have a look at your car. But if you've got someone else to do it for you, say some law enforcement type, I'll mosey along home."

Emily wasn't certain Donald had a home. She'd never seen it, but he had to live somewhere, park his bass boat somewhere, shower somewhere...

"Sorry, Donald. I'm in a really bad mood today."

"Your boyfriend give you a hard time last night?"

"I thought you came to help me, not harass me."

She opened the door to Donald and waved him in. He peered closely at her face as he passed her and took a seat at the kitchen table.

"You look like you spent the night wrestling a gator. What's wrong?"

Emily was about to tell him to mind his own business, but she caught a note of true concern in his voice.

"Do you know anything about fixing cars?" she asked.

He nodded. "I know everything about engines no matter what kind. Why do you think I'm here if not to help?"

Well, she thought to herself, maybe you are here to help, but I also think you're checking to see if Lewis spent the night, you old reprobate.

On the way to the country club, Emily talked Donald into stopping by the Blue Heron Retirement Home. She hoped to find Hap there playing cards or watching television or romancing one of his lady friends. And she hoped the romancing was being done with their clothes on. Donald wasn't keen on accompanying her into the Blue Heron, but the day was so humid and hot, he also didn't want to run the air conditioning in the truck while he waited.

"Don't be such a grump. It'll only take a moment, and you can see the steer horns hanging on Hap's bulletin board."

"Why would I care about that?"

"Humor me." She pulled him into the recreation room where the residents were gathered at tables playing cards or sitting on couches on the other side of the room watching television or reading. Hap was not there.

Emily grabbed Donald's hand and led him down the hallway to Hap's room. He dragged his feet and looked as if the short walk was torture, but when they got to Hap's, Donald dropped her hand and stood in front of the door, his mouth hanging open.

He stared at the five-foot expanse of horns decorating the message board.

"Jethro," Emily said. "Big fella, musta' been."

The door swung open and Hap's head of unruly white hair appeared.

"Emily. And Donald. Come on in."

"We don't want to disturb you if you've got company." Emily noted the bed was made and empty, but she scrutinized the rest of the room as if she expected a nude octogenarian to emerge from under the bed or behind the desk.

"Sit?" he asked.

"No. We have to go see about my car. I stopped by because I'm following up on some information for Detective Lewis." Emily caught Donald's look of disgust out of the corner of her eye. Hap plopped himself into the wheelchair he usually parked in the corner of the room when he wasn't giving rides in it to the residents or an occasional nurse.

"You think the detective needs your help, do you?"

"Not at all. He's quite capable of solving this one on his own, but you know how he is. He insisted I help him out."

Hap smiled then cackled, slapping his knees with his hands. "You're a bad liar, Emily Rhodes, almost as bad as Detective Lewis."

"What do you mean?" she stammered.

"He left here not twenty minutes ago. Said he was stopping by to say hello, see how I was doing, but I figure from the way he steered the questions around to the murder he thought he could use me to find out where you or my daughter got your information on Mrs. Pratt."

Emily sunk wearily onto the edge of the bed. She hadn't duped anyone. She simply made a fool of herself with Lewis, and now, with Donald hearing the story too, he'd put his own unsavory spin on it. Which he'd hit her with as soon as they got into the car.

"Don't you want to know what I told him?" Hap's face had that cunning look on it, the one where he wanted something in return for what he was offering her.

"Want to go to lunch?" she asked.

Hap slapped his knee again. "Do I! The food around here is awful. Let's go to the ice cream shop."

"They don't serve lunch." Donald seemed almost happy to announce this disappointing news.

"Ice cream is lunch." Hap got up and opened the closet door. He grabbed his white Panama and clapped it on his head. The smell of naphtha wafted out from the depths of the closet.

"You don't mind taking Hap out to lunch, do you?"

Donald rolled his eyes at Emily's question.

"Think of it this way, sonny," Hap said to Donald. "She's a pretty woman, and you get to spend time with her. Course I'll be chaperoning. Unless you'd like to give me your keys, and I'll go. You two

can stay here. I just changed the sheets on the bed."
Hap winked at Donald.

"That does it. You'll get a small dish, no hot
fudge, you old gigolo." Emily grabbed his arm and
led him from the room. Donald followed after giving the bed a long look.

"What did the detective want you to ask me?"

"Oh, forget it, old man. You know darn well he
doesn't want me interfering on this case, but I remember you introduced me to a lady whose last
name was Pratt. Any relation to the victim?"

Hap stopped in the middle of the hallway and
placed his finger to his forehead as if trying to nab
a thought from his brain.

"I forget. This old mind doesn't work too well
unless it's properly fueled." Hap gave her a sly look
from under his bushy eyebrows.

"Fine. You can have two scoops, hot fudge sauce
and peanuts. That should sky rocket your blood
sugar."

CHAPTER 11

"**D**on't dribble any on your suit or tell Clara I fed you ice cream." Emily handed Hap another napkin to wipe the chocolate off his mustache. "She'll have my hide, what with your diabetes and all."

"She worries too much." Hap dropped his spoon into the empty sundae dish and settled back into his chair with a sigh.

Donald crossed and re-crossed his legs while he stared out the shop window. When that gesture didn't seem to get Emily's attention, he checked his watch, then tapped the crystal and peered at it with a scowl on his face.

Emily continued to ignore him.

"Now about your friend, Mrs. Pratt." Emily leaned across the table toward Hap.

Hap's chin dropped onto his chest and another sigh escaped his mouth followed by a snore.

"Don't try to fool me. I know you're not asleep. I need an introduction, sooner rather than later."

"You're awful impatient, aren't you? That's the trouble with you little Yankee gals. Too het up on getting somewhere."

"Hap, we're talking murder here. I'm no more 'het up' than the detective. He's got a man in jail he knows darn well didn't commit the crime. He's looking in the wrong direction, but will he listen to me? I'm just one of those little 'het up' winter visitors who expects law enforcement to work in a timely manner. It's personal, like most murders are. Besides, even if I'm wrong, any idiot knows when you get your tips from Toby, something's amiss."

Suddenly Donald seemed to be all ears. "You mean Toby was in on this case? Now that's just plain dumb. I thought Lewis was smarter than that."

Emily might criticize Lewis, but she felt defensive when Donald did. "Well, he didn't want to involve Toby. It was the county's idea. Some kind of plea deal, I guess."

"Still, Lewis should know better." Donald shook his head, but his face said he was pleased Lewis fumbled the case.

Emily ignored Donald and turned her attention to Hap once more. "Have you talked to Mrs. Pratt since the murder? How's she related to the victim anyway?"

"He was her brother-in-law, and from what she told me, she wasn't grieving at his demise. She said he was a no account and a skirt-chaser." Hap stopped talking and looked pensive. "Say, honey, maybe you got something there. Maybe it was personal. One of his women got jealous of the others."

"Or his wife might have. I've got to talk to her."

Hap picked up his spoon and licked it. "Okay, I'll get the two of you together, but it's gonna take more than a puny dish of ice cream for me to make introductions."

A shadow fell over the table. Emily looked up. Behind Hap stood his daughter.

"Hi, Clara. Join us in a cone?" Emily smiled up into her friend's face, but Clara's lips remained drawn across her teeth in a grim line.

"Whose idea was it to get my daddy to eat ice cream? I've got enough on my plate working at the country club and seeing to my son's inheritance suit. I don't need a father in a diabetic coma."

Some words of apology on Emily's part, the promise not to do it again on Hap's and everyone's heads together over the empty dishes finally led to a settlement: Donald, Emily, Clara, Hap and Mrs. Pratt would have dinner together on Saturday night. We're going to give Detective Lewis a group to reckon with, thought Emily, a posse made up of two octogenarians, a lawyer, one amateur sleuth with actual detecting experience, albeit it minimal, and a mean old bass fisherman. Emily mentally pumped her fist in the air. Her only concern was why Donald wanted to be part of it all.

Clara winked at her, then leaned over and whispered in her ear. "You've got a date with Donald."

Emily returned the wink with a look of horror. "I do not."

"You do not what?" asked Hap.

She stared at the tabletop for a minute, then sneaked a look at Donald. Clara was right. She'd never seen Donald look so happy. He was glowing as if he had a big ole bass on his line, and the glow continued long enough for Donald to determine she needed a new battery for old Stan. By the time he'd taken her to buy one and back to the club where he removed the old one and put in a new battery, Donald was back to his grumpy self.

On Saturday night three couples sat on the outdoor patio at the Sand Shark. Clara brought along her son Darren, an even six at the table.

Hap made the introductions. "This here is my bridge partner, Mrs. Lorelei Pratt." The older woman, dressed fashionably in a silver pantsuit, flashed a dazzling smile.

"Please call me Lorelei." She ordered a Cosmo, a double, and leaned her elbows on the table. "I hear you're somewhat of a detective." She scrutinized Emily with clear hazel eyes. "Hap says you'd like to pick my brain about the murder."

Well, that got right to it, thought Emily. At this rate she'd be out of here before the waiter came around again to take their dinner orders. Emily glanced at Donald who had slipped his arm around the back of her chair. She leaned away from him and focused on Lorelei.

"First, let me say how sorry I am about Everett's murder."

The waiter placed a large martini glass in front of Lorelei. She took a long sip and smacked her lips. "Too much cranberry juice, but otherwise acceptable, which is more than I can say about Everett. I thought about killing him myself on many an occasion. He was so mean to Melanie and her so long suffering. I told her to get rid of him years ago."

"Did you tell her how?" asked Emily, then clapped her hand to her mouth. "Sorry. That was rude."

Lorelei narrowed her eyes. "Am I a suspect? Cuz if I am, I guess I have a choice of whether to hire Hap or you, Clara, as legal representation."

"Emily's from New York." Donald spit out the name of the state as if declaring her origins somehow explained her lack of manners.

Everyone at the table nodded and looked sympathetic.

"I can't help where I'm from." She took a slug of her wine and choked.

"Of course not, and we forgive you." Lorelei handed Emily a tissue to stop the flow of tears.

"Thanks." Emily blew her nose and reached for her water glass. "You're not responsible for where you were born." Donald encircled her shoulders and gave her a squeeze.

Everyone nodded again.

"There's nothing wrong with being from New York." A defensive note had crept into her voice.

Donald had to be lying. She knew he thought it was almost criminal to be born outside of Florida. She quickly corrected herself. To Donald, it was a sin to be born outside this county.

"How can you stand all that concrete?" Lorelei wrinkled up her nose.

"I'm from the state, not the city."

"What's the difference?" Hap winked at her.

Emily decided it was time to get off her Yankee origins and get back to the murder. "Never mind. You were talking about Everett. How are you related to him?"

"Melanie and I married the Pratt brothers. One was a drunk and a womanizer, the other, my dear departed Charles, the best man in the county. A good provider, loving husband and father, a good Christian man. Not much to brag about in the sack. Not like you, huh, Hap?"

Hap raised his glass in a salute. Lorelei smiled at him, then slid her eyes in Donald's direction.

That's more than I needed to know, thought Emily, and less than I need to solve this murder.

"Everett took after his scallywag of a father and Charles after his mother, a real gentle soul. Everett was the youngest in the family, the baby and spoiled rotten."

"Did you know he was such a great cook?" asked Emily.

"The man couldn't cook his way out of a tunnel with an exit sign pointing toward the door."

"He won a lot of contests to be so bad at it." Donald signaled the waiter for another round of drinks, but the waiter dashed by the table without a momentary sideways glance.

"I'll tell you who the cook was. It was Melanie. And I'll bet the recipe was her daddy's. Everett was probably a thief as well as philanderer." Lorelei slammed her empty Cosmo glass on the table. "Where's a darn waiter when you need one?"

Oh, oh. This wasn't going to be as easy as she thought. She wanted to talk to Melanie without Lorelei suspecting Emily had her at the top of the list as a murder suspect. Maybe she'd go at it another way, the way a Yankee with no manners would.

"Here's my theory about the murder. I think one of his uh, women, did him in, probably got tired of waiting for him to get rid of Melanie or got jealous of one of his other women. Doesn't that seem possible? I'd sure like to know what Melanie thinks about this whole thing, but Detective Lewis wants to see the motive as related to barbecue competition." Emily sat back in her chair and watched the reaction on Lorelei's face.

"Why wouldn't you think of the wife first? Isn't that what all the television shows say? You wouldn't be wanting to back poor Melanie into a corner and pin this murder on her, would you?" Lorelei's hazel eyes took on the color of storm clouds.

That's a possibility, thought Emily, but she shook her head and tried to look shocked at such an idea. "I met Melanie the night of the murder. She sure didn't seem like a woman who had just killed her husband. She appeared to be in shock to me."

Lorelei nodded in agreement. "Just so."

Emily's attention was drawn away from the table by a couple entering the restaurant. It was Lewis and his wife, er, ex-wife, Emily corrected herself. *What was she doing in town?* Emily waved at them. Dumb, Emily, she said to herself. *Why did she do that?* The last thing she wanted was to get up close and personal with the ex-wife. And she was the ex-wife, Emily reminded herself, emphasis on the *ex* part.

He took his *ex*-wife's arm and led her over to Emily's table. Hap stood and made the introductions.

"You're Melanie Pratt's sister-in-law, aren't you?" Lewis' eyes had taken on the look of a predator about to pounce on his prey.

Maybe Lewis was working the personal angle as well as the business competitor angle, thought Emily. *Best not to underestimate the man.* "Don't let us take you away from your evening out." Emily wanted him gone from the table so she could pursue her line of questioning without the detective horning in on her act.

"Why don't you join us, Detective Lewis?" Lorelei patted the seat next to hers. "There's lots of room, and Emily here was asking me about Everett. I won't have to tell my story twice."

"I'm sure the detective wants to get away from work on his night out." Donald spoke through clenched teeth. "All work and no play, right, Mrs. Lewis?"

"I took back my maiden name. It's Milford, but call me Adrienne." She slid into the empty chair beside Donald and smiled at him with more intimacy than Emily thought called for in public. Emily suddenly found herself leaning toward Donald. Earlier she had wanted to sit as far away as possible, but this woman seemed to make Emily's estrogen boil over.

Lewis ignored the chair next to Lorelei, but pulled out the one nearest his ex-wife. Before he could sit, Adrienne touched his shoulder and shook her head.

"Be a dear and get me a gin and tonic, would you? You know how slow the service is in here."

Lewis reddened a bit, but headed toward the bar.

Adrienne locked eyes with Emily. "I hear you and my ex had to share a shower the night of the storm on Jekyll Island."

Well, that did it, thought Emily. She hated the woman.

"You what?" Donald withdrew his arm from her chair.

"Could we just talk about murder?" Clara had been silent for most of the conversation, but her face said she'd gladly change her birthplace to somewhere north of the Mason-Dixon Line just to get some information out of Lorelei. "It's so much simpler."

Adrienne wrinkled up her nose, but Clara dismissed her obvious distaste with a flap of her hand. "You don't have to listen if you don't want to, but, as a member of the court, I am intensely interested in solving this case."

Adrienne looked at Clara for a moment as if she was thinking about saying something, but she shifted her gaze back to Emily.

"What's your interest in the case? Other than my husband, that is?"

"Your ex-husband, you mean. And other than him, I stumble onto dead bodies with some regularity, and I just like to hang out with cops, I guess." Emily thought she heard Donald growl. "Oh, and bass fisherman, too, especially when they go after fish and find a dead body."

"You did that? You found a dead body too?" Adrienne batted her eyelashes at Donald.

"Once, just once, and it was Emily who caught it on her line. That was last year. We wrapped up that case long ago, but if you're interested, I can take you out in my boat and show you..."

Without a word, Adrienne got up from the table and walked off toward the bar where Emily watched her grab Lewis' coat and pull him toward the door.

"Damned short attention span. She was married to a detective. I thought she'd like talking about cases." Donald looked genuinely sorry to see her go. Everyone else seemed to welcome her absence.

"I apologize for asking the two of them to join us." Lorelei's voice sounded sad for only a minute, then changed. "Where is that waiter? I am dry as a gator hole in a drought."

"You said you thought of killing Everett yourself on occasion."

"Tenacious little thing, aren't you?" Lorelei narrowed her eyes at Emily. "But I like your honesty. The man was killed with a barbecue poker, I understand."

Emily nodded.

"Well, that's not the way I'd do it."

"It's not the way most women would murder someone," Clara added.

"I'd kill him slowly. Make it look like he was sick of something. Poison, of some kind, that's what I'd recommend."

"Poison? Like rat poison, maybe?"

Everyone looked up from the table toward the man who spoke. Detective Lewis stood there, hands on his hips and a scowl on his face. His gaze travelled around the table and came to rest on Emily. A slow smile replaced his earlier frown.

He leaned down and whispered in her ear. "You think you can find out who the poisoner is before I can? I'll bet you a bottle of shower gel."

※

"What did he say to you?" Donald hadn't spoken a word since they left the restaurant and got into his truck. She knew the evening wasn't quite what he had planned, but she'd be darned if she'd try to make it up to him by sharing Lewis' snide comment.

Despite Lewis' put down of her sleuthing skills, her evening wasn't entirely a bust. She and Lorelei had arranged for lunch tomorrow without the others. Emily wanted to know more about the family. She didn't believe Lorelei was the one who was lacing Everett's food with poison. *It had to be someone close to him. Like Melanie. Or one of his lady friends. Or someone in the family. Surely not the basset hound.* Naomi ran into the son at the festival on Jekyll Island and said he was an unfriendly guy. She wondered who lived with Everett and his wife. Was there poison in the house, perhaps in the gardening shed or storeroom or under the sink? Did the poisoner get impatient with how long it was taking to kill Everett and decide to bash him in the head to get the job done faster? A million questions pounded in her brain. Lewis would know some of the answers, but she wasn't going to ask him.

"You're mighty quiet." Donald looked away from the road to gaze at Emily's face.

"Watch it!"

Donald turned his attention back to the road ahead just as a large creature crossed in front of the truck. He slammed on the brakes and swerved into the left lane, missing the retreating form as it dashed off into the palmetto and scrub on the other side of the highway.

"What was that?" Emily's voice shook and her fingers tingled with residual fear at having almost collided with the animal.

"Feral pig. I missed it. Good thing too. This one was big. It might have caused a lot of damage to the truck if I'd hit it."

"What about damage to the people in the truck?" Emily shivered at the thought of lying injured on the dark road at this time of night. Not many people came this way.

"Oh, sure. That too." Donald slowed the truck and sneaked a look at her. "You okay?"

"I'm fine. Where do those things come from? Some farmer's field? They ought to have better fences."

Donald laughed. "They're feral, wild pigs. No one owns them. There are thousands of them around here. A few are pure bred Eurasian boars, but most are hybrids, a cross between the boars and domestic pigs."

"Just when I think I'm getting used to this place, something pops up to make me uneasy. Gators, and now feral pigs."

"Well, this land belongs to the gators, but the pigs, well, they were brought in by the Spaniards."

"When I was a kid we visited my uncle's farm. One of the sows had a litter of little ones. They sure were cute."

Donald snorted. "Stay far away from these pigs. They grow four large incisors, razor sharp, and the mamas get very upset if you come between them and their little ones."

It was always something, thought Emily. If the gators, mosquitoes and the pigs don't get you, then a dead body might. She sat back in her seat and longed for the comfort of her little apartment up north where the only pigs were the ones at the market in the form of pork chops. She sighed. *Might as well admit it. I'm Yankee through and through.*

CHAPTER 12

Toby was uncomfortable at the marina in Stuart. He was not fond of water or boats of any kind. Although he was at dockside and the depth there couldn't have been more than six or so feet, looking down into the water gave him the jitters. It wasn't just the night and the water. Face it, Toby, he said to himself. *Mr. Smith gives me the jitters*.

A hand grasped his shoulder and squeezed, then squeezed harder.

The person crushing his shoulder let go abruptly, laughed and slapped him on the back as if they were old friends. They were not friends, but old business acquaintances in a deal that didn't quite work out for either of them. Toby didn't know who he feared more, Mr. Smith or this cop gone bad, a rogue with a zeal for humiliating women.

"You know, Toby, you get uglier every time I see you. Anyone ever tell you you look like a troll? And the beard. There's a nice addition to your sickening appearance." Barry Montrose made him nervous. Montrose was a dirty cop, and although some might put Toby in that same category, Toby didn't think of himself that way. In fact, he disliked cops on the take. Toby wasn't a bad cop, merely one who was misunderstood by his colleagues.

To prevent Montrose from seeing the disgust and fear on his face, Toby raised his hand and stroked his beard. He was glad he grew it. Playing with his mustache and fondling his beard made him feel manly, courageous even. Most of all, he thought it made him look distinguished.

The man who spoke disparagingly of Toby's growth was Naomi's ex-husband. Toby had once done him a favor expecting to be paid well for it, but most of the money hadn't materialized even though Toby had handed over Naomi to him as agreed. The young woman had gotten away from her abusive husband, shooting him to make her escape. Toby knew she humiliated him. A girl shooting a cop. Toby thought about how he'd lost out on that deal and wondered if Montrose was foolish enough to stiff him again. Or was Toby fool enough to let him? Nope, thought Toby. I'm on my guard this time.

"Bungled it again on Jekyll Island, didn't you, you twisted little man?"

"Blame the weather, not me, or better yet, blame your Mr. Smith for being too chicken to hang around in a little blow to do the job."

"'A little blow.'" The words came out of the darkness behind Toby, no more than two feet away from his ear. They sent a tremor into his soul, and for a moment, he wished Naomi's husband was crushing his shoulder instead. "Perhaps we should take the troll with us when we set sail with our cargo. Take him prisoner also. We don't need him. I'll make some arrangement to get her."

"You don't have the connections. Toby does. Do you realize how out of place you'd look in cow country here? No, Toby's our man." With this, he grabbed Toby's shoulder again and squeezed. Hard. "Huh, Toby? You'll do the job right this time. Or I'll never use you again. And no one else will either."

Smith said nothing, merely looked down at Toby, his cold eyes paralyzing any response Toby might have given.

Toby hated both these men, and someday, he vowed, he'd get back at them for treating him like a cretin. For now, he'd just play along. And live through another night.

⚜

Emily waited for Lorelei at the Cattleman's Ranch, one of the area's newer and better restaurants. Unfortunately, its specialty was barbecue, and the odors emanating from their kitchen made Emily nauseous. Just as well, she thought. *I think I'm putting on a little weight. It must be investigating these murders. I always seem to be questioning someone in a restaurant.*

"May I join you?"

She looked up and straight into those piercing eyes of Detective Lewis.

"No, you may not. I'm meeting someone, and the conversation is private." She crossed her arms in front of her chest and stuck out her chin at him.

He ignored her and sat. "Thanks."

"Are you following me?"

"I've got better things to do than to tag along behind some little gal who thinks she's smarter than me."

Emily harrumphed and tucked her arms more tightly against her chest. She was more than a bit tired of men referring to her as "a little gal."

"You might be interested to know I talked with Melanie Pratt this morning."

Emily's face brightened, she dropped her defensive pose and leaned forward. "What did you find out?"

The look of triumph left the detective's face. "Nothing much."

"You need a warrant to search her house, under the sink, or in the garage, storage shed, whatever."

"You think I don't know that? I'm working on it."

Emily smiled, a tiny muscled twitch that twisted only one corner of her mouth up. "Me too."

Storm clouds gathered on Lewis' face. "Emily, Emily, Emily. When will you ever learn? This work is for a real detective." He got up without another word and walked away.

He tipped his hat to Lorelei Pratt who entered the restaurant as Lewis walked toward the door. Before he exited, Emily saw him turn and give her a final severe look.

Pig-headed cop.

"So what was our friend, the detective doing here?" Lorelei slid into the chair opposite Emily's.

"I don't know. Maybe he took an early lunch."

"He stopped by to talk with you?"

Emily hesitated before she replied, knowing that what she was about to do didn't feel quite okay with her conscience.

"Yeah, he did." She leaned forward and grabbed Lorelei's hand. "He's looking at Melanie for the poisoning and for the murder. We need to do something. Maybe, if I talked to her, I could change the detective's mind."

Lorelei scrutinized Emily's face. Whatever she saw there convinced her to trust Emily. "Right. Let's grab something to go and visit Melanie. I love that gal, and I'd sure feel bad if the detective railroaded her into jail."

"So would I." Emily crossed her fingers. It wasn't exactly a lie, especially if Melanie wasn't guilty, but if she didn't poison her husband, who then?

⸻

Emily had second thoughts about driving Lorelei to Melanie's house as she steered recalcitrant Stan the Sedan down the potholed sandy route.

"Turn here." Lorelei gestured to a driveway that was even more bumpy than the road. "Right, there it is."

Emily applied the brakes to Stan who came to a stop with a shudder, the automobile equivalent to a sigh of relief. Directly in front of them the oldest trailer Emily had ever seen. In places the aluminum siding hung to the ground as if someone tried to strip the siding bare, but failed, leaving the structure looking as if it had been unsuccessfully skinned. An air conditioner, tipped precariously out one of the front windows, stuttered and droned. Water dripped from the bottom of the unit and ran down the side of the trailer in a rust-colored stream.

This was the home of the winner of barbecue contests throughout the southeast? Emily couldn't believe it.

Melanie slammed open the front door. It threatened to fly back in her face, but she caught it in time. She nodded at Lorelei, giving little hint they were sisters-in-law. "I'm not prepared for visitors."

And I'm not prepared to question this woman in what she calls her home, Emily thought. The place appeared as if it might collapse under the weight of visitors. Maybe that's what Melanie meant by being unprepared.

As Emily searched for some excuse to leave, another woman appeared in the doorway. This one was younger than Melanie. Where Melanie looked as if she carried the burden of the world upon reluctant shoulders, her companion, a smile on her full lips, slipped her arm around Melanie and waved gaily for the two visitors to come in.

"Hi there, Lorelei. Haven't seen you around here much. C'mon in. I just fixed a batch of sweet tea."

"I'm Emily Rhodes." Emily held out her hand, and the younger woman shook it with enthusiasm.

"This here's Melanie's daughter-in-law, Stacy. Emily and I are here on business. We think that detective may want to arrest your mamma for murder, and Emily thinks if she talks to Melanie, she might convince the detective he's wrong."

Melanie's hand flew to her throat, and for the first time since Emily had met the woman, her face registered other than fatigue and depression. Now her expression was one of fear.

"That's just silly." Stacy drew her mother-in-law closer to her. "Mama wouldn't harm anybody, even Everett, though he sure deserved what he got."

"Who's there?" The voice was male and filled with suspicion.

Oh, oh, thought Emily. This had to be the son, according to Naomi a real unfriendly sort.

A man Emily recognized from her daughter's description of him pushed into the doorway. "Oh, it's you, Lorelei. Seems the only time you come visiting is when someone's died."

"My husband, Jasper, Everett's son. He's taking his daddy's death real hard."

To Emily's eye the man didn't look sad, rather his face conveyed hostility.

"Uh, maybe this isn't a good time." Emily took one step backward.

"Who're you?" Jasper spit out the words and leaned forward as if he contemplated launching himself at her.

"This is a friend, Emily Rhodes. Jasper. Your mamma's in trouble, and she's here to help." Lorelei certainly had chutzpah. She didn't appear frightened of the man at all.

"Help? How?" Jasper's anger didn't diminish, but seemed to increase in intensity. Emily watched a red flush color his face and spittle fly from his mouth. He reminded her of an enraged bull.

"I know Detective Lewis and..."

"He's got the killer in jail." Lorelei said.

Another man appeared behind Jasper in the trailer doorway. He was as lean as Jasper, but short. His face reminded Emily of a bat's with its long pointed nose and small mouth filled with tiny teeth.

"Elmer, my partner in the barbecue business." Jasper said.

The appearance of another male seemed to calm Jasper. He reached in his shirt pocket and pulled out a cigarette.

"Outside," said his wife.

"I am outside."

"No, you're standing in the doorway. That smoke is just gonna drift back into the kitchen, and the house will stink for days. Besides it's not good for Riana. She's only eleven. I want our daughter to grow up in a smoke-free house."

He pulled the cigarette out from between his teeth and slid it back into the pack.

"Elmer's right, isn't he? The killer's in jail?" asked Melanie. "I didn't kill him."

"Well, there's another issue the detective's looking into," Lorelei said. "We're here to explain, and Emily thinks she might help out."

"I gotta get to work." Jasper reached into the house and grabbed a denim jacket.

"You're cooking tonight? I didn't know there was a barbecue festival around here except for one rescheduled because of, uh, your dad's, uh, you know," said Emily.

Jasper gave her a look that said her comment was about what he'd expect from a dumb blonde, probably a dumb little gal blonde, thought Emily.

"I work at the box factory. Barbecuing is a hobby. Can't make no money cookin' meat." He and Elmer strode toward a pickup parked at the side of the trailer. The truck was as battered as the trailer. Man these folks were hard on metal, thought Emily. He and Elmer got in, Jasper taking the driver's seat. He hit the gas, spinning the wheels on the sandy drive.

"Never mind him. He's..."

"Grieving for his daddy," Emily finished for Stacy. *Yeah, that would make me crusty, too.*

"C'mon in." Melanie stood to one side and let Emily and Lorelei into the trailer. The inside surprised Emily. Everything was old and threadbare from the curtains hanging limply on the windows to the plaid couch, whose upholstery was worn thin by years of use, but the place was neat, clean, and nothing seemed out of place. The old hound dog slept on the floor in front of the couch. At their entrance, he raised his head and looked hopefully toward a dog dish on the kitchen floor, then turned his attention to the torn, but mended recliner that sat in the far corner of the living room.

"No food now, and you stay put, Milo." Stacy waggled her finger at the dog, who lowered his head with a sigh of disappointment, then scratched his stomach and returned to his slumber world of rabbits, squirrels and other creatures who would flee before his ferocity. Even dogs had their dreams, Emily conceded.

Emily settled herself on the sofa. When Melanie handed her a glass of tea, it slipped through her fingers and dropped to the floor.

"Oh, I'm so clumsy. I'll clean it up." Emily popped off the couch and dashed for the kitchen. Before either Melanie or Stacy could follow, she opened the door under the sink.

"I assume this is where you keep your cleaning rags." Emily stooped down as if to look for something to mop up the tea. Instead she explored the contents of the cupboard looking for anything like rat poison.

Melanie stooped down behind her. "Here. Let me. You're company. I'm out of rags here. There are some left in the bathroom, I think."

Emily pursued her down the hall, knowing now was the only opportunity she'd have to see what was stored under the bathroom sink. Melanie grabbed a cloth rag and turned to face Emily.

"It might stain. You know how tea is. Don't you have any cleaners there?"

"Cold water will take it out of the couch, and it don't' look like any of it spilled on you." She gave Emily an unfriendly look, as if she knew what Emily was up to.

Emily refused another glass of sweet tea, and by the time she and Melanie returned to the living room, Lorelei had finished hers.

Lorelei looked toward Emily. "You ready to go?"

Melanie led them to the outside door. "I guess you've seen what you need to."

Emily nodded in embarrassment. Her attempt to look into the trailer's cupboards and storage places was bumbling.

"You can tell Detective Lewis there's nothing here of interest to him." Stacy spit out the words and put her arm around her mother- in-law's shoulder. "You can also tell him not to send an amateur to do his job for him. I'm ashamed of you, Lorelei, for believing this woman's tale she wanted to clear Mama's name."

Lorelei delivered a look of disgust at Emily. "I surely am ashamed of myself." She opened the car door and got in. Before she joined her, Emily turned toward the trailer for a final look at the place. Despite her embarrassment at how lousy her detecting skills were, she wondered if she'd missed something. Maybe she had, but now was not the time to explore any further.

"Nothing, was there?" Lorelei looked at Emily with a smile of satisfaction on her face. "You are a traitor. That'll teach me to believe in a Yankee." Lorelei stared out the side window the entire way back to her place, then got out of the car and without a backward look, stalked up to her front door.

Emily drove off, feeling as if the entire endeavor had set the investigation back several steps. Instead of gaining Melanie's trust, she'd alienated the woman with her graceless attempt at finding the poison. How could she face Detective Lewis? She'd face him, she told herself, but only after she'd satisfied her curiosity about those storage hatches she'd seen under the trailer. All she needed was someone to help her.

Emily hummed tunelessly all the way back to her place. She'd almost decided to get in touch with Donald, but her daughter's voice on her answering machine back at the house told her she could skip putting herself in Donald's hands. It was just as well. He'd get ideas, and she didn't need that.

"Hi, Mom," said Naomi's voice on the machine. "I got a great job. I'm dying to tell you about it, but it doesn't begin for two weeks. I thought I'd come visit, and we could attend the barbecue cook-off together. Unless you're still off smoked meats. Call me."

She could do smoked meat if that's what Naomi wanted, but she was more interested in a smoker's storage area, and she wondered if Naomi was too.

She was about to return her daughter's call, when the phone rang.

"Hi, honey. I know this is short notice, but it's me, Daisy DuBignon St. Simonton. Hubby and I took a drive down here on a lark and thought we'd look you up. You gonna be home tonight?"

How fortunate. Daisy seemed like a woman with adventure in her soul, and Rodney might be just right for the position of look-out. No sense in getting Naomi involved if she could help it.

<hr>

"You want to do what?" Daisy and Rodney were seated on her couch each sipping some Maker's Mark.

"I have to work tonight, the late shift, but I'm sure it'll be a slow evening. We can get out of the country club around nine and drive on over to Melanie's place. I found out there's a meeting of the contestants for the contest, and it starts at nine. It shouldn't be over until ten or so. Plenty of time."

The information on the meeting came from the cook-off's manager, Big Chuck. She'd called to chat with him about working the event this weekend. He wasn't exactly suspicious of her call, but in order to get her information, she did have to promise him free drinks next time he came into the country club. She figured him for an old horse trader who never gave anything away for free.

Emily knew she was taking a chance on many levels. There was the possibility she would get caught. Or maybe she'd misjudged the St. Simontons, and they were more law-abiding than she was or less interested in getting to the root of a killing they had no interest in.

Daisy and Rodney exchanged glances.

"Well, heck, yes. We're in, aren't we honey?" Rodney seemed about to jump out of his wheelchair, and Daisy looked as if she might just help him do it.

"Sounds like fun and I haven't had a real adventure since the time last year we hid Bradley Murphy's Cadillac behind the local house of pleasure. You should have seen his wife's face when the police found it. 'Course Bradley had it coming. He was a real rounder." Daisy chuckled and slugged down the rest of her whiskey.

"No one suspected you two did it?"

"Honey, I'm in a wheelchair and my wife is a lady of some standing in the community." Rodney winked at Daisy.

⚓

By the time they got to Melanie and Jasper's place, it was after nine and there was only one light burning in the trailer.

"I think we're in luck. The entire family is out."

"They got a dog?" asked Daisy.

"Yep, but he's usually too tired or depressed to bark. I got this if we need it." Emily held up a thick steak.

"I'll stay here and signal if anyone comes. One if the cops, two if the residents." Rodney held up a large flashlight.

Emily and Daisy left him in the car which they parked by the side of the road in a thicket of Australian pines. They made their way up the asphalt and turned into the driveway. The moon was out, and there were no clouds in the sky. It was easy to find the driveway and to see the trailer ahead. Of course, admitted Emily, the light made it easy for them to be seen by anyone inside the trailer too.

"See those hatches underneath? We need to get in there and take a look. I hope they're not locked." Emily led the way toward the dwelling and stopped a short distance from it. Something or someone was moving around inside. As she stopped to listen more closely, she smiled.

"It's the dog. He just resettled himself." Probably in the forbidden chair, Emily thought. "Hear him? He's gone back to sleep."

Sure enough, canine rumbling noises came from within followed by several short snorts and a return to snoring.

Emily tiptoed up the front steps and onto the landing. She looked through the window and into the dimly lit living room. The basset hound, sleepily ensconced in the recliner, raised his head and looked back at her, then lowered it again and gave forth a moan of sheer doggy tiredness.

"We won't need the steak. He's more interested in sleeping than eating." She climbed down the steps and tossed the beef to one side to free up her hands.

While Daisy held the flashlight, Emily opened one of the doors. A tide of trash tumbled out into the yard. If the other hatches contained similar items, there would be enough junk underneath the place to fill a small garage. Everything appeared to have been tossed into the storage area without regard to function.

"We have to sort through all of this?" Daisy sounded dismayed. "Let's hurry."

Emily tossed paint cans, sections of broken ladder, and what looked like parts of an old riding lawn mower out into the yard so they could examine everything more closely. Once one hatch was empty, Emily began on another while Daisy, juggling their flashlight in one hand, replaced the articles in the first.

"I'm assuming we don't need to be too neat. They probably won't notice if things are a bit jumbled." Daisy tossed a mower wheel into the hatch and jammed the door closed.

"Here we go. Finally." Opening the door on a third compartment revealed gardening tools, rusted, broken or covered with caked dirt and a collection of plastic containers—plant fertilizer of various kinds and bags of potting soil, but no rat poison.

"With all this trash, you'd think there would be a lot of pests around here. Why wouldn't they have rat poison? I can't see the basset hound as much of a ratter. I'll bet he thinks dog food only comes in a can." Emily wiped perspiration off her forehead and stuck her head farther into the hatch.

Daisy stood up to move closer to Emily. When she did, she swept the flashlight across the yard. She let out a short gasp. "Oh, I think they have plenty of pests around here."

"Hey, I can't see a thing. Shine the light back here."

"Just close the door and let's go."

"But..."

"Now. We've got a visitor." Daisy's voice took on a note of fear.

Oh, crap, thought Emily, it's probably Detective Lewis. *He always shows up when I don't want him around.* But Rodney hadn't signaled them. What was going on?

"Who?" asked Emily.

"It's a what."

"What what?"

"As in reptile, large, behind you about ten feet. Let's move, Emily."

Emily turned around to look into the predatory eyes of a twelve-foot gator. "Oh, boy."

"Run!" yelled Daisy. She grabbed Emily's arm and the two of them fled across the yard toward the drive.

Emily glanced over her shoulder. "I don't think we have to worry. He's not interested in us." She grabbed the flashlight and shined the powerful beam into the yard to watch the large reptile make a one-gulp meal out of the steak Emily had tossed there.

"Don't be silly. That steak is simply the appetizer. We could be the main course." With her long legs able to cover more ground than Emily's short ones, Daisy almost lifted her off the ground as she pulled her toward the car.

"Wait a minute." Emily stopped short and turned toward the animal. "Shoo."

"Are you crazy?" Daisy tugged at her arm.

The reptile looked at the two women, then opened his mouth and moved toward them.

"Damn. It worked when Donald did it." Emily let herself be tugged toward the car.

"This Donald some kind of a gator whisperer?" Daisy was nearly out of breath.

"No, he's some kind of a mean bass fisherman with real attitude. He scares gators."

"You should have invited him along tonight, or, better yet, not tossed that delicious steak into the yard."

"It was one I had forgotten in the back of my freezer. I thawed it and found it was freezer burned." Emily panted between words.

"And you were going to feed it to that poor dog?"

"He's a dog, not a gourmand." Emily pulled open the car door and jumped in. Daisy slid into the driver's seat.

"You find it?" asked Rodney.

"We found something." Emily slid down in the seat in despair. Someone close to Everett had to have been feeding him that poison. It had to be someone in the family. Where would they keep it?

She thought back on what she knew of the family. Hap seemed to know of them before the murder. Hap knew everybody around the area.

She sat up and poked her head into the space between the front seats. "You two busy tomorrow?"

"Honey, we are not going back to that place. The family will come home and know someone was searching through their storage area." Daisy turned onto the main highway.

"No, not the house. I thought we might go for a stroll through the woods. I'll have to leave you out of this one, Rodney. Sorry." Emily leaned toward Daisy to try to catch the expression on her face.

"What do you have in mind?" Daisy sounded interested.

That's my girl, thought Emily.

CHAPTER 13

The next day Emily took Daisy with her when she stopped by Hap's room at the Blue Heron Retirement Center.

"You're gonna do what?" Hap sounded surprised, but not horrified at her idea.

Emily shook her head up and down. "But I'm not wasting my time if you think I'm on a wild goose chase."

"Likely not. The Pratt family, at least Everett's branch of it, has been around here for generations, and they have a reputation for ignoring the law. I can't say for certain, but I'd guess this would be one of those times the family would want to stick it to the system. And it would make them money on the side."

Someone knocked on Hap's door.

"You expecting company? We'll leave." Emily got up from the bed where she'd been sitting.

"Lorelei's coming to take me out to lunch. You could join us."

The door opened, and Lorelei stepped in. Today she wore a red warm-up suit and her shiny white curls were drawn back into a ponytail. She looked twenty years younger in this outfit. The frown on her face when she spotted Emily put the twenty years back on.

"Oh, it's you." Lorelei walked across the room and put her arm around Hap.

"Let me introduce you to my friend Daisy St. Simonton."

Lorelei hesitated a moment, then stuck out her hand. "You aren't from around here, are you?"

"No. My husband and I live in Brunswick, Georgia. We're here to visit Emily and take in some of the sights."

Lorelei let out what sounded like a snort. "Sights! Not much to see in this place, unless you like cattle and cowboys."

"Well, we do." Daisy smiled.

"I asked the girls to come to lunch with us." Hap opened the closet door to pull out his white straw hat.

"But we already have plans." Emily thought Lorelei looked relieved they wouldn't be joining Hap and her for lunch.

❖

"I wouldn't have minded having lunch with them, but you sounded as if you didn't like the idea." Daisy slid into the passenger's seat of Stan.

"I want to like that woman, but there's something about her that bothers me. I can't put my finger on it." Emily waved to Hap and Lorelei as she steered the car past them and onto the road.

"Maybe I can help."

Emily looked at Daisy with curiosity. "How?"

"I think I met her years ago, and what I know of her isn't good, although it's mostly rumor, one you might want to explore some."

As they drove back to Rodney and Daisy's motel, Daisy began her tale.

"You might say we were white trash, but Mama wanted me to be raised as a southern lady, go to the best schools, have my coming out party, meet all the right people, so she sent me to a women's college in Milledgeville, Georgia—a finishing school That had to cost her a bundle. Luckily she sold all that land to the developers when I was in my teens or we couldn't have afforded it."

Emily glanced at Daisy and chuckled.

"What's so funny?"

"I'm having a heck of a time imagining you as a 'finished' southern belle."

Daisy tried to put on an indignant look, but Emily could see it failed as one side of her mouth lifted. Soon laughter poured out of Daisy's lips.

"I guess I did get into a bit of trouble there."

"Tell me."

"I thought you wanted to know about Lorelei."

"I do, but I'll bet your days at that school are far more interesting. Lorelei can wait."

"Well, okay. One story about me and then back to Lorelei."

Daisy settled herself into the seat more comfortably. "The head mistress was a real pain. Rules, rules, rules, and she intended to enforce them. The curfew was nine o'clock on weekdays and eleven on weekends. I thought that was just stupid. When I was home, Mama let me stay out on the weekends as long as she knew where I was. I was a wild one, true, but I was smart, too. At school I kept accruing late minutes by coming in after curfew. The punishment was spending an entire weekend in my room."

"I'm certain you found a way around that." Emily sped up and passed a Cadillac with two white-haired folks in it.

"It was a challenge. Whatever I did to get out of my room had to be clever enough that I wouldn't be caught or eventually I'd be expelled. Mama's money would be wasted."

"What did you come up with?" Emily turned into the motel parking lot, eased Stan into one of the open slots and let Daisy continue the story.

"There were two women who were assigned the job of checking to make certain I was in my room. The monitor spies, we called them. I found out their weakness and simply bought them off."

"With what?"

"Godiva chocolate. It took a good bit of my allowance, but it was worth it. Anytime I got stuck in my room and decided to sneak out, I could count on their ignoring my absence if I slipped them a box of chocolates. That took care of that, but how could I find a way to get around coming in late? I knew if I did it many more times, the head mistress would finally recommend my expulsion."

"Somehow I doubt your choice was to come in early."

"Not me. I set up a committee. Anyone needing to stay out late on a weekend submitted their intentions to the Late Minutes Committee. Of course I was the head of it. Then we developed a plan for getting them back into the dormitory without being noticed or using up their allotted minutes. It took planning and forethought. No one could just pop in late and expect us to rescue them."

"That was the smart part of your wildness, right?"

Daisy nodded and continued her story. "Sometimes it was as simple as someone else signing them in when the head mistress wasn't looking and bribing the monitor spies with chocolate when they came around to do bed check. On one occasion so many girls wanted to stay out for a dance at the boy's school down the road, someone set the head mistress's wig on fire, and the fire department arrived. There was so much chaos, she never knew who came in that night. We used so many ploys to get extra time out, and they were so clever, we wrote them up in a book and gave them to the school when my class graduated. I think the book is still in the library." Daisy broke out in laughter and Emily joined her.

"I certainly picked the right partner for my stroll in the woods." Emily laughed and slipped her arm around Daisy as they walked to Daisy and Rodney's room. As Daisy inserted the key card in the lock, the door opened and Detective Lewis stood there glowering at them.

"What're you doing here?" Emily's good mood fled.

"The Pratt's reported a break-in last night."

"Oh? Anything of value taken?"

"Nothing taken they could determine, but their storage area below the trailer had been riffled through. But why am I telling you this? You must already know about it."

Emily batted her eyelashes at Lewis. "I'm not the kind of little gal to steal."

"I know that. As I said, nothing was taken. Someone was simply looking around. That couldn't have been you, could it?"

No one said anything.

"Here's the odd thing. When they got home, not only was there, uh, stuff, all over the lawn, but a big ole gator was sitting there acting as if the place was his."

"So it was the gator's doing." Emily couldn't keep the sarcasm out of her voice.

"Someone saw a car parked on the road up from their place. You think the gator drove there?" Lewis wasn't smiling when he spoke, and his clenched jaw forced his cheek to jerk. The guy had no sense of humor, thought Emily.

He sighed, strode to the door and clapped his hat on his head. "Don't make me mad. And don't make the mistake of thinking I'm not two steps ahead of you. I could have told you there was nothing in those storage compartments."

"How do you know that?" Emily was getting the feeling Lewis really was two steps head of her. *Damn.*

"We executed a search warrant yesterday afternoon." He smiled, tipped his hat to both of them and turned to leave, but stopped before he opened the door. The twinkle left his eyes, and his expression was once more serious. "You're playing around with murder. Stay out of my investigation, Emily."

"Or you'll do what? Arrest me?"

"Worse, much worse." A tiny smile moving its way across his lips broke up the stormy expression on his face. "I'll tell Donald Green you have a crush on him." He left, slamming the door behind him.

Rodney and Daisy exchanged looks.

"That man has got it bad for you. He's acting as stupid as I did when I courted Daisy."

⁂

Back in her park model, Emily realized Lewis' visit swept away all thought of what Daisy was going to tell her about Lorelei. Well, no matter. They could talk on the way to their rendezvous later this afternoon. She checked her watch. Time to jump into her work clothes and head for the country club. She ground her teeth together in frustration when she remembered she'd scheduled Donald to work afternoon and evening shifts. Fortunately she'd see him only when she set up. It was the Twelve Oaks RV Park's tournament dinner, and the bar would be swamped. That would be Donald's problem to handle.

As she drove toward the country club, she thought about Lewis' remark about telling Donald she had a crush on him. She hoped he was kidding. If Donald believed that, she didn't know if he'd drool over her or find the idea of romance beneath him. What did she care how he felt? Liking Donald was not an easy thing since it was never clear if he liked her back or merely tolerated her company. He had tried to kiss her once, but that was only when they both thought they were going to die. Imminent death did funny things to people, Emily thought.

Seated on a stool in the empty country club bar was Lorelei Pratt.

She and Donald seemed to be having a laugh together. The woman must have something going for her, Emily decided as she entered the room and grabbed her apron from behind the bar. Donald was not easily amused. Or at least, it was difficult to tell if he was ever amused since his expression rarely deviated from dour, but Lorelei whispered something in his ear as he leaned forward and the two of them grabbed hands and laughed loudly.

"Hi there, Donald. I'm surprised to find you here, Lorelei."

"I came to see you."

Odd, thought Emily. The woman did not like or trust her. With good reason, of course. Emily had lied to her about helping her sister-in-law, Melanie.

"And here I am." Emily started prepping the bar for opening.

"Could we talk, somewhere more private?" Lorelei threw Donald a look. "Girl talk."

"I'll finish setting up. You gals just babble away." *Babble? Donald said babble?*

Emily gestured toward a booth in the corner. "This is as private as it gets here. And we're expecting thirsty hoards to descend in less than a half-hour."

Lorelei slid into the booth and looked across the room at Donald. She waved a pinky at him, and he winked at her. Wow, thought Emily, the woman sure had a way with men if she could take on curmudgeonly Donald.

"I know we got off on the wrong foot, dearie."

Emily hated to be called "dearie" as much as she disliked the term "little lady."

She said nothing, simply nodded for Lorelei to continue.

"I'm very protective of Melanie. She's had a rough life with that husband of hers. What a bum he was. I thought you were being honest with me when you said you wanted to help her, but when I talked to Detective Lewis this afternoon, he said you were simply trying to win some kind of bet with him."

"There was no real bet. I'm trying to point out how wrong he can be about human nature." The woman sure had a busy afternoon, thought Emily.

Lunch with Hap, a tete-a-tete with Lewis and now a rendezvous with Donald.

"You mean about how jealousy and love can be powerful motivators for criminal acts? As important as greed?"

"Yes. Why were you talking to Detective Lewis? And why mention me?" Emily found the woman's behavior puzzling.

"I went to him because I think there's a relationship between the murder and the attempted poisoning. I wanted to tell him so. He told me that's what you thought."

"So you think your sister-in-law tried to poison her husband and then got impatient and bopped him with the fire poker?"

"No! I don't think Melanie was the one, but it was someone close to the family, someone Everett saw frequently."

Emily sighed in frustration. "Lorelei, you're making a case for Melanie. Who was closer than she and cooked his meals?"

"He ate only half his meals at home, Melanie told me. When they were at the cook-offs, he ate there, and no one would take the chance of poisoning barbecue meant for everyone. I told the detective to take a look at his women, and there were a lot of them over the years. The man was a satyr. Melanie said so."

"I can guess what Detective Lewis said. He's got his man and the poisoning issue is secondary now."

"Well, he hinted he had some questions about his case."

Did he? Emily was not surprised. Bill Harper certainly had motive to kill Everett since the man beat Bill at every contest in the last six months, but Toby had found the fire poker in Bill's truck. Where Toby was involved, there had to be something wrong.

"Did Melanie tell you their names? And why wouldn't she give them to the detective?"

"Well, I guess she did, but until now he wasn't real interested. I think he still thinks the murderer was one of the barbecuers."

"Where do you fit in this, Lorelei?"

"I know Melanie didn't poison him because she saw the hell I went through when I was accused of killing my husband. Not only is Melanie not a violent person, she's seen firsthand what false accusations do to a family. She'd never do that to her family. Not Melanie."

Emily gulped. "You were accused…"

"My first husband died under suspicious circumstances. They never determined the cause of death, but the authorities suspected me although they never brought charges. I finally moved away from Milledgeville. I'm sure your friend Daisy told you all this. She must have recognized me."

"Uh, no. She didn't." Emily kicked herself for not insisting Daisy tell her about Lorelei.

"Anyway. Here." Lorelei handed Emily a piece of paper with several names written on it. "You can get the jump on your detective friend. Between you and Detective Lewis, I like you better. I'm not fond of cops after what the authorities put me through with my husband's death. Besides, women need to stick together."

Lorelei got up from the booth without another word and wandered back to the bar. She and Donald took up their conversation where they'd left off. Soon the two of them were laughing. He reached over several times and patted Lorelei's shoulder.

The woman certainly was full of surprises. She had to be twenty years older than Donald, yet she exuded a sexual attraction as alluring as a minnow for a fish. Emily dropped her glance to the paper in her hand. Five names. Emily raised her eyes to the twosome at the bar. She wondered if those were the only women Everett pursued.

⚜

"It was nice of Rodney to come along." Emily and Daisy were a good quarter of a mile north of the Pratt's trailer, but according to the records in the county clerk's office, they were on land owned by the family.

"He's a dear man, and he likes to feel useful."

"Right, but I also think he's worried about this adventure and wants to be close by if we need help." Emily stopped walking and peered off to the right.

They left the car parked at the beginning of a gravel road set up by the county for hiking and bicycling. The trail wound through hammocks of pine and clusters of oak trees and meandered around a pond populated by a few gators, turtles and abundant birdlife—herons, egrets, mud hens. People, mostly snowbirds who had the time and interest in species alien to northern climes, preferred to observe rural Florida's wildlife here in their natural habitat rather than in the more intimate vicinity of swimming pools, backyards or under cars.

"Here's the path. Clara told me teenagers used to come back through here to find hideouts for their beer parties." Emily stepped into the shadow of the trees.

A few feet up the pathway, they encountered discarded food wrappers, beer cans and bottles and even a pair of girl's panties. Emily chuckled as she held up the underwear on the end of the walking stick she'd borrowed from Hap.

"Looks like they still party around here." Daisy passed Emily and continued up the path.

"According to Clara, we should find another path leading off through that stand of oak trees on the small hillock in front of us."

As they approached the trees, the brush seemed to close in around them and the vegetation grew heavier, palmetto making it difficult to walk. Emily caught a movement out of the corner of her eye. A snake slid silently into a heavy clump of vegetation.

"I'm not crazy about snakes." Emily shuddered and was thankful she thought to wear her heavy boots and borrow the walking stick. Daisy was similarly shod, but carried no stick to help her prod underbrush as they wound through it.

"If there's a path through those trees, I don't see it. Maybe it's overgrown. We'll have to make our own way, I guess. Maybe this will help." Daisy set down her backpack and extracted a machete from it.

"Wow! Where did you get that?"

"Heck. I always carry this in the car under my seat. I thought it might come in handy today." She brandished the huge blade in front of her and began to slash through the heavy brush.

Gosh, thought Emily, it was bad enough everyone around here sported some kind of gun, but a machete? The sight of that huge blade sent a shiver through her body.

"Well, I'll be dipped in honey and fed to the bears, there it is." Daisy pointed ahead at a small clearing among the trees.

"Shh. Let's make certain no one's around here now."

A ramshackle shed stood next to the apparatus, a large metal container, which narrowed at the top. Metal tubing came off it and into another container, and from this one, the tubing coiled around the inside of a galvanized bucket. It was a moonshiner's dream, an old still.

"It doesn't look like it's been in use for years." Daisy fingered a piece of tubing that dangled from the first container. "Bone dry."

"Maybe the barbecue business is more lucrative than Jasper led us to believe, and they abandoned the still."

"Or they found out the Tobacco, Firearms and Alcohol people were on to them. Good God, there's a cobweb here the size of a small boat." Daisy pointed to the gauzy home of a spider, which rested in the middle of it.

"Beautiful. A golden orb, I'd guess. Leave her alone."

Emily swiped her hand across one side of the vessel. Copper shone through the area she'd wiped clean. The narrow neck with the wide bottom gave it a grace despite the grime.

"Shine it up, and it would be a work of art," said Daisy.

"I wonder if the Pratt family even knows it's here. Maybe it doesn't belong to them." Emily walked up to the shed and opened the door for a look inside. It was filled with old jars, many of them broken, buckets dented and stacked in one corner and a maze of tubing, which curled its way around the floor of the building. Emily stooped over to pick up one end, but quickly pulled her hand back.

"Yowwee. It's alive."

Daisy brandished her machete toward the writhing tubing. "Aw, it's just an old corn snake. Won't hurt you." She touched it with the end of the weapon, and it slid out of sight into the back corner of the shed.

"There's nothing here. I was so certain this was the answer." Emily sank down on an old wooden stool that sat near the door. As quickly as she dropped onto the three-legged seat, she popped back up and looked carefully at the ground near it.

Daisy laughed. "No more snakes."

"Good." Emily remained standing. "I was sure the Prattts were moonshiners, and so was Hap. He knows everything about this county. How could he be wrong?"

"Might as well return to the car." Daisy led the way back down the path they'd followed. "Look at it this way. If you were slowly killing someone with poison, and it was discovered, would you keep it around? And even if you did have poison in your shed or under your seat, that doesn't mean you're guilty of trying to kill anything other than varmints."

"From what I hear, Everett Pratt was a varmint." Emily pushed damp tendrils of hair off her face. Summer was descending upon the county with a vengeance.

She gave some thought to what Daisy had said.

"If you thought this trip was for nothing, why'd you come along on this jaunt then?"

Daisy turned to look back at her. "Because you might have been right. And it sounded like fun."

CHAPTER 14

Daisy and Emily continued to make their way back to the car. "Hotter than a branding iron." Daisy wiped her forehead with her hand. Emily nodded and continued to trudge along the path.

"Honey, I'm real sorry this didn't turn out better. I know you wanted to show up Stanton, but Rodney and I need to get back to Georgia. I miss those coastal winds."

"Stanton? No one calls him Stanton." Emily slid the name across her tongue to try it out. It felt odd and sounded worse.

"His ex calls him that. I guess I picked it up from her."

"Did he spend much time in Brunswick with her? The four of you socialize?"

"God no. To both questions. She couldn't stand rural Florida and moved back to Brunswick less than a year after they married. He visited some, tried to live there for a while I guess, but then came back here. She and I ran into each other at some community events. She always talked as if he was some big shot in an urban police department. She led everyone to believe it was Tampa or Orlando. They were a mismatch from the beginning."

"There's the car." Emily strode out of the woods and onto the gravel road where the sun beat down more fiercely. "I kind of wish I was coming with you."

"You know that's a big lie. You like this detecting business even if you aren't one officially. And don't you worry about Stanton. He'll come around."

Emily was about to ask Daisy what she meant by "come around" when Rodney yelled at them from the car.

"I thought you girls would never come back. Let's get out of here and get some cold ones. We passed a bar down the road."

At the Owl's Nest Bar they grabbed three drafts and took a table in the corner away from the pool table where three young men were shooting a game. Rodney rolled his wheelchair around to watch the men while Emily and Daisy chewed over the afternoon's adventure.

"I'm going to forget the moonshine idea and have a talk with the women whose names I got from Lorelei. They're supposed to be the ones Everett was messing around with." Emily took a long draw on her beer, then set the frosty mug down on the table with a sigh of contentment. "Hot work."

"I wish I could go with you, but I think Rodney and I will leave early tomorrow for Brunswick. You'll keep us posted on what's happening, right?"

"Sure." Emily stared across the bar and out onto the wooden patio.

Daisy's gaze followed her friend's. "Something bothering you?"

"Can you imagine how Melanie must feel? She even knew the names of the women he was fooling around with. He obviously didn't try to hide it from her."

In Emily's eyes it was looking more and more as if Melanie had reason to want her husband dead. The look Daisy gave her said she'd come to the same conclusion.

"That's got to be the strongest motive for murder. Slow with poison or fast with a barbecue poker, either way the wife of a philandering man has to be a top suspect in his murder. I'm probably wasting my time." Emily tossed down the rest of her beer, looked at Daisy's mug and Rodney's and signaled the bartender by holding up three fingers.

"Hope you gals don't mind, but I haven't played pool in a long time." Rodney wheeled the chair up to the table and placed two quarters on the corner of it. One of the players lined up his shot at the eight ball, drew back on his stick and sank the ball. He also sank the cue ball. The other man let out a whoop of glee.

"Let's lay some money on this game, pops," said the youngest of the three players and default winner of the last game.

Emily watched him give Rodney a condescending smile and turn to wink at his companions mouthing a "Let's get this old man's money." His hair was bleached blond, not from working outdoors, Emily suspected, but from follicle familiarity with a dye bottle. On his face was the beginning of a mustache, which Emily knew would only grow in when he was much older. He was a kid with a snotty attitude, and Emily wished someone would take him down a peg. Too bad Lewis wasn't here. She bet he could handle a pool cue with finesse.

Rodney broke, dropping two striped balls into a side and a corner pocket, but he missed a bank shot for his next ball.

"Watch this, pops." The kid scored three balls and looked as if he would run the table, but he failed to put backspin on his next shot and the cue ball chased the three into the corner pocket. He slammed the butt of his stick onto the floor, then smiled. "I'll get it back after this shot," he said to his companions.

"Pops" never let him take back the table. With a flair that belied his seat in the wheelchair, Rodney ran his stripes and sank the eight.

"How about another one? You can get even with this old man."

Daisy leaned across the table and whispered in Emily's ear. "He'll beat the pants off him in this one too. We'd better be prepared to blow this place. These young whippersnappers will be mad."

"Okay, but I've gotta pee first."

"I'll come with you."

Daisy and Emily left for the bathroom. When they returned, Emily caught sight of a familiar back at the pool table. The presence of the detective had obviously settled the young men down, and they seemed content to have the table back with no more damage done to them than the loss of several fives from their pockets.

Lewis did not hear the women approaching.

"Thanks for watching out for them the other night and today."

"Rodney did what?" Daisy's voice was coated with steel.

Lewis whirled around to face her and Emily. Rodney, his view of the women blocked by the big detective until now, reddened.

"Sorry, honey, but he asked me to keep an eye on you gals. Just to make sure..."

Emily finished the sentence for him, "Just to make sure we didn't find anything that might make the detective look bad. Right?" Her face looked as if she had bitten into a bag of nails and was about to spit them into Lewis.

"Men," the two women said in unison. They turned on their heels and walked out of the bar.

Daisy then turned and stuck her head back in the door. "I'm sure Detective Lewis will be more than happy to give his little spy a ride back to the motel."

Daisy and Emily jumped into the Cadillac and sped off, gravel spraying from the back wheels.

⬧

"I heard from one of my contacts that the Rhodes woman's daughter was coming here for the barbecue festival. We can take care of them then." Toby sat in the driver's seat of his beat-up truck parked driver door to driver door next to the silver Lexus driven by Naomi's ex-husband, Barry. Mr. Smith sat in the passenger's seat, rethinking his decision to transport Barry's ex-wife and her mother to North Africa to be sold into slavery. *A cold fate for the two women, worse than death.* While it was the only thing about Barry that Smith respected, he still found that Barry along with Toby made his head hurt. They were so inept, clumsy, such rubes. He was bored. And very unhappy. Unhappy made him want to hurt someone, and he didn't care who.

Their rendezvous took place under a large palm tree at the edge of highway 710 outside Indiantown.

"Where the hell are we?" Mr. Smith had said little at this meeting, but he telegraphed his attitude about the location and Toby's plan to kidnap the women by sighing and rolling his eyes. Neither of his companions was smart enough to understand how close he was to exploding.

He tried a more direct approach. "It's hot sitting here. We could have met on my boat. We could have lured them over to the coast instead of trying to play cowboys and Indians in this wasteland." He swept his long fingers in a disparaging motion toward the fields of grazing cattle that bordered the roadway.

"Too complicated." Barry's curt dismissal of Mr. Smith's objections to the plan further irritated the international criminal. *I'm dealing with two ex-cops, and I'm beginning to see why they no longer hold their positions.* He sighed, this time loudly. *But the money's good, I'm unknown around here, and I'm between jobs.*

"I've got this covered. You two stay out of sight until we make our move. Then we can meet up and head for the boat." *Toby the toad had spoken.* Smith imagined killing him by throwing him into the canal that ran along the road. If the alligators didn't grab him, thought Smith, perhaps pond scum, giardia, or other bacteria would slowly eat away at his intestines or his flesh. The image these thoughts conjured up in Smith's brain amused him. He chuckled.

The two other men stopped talking, puzzled looks on their faces. Perhaps he should just throw them both into the swamp and make for the coast, sail out of here on his boat and head for the warm waters of the Caribbean. Smith was suddenly very tired of this caper. He despised the other men, hated how Toby smelled and had no respect for Barry. *He was simply a thug. No class.* Smith was used to dealing with criminals whose rap sheet included more than hitting their wives. Most of his friends were known to Interpol. These guys barely caught the attention of the county authorities.

Not only did he think Toby was an idiot, but he also knew he was hiding something. He was cooking up some half-assed plan of his own. What it was, Smith didn't know, but he suspected Toby had in mind to make some money other than what he was taking off the husband. Should he tell Barry or let it go? Smith didn't really care what Toby had in the works. He was confident he could handle either or both of them. He swatted a fly off his arm and again gazed out at the cattle. *Damn funny-looking creatures with their floppy ears and neck humps.* Yet he found them a lot more appealing and interesting than the two-bit criminals he was in league with. *Morons.* The men, not the cows, he thought.

⁂

Emily saw off the St. Simontons the morning after Daisy's and her unsuccessful attempt to find the Pratts' still. As she hugged them goodbye at the motel on her way to work that morning, she couldn't help but notice there was a feeling of chilliness in the air, and it was not due to the weather. Daisy was still pissed at Rodney for being Lewis' spy. She wondered how much of their exploits Rodney revealed to the detective.

Emily had hung up on Detective Lewis when he called last night. She was still aggravated. She knew Daisy's anger at Rodney would pass, but Emily intended hers at Lewis to be lifelong.

"Call me when you get home." Emily waved as the Cadillac pulled out of the parking lot. When she turned to get into Stan, Lewis pulled up.

"Oh crap," she said.

"It is a wonderful morning, isn't it? But it's going to get hot, hotter than yesterday." Lewis appeared to be in some kind of pleasant mood today. That made Emily suspicious.

"What do you want?"

"If you have the time, I'd like to buy you coffee."

"I'm on my way to work."

"And I'd like to apologize."

She continued toward her car and opened the driver's door. "You know it isn't just your setting Rodney up as a spy. It's your whole attitude on this case. You think you've got it solved, and you don't think anyone else has a pea of an idea."

Lewis' smile faltered a bit, but he plastered it more firmly on his face and tried to speak.

"Shut up. I'm not finished. I also know you think I'm an idiot, that I haven't a clue about who did what to whom, but I think I do. Ask yourself, detective, how tight your case against Bill is if your only evidence is his motive, the same one all the barbecuers had, and the barbecue rod, the one Toby, your oh so reliable informant, delivered to you."

Lewis cast his eyes downward as if to make humble, thought Emily, but I'm not fooled.

"Okay, let's say I'm wrong. To be honest, Emily, I've got nothing else except a boss who's breathing down my neck to make certain the community knows we've made an arrest and the festival and the town is once more safe from murderers."

He looked so depressed she almost felt sorry for him.

"You could interview those women Everett Pratt was making whoopee with."

"I already did that. Nothing."

"See there you go again. You think because you had a chat with them, you've taken care of things, but I'll bet they'd be more comfortable talking with another woman. Did you think of that?"

"No, of course not. I got my detective badge out of a cereal box."

Lewis glanced at her with a sly look on his face, and Emily realized she'd been had. *Manipulated. Run around by a tall, sexy detective who was smarter than she gave him credit for.*

"Call me after you talk to them." Lewis winked at her and tipped his hat as he got into his cruiser.

Emily could only gaze at his taillights with an open mouth.

⊰⊱

Emily read the first three names on the list Lorelei gave her. Faith Walters, Hope Coldwell, Charity Levre. Faith, Hope and Charity. *Cute.* She checked a phone book and located all three of them in one of the struggling fish camp trailer parks along the rim canal, the canal that ran most of the perimeter of the Big Lake. At one time years ago when the fishing was better, before hurricanes had churned up the lake, these so called "fish camps" were places winter visitors came to rent an inexpensive place, hire a guide and boat and fish the waters of the lake. With the damage to the quality of the lake's water, the fishing had changed. Coupled with the economic downturn that hit rural Florida harder than coastal areas preferred by tourists, camps closed or were reduced to less than half their size. The one listed as the address of the three women was south on Highway 441 and 98, several miles outside of town and located close to Emily's place.

"Jammer's Fish Camp" read the weathered sign as she drove Stan down the gravel driveway toward the tumbled-down fish-cleaning station that stood at the canal's edge. More old trailers with sagging metal skins lined the road into the camp, their condition worse than that of the Pratts'. No matter how battered and old, they all sported a window air conditioner that sometimes worked, Emily knew, but often did not. Some of the mobile homes were abandoned, left to continue their decay alone under the brutal Florida sun. Emily suspected their former occupants hadn't moved out for better housing on the coast.

She checked the paper in her hand for the number of the first trailer, 464. The others were 10 and 11. When she located the first one, it sat on crumbling cinder blocks at the water's edge. A gravel patio area peeked from around the back of the dwelling. Emily could see it once had been a humble lakeside abode, a small casita on the canal, surrounded by several ponytail palms and bougainvillea. Now the yellowed palms drooped unhappily for lack of water and the bougainvillea exploded over the trailer's roof and sun porch, making a tangled, impenetrable jungle of green. Here and there a few flowers bloomed in showy reds and purples, but the recent drought made the thorns on the plant more prolific than the blooms. Emily shuddered to think of what critters made homes in the mass of vegetation and awaited a door left open to take up more sumptuous digs inside the trailer.

Interesting numbering system, thought Emily. All three trailers sat next to one another. The other two were even older than the first. No plantings around them, only sand mixed with the black dirt of the Okeechobee basin.

She got out of her car and went up to the screen door of 464 and knocked sharply on it.

"We're around back," called a female voice. "If you're a friend, grab a beer from the fridge and come on out. If you want money, leave now cuz I got a gun and a trigger finger that yearns to put holes in bill collectors."

Emily heard laughter coming from the gravel patio area. She shrugged her shoulders and opened the screen door. The inside was what she expected, cracked linoleum, cabinet doors with hinges missing, and when she opened the fridge, she found nothing in there but several six packs of beer and a lonely piece of pizza, edges curling up, cheese dried and cracked. She grabbed one of the beers, opened the screen door to the back and stepped outside.

"Hey, I know you," said one of the women seated on a straight-back kitchen chair.

"Emily Rhodes. I'm the bartender at the Big Lake Country Club."

All of the women looked alike, bleached blonde hair, teased in a manner not seen since 1965, spaghetti strap tops covering large breasts and substantial muffin tops. Yet the smiles on their faces said they were friendly and happy to have company.

"Here, I'll get you a chair." One of the women ran into the house and extracted the mate to the one already outside.

"You can take mine. It's more comfortable." The woman gestured toward the lawn chair she'd been in. Emily was reluctant to sit in it. Its seat was made of plastic straps, half of which were missing.

"Maybe not a good idea, Charity. Her butt's so little, it'll sink right through."

"Try 'er anyway."

Emily did, and sure enough, her jeans-clad rear end slid between the straps and headed south. "I can just stand."

"No way. Get comfortable." Charity, the runner for the chair, grabbed a chaise lounge from a corner of the patio, dislodging a grey cat. At least Emily thought it was a cat. It could have been a raccoon or an opossum.

"Shoo, you lazy old thing."

Okay, Emily said to herself, *it's a thing.*

The women dragged the lounge toward the group. The pad on it was mildew-covered.

"It's a little dirty, but it's comfy. Sit back and relax." The woman identified herself as Hope and introduced the others.

Emily gingerly placed her butt on the edge of the lounge. The three women looked at her expectantly.

Oh, what the hell, she thought. She settled back into the lounge and put her feet up. *I can wash my jeans when I get home.* She leaned her head back and popped open her beer. A lizard slipped out from behind the headrest and dashed for safety.

"Cute little buggers, aren't they?" she said.

"They poop all over the place," said Faith. Or was it Hope?

"Not as much as those damn palmetto bugs. I'm forever cleaning bug crap off my table and stove."

Spoken like a true Floridian, thought Emily. Winter visitors hired exterminators. The natives just swatted the damn things.

"You didn't come for the beer and the sunset now, did you?" asked Charity or Hope or Faith.

Emily gazed over the canal waters. The sunset might have been beautiful here, she thought, and said so.

"It's nice." All three women nodded their heads.

Emily searched for a way to begin the conversation. "Uh, you said you know me?"

"Well, not know you, exactly, but I saw you once at the Burnt Biscuit. You were tending bar there and got sacked I hear." The smallest of the three women said this. That was Hope, thought Emily.

"That was my first job, Hope, and it wasn't a good fit for me."

"I'm Charity."

"Right. I went to the Big Lake Country Club."

"Yep, I heard you got fired and then went off and killed that rich rancher."

"No, no. That wasn't me."

The three women exchanged glances. One spoke, but Emily couldn't get the names straight yet.

"Like a friend of mine said, maybe he deserved to die."

The women sipped their beers and continued to look at her.

"Uh, he was a mean one." Emily took a sip of her beer to wet her throat. This wasn't exactly what she had planned. She was supposed to interrogate them.

"I found the body." Another sip. "The other day I found another body." *Why was she telling them all this?*

"You sure you ain't bumping off these folks?"

"I think the victim was someone you knew."

"Everett Pratt. We knew him alright. Used to party with him," one of the three said.

"All of you partied with him?"

"All of us. Together. We had us some great times. He brought us moonshine. He made the best in the county."

"When was the last time you and Everett got to-gether?"

"Hey, that's what that detective asked us the other day."

Their faces changed from open friendliness to suspicion. "You're not a cop, are you?"

"Oh, no, I just…"

"Find bodies, right?"

Emily nodded. "You know Everett's wife, right?"

Three heads again nodded, but slowly now and with some reluctance. They had stopped sipping their beers, and Emily knew it wasn't because the bottles were empty. She was about to be thrown out on her ass. She had to recover the creds she had when she came in.

"See, I kind of follow what the cops do, but I do it different. They come here and try to see if you had reason to kill Everett. I come here because I think you might know something to help poor Melanie Pratt. The cops seem to think she might have killed him."

"Melanie? Melanie wouldn't hurt a soul." Faith stopped for a minute, then continued. "Not unless that person was hurting on her family. Then she might do something."

"So you're sure Melanie wouldn't have done in Everett because he was playing around…"

"With us? Hell, no. She was grateful he wasn't crawling into her bed. Aside from his great moonshine, Everett wasn't much to talk about. Besides we stopped partying with him a long time ago."

"Why was that?"

"I think he found someone else."

CHAPTER 15

"Everett Pratt found someone else? Do you know who?"

Faith grabbed up the beer bottles, now empty and headed into the trailer. "Let me think a bit."

When she returned with a beer for each of them, Emily included, she sat and stared over the canal for several minutes.

"You two remember her name?" she asked her companions. They shook their heads and laughed. "We must have burned out some brain cells on Everett's booze."

Emily drew the paper with the names of Everett's women friends out of her back pocket. "Let me read you a few names. Maybe you'll recognize one of them." She set her beer bottle on the ground and looked at the names.

"Terry Blanchard?"

The women shook their heads.

"Mimi Presco?"

"I know Mimi," said Hope. "She came to my bible study class a couple of times. I can't believe she'd be involved with Everett."

"Her sister then," said Charity.

"Oh right. It wasn't Mimi who had a thing with Everett. It was her sister, Connie. Connie was one wild gal. But that was before us."

The three women continued to suck on their beers.

After several minutes of silence, Emily got up. "I don't want to take up more of your time. If you think of the name of the woman or anything else that might help me, would you give me a call? Here's my cell." She scribbled her name and number on a slip of paper and handed it to Faith. Or was it Hope? "Thanks for the beer. I'll let myself out."

She drove Stan out of the camp and headed home. Naomi would be showing up soon, and Emily had some laundry to do. It was a dead end on the women, and one of the names Lorelei had given her wasn't even one of Everett's girlfriends, but Lorelei claimed Melanie gave her the names. Maybe Everett's wife got them wrong. Or there could have been more. She'd have to go back to Lorelei, or better yet, Melanie.

※

"You and Daisy did what, Mom?" Naomi sounded worried. "You could have waited for me to show up. You have all the fun."

No concern for my escapades after all, thought Emily. Naomi expressed only curiosity. Like mother, like daughter. Emily smiled. *The gal had a nose for adventure.*

"Sorry, honey. I thought we had to move fast. Anyway, what's fun about going through the contents of an old trailer or checking out a still that isn't operating now? Emily drove her car down the road toward the Pratts' trailer. She wasn't sure Lewis would approve of this move, but he did want her to question the women. And Melanie was a woman.

Emily hoped none of the men was at home. She wanted to get Melanie alone, thinking she might be more open without testosterone circulating around her head. There were no cars in front of the trailer when she pulled up, but she could see movement through the windows.

Melanie answered the door, the same hang-dog look on her face as the other times Emily had seen her. When she saw it was Emily, her expression drooped even more, and her sorrowful eyes filled with fear.

"Oh," was all Melanie said. She stuck her head out and looked into the yard.

"It's just us. This is my daughter Naomi."

Naomi smiled at her. "I'm sorry to hear about all your trouble, Mrs. Pratt."

As if placated by Naomi's expression of sympathy, she held open the door and gestured them into the trailer.

"I know what you're thinking, but I'm not here because I think you killed Everett. I'm here because I think you can help us find who did." Emily rushed ahead before Mrs. Pratt could say anything. Or throw them out.

"You gave your sister-in-law Lorelei the names of women Everett was, uh, friendly with…"

"He was having his way with them." Melanie said this with no expression in her voice, not anger, not sorrow, not even judgment of his betrayal of her.

"Right. But that was a while ago. I hate to ask this, but was there someone more recent?"

"You think he stopped seeing his women?" asked Melanie. It wasn't really a question, but a statement filled with sarcasm, almost the first emotion Emily had observed in the woman.

Time for Emily to be completely honest. "No, I don't, and neither do you. Are you protecting someone?"

"No." Her answer came quickly, so quickly Emily knew she was lying.

"Mrs. Pratt, if you don't level with me, the chances are Detective Lewis will have no choice but to take you in for questioning and then perhaps arrest you." Emily let silence hang between them.

Melanie repeated the names Lorelei had given Emily.

"I have those names already. Come on, Melanie. Give me something."

"I don't know if Everett had anything going with her, but he talked a lot about a woman who joined our church about a year ago, Amy Bushnell, a divorcee. She seemed real lonely."

The sound of tires on the gravel driveway drew Emily's attention. A pickup pulled in and Melanie's Jasper and his friend, the skinny, short guy got out.

"You better git on out of here now. Jasper and Elmer don't seem to like you snowbirds hanging around here."

That was the friend's name, Emily remembered. *Elmer.*

"We're just leaving," Emily said to Jasper who stomped through the door and into the trailer.

"That's about right. And don't come back here bothering us folks. We're..."

"Grieving for your father. Sorry." Emily slid past him and out the door. Naomi followed. Elmer leered at her as she passed, then reached out and ran his hand over her rear.

Naomi turned on him and smacked him across the chin. "Hands off, you hairy creep!"

Elmer chuckled and licked his lips.

"Leave her alone," Jasper said. "She's nothing but Yankee trash."

As Emily and Naomi made their way back to the car, Emily could hear Jasper begin questioning Melanie. "What did she want? You didn't tell her nothin', did you?"

Emily couldn't hear Melanie's reply.

"Don't you know better than to talk to them people?" Again Melanie's voice was too low to be heard.

"Help us? She has no interest in helping us." Jasper turned his head and looked through the open window. When he saw Emily standing at her car, he reached up and slammed the window closed.

"I think we made more trouble for that poor woman than did her any good." Naomi shook her head. "Jasper and that Elmer slug are trouble. Jasper probably takes after his father. I'd like to have done a bit more damage to that scrawny one, but it was Melanie's home."

"Yup, I watched you pull that punch to his face. I'm glad you minded your manners in there. Keep the demonstrations from your karate class in reserve for another time." Emily shifted into reverse and pulled the car out of the drive and onto the road.

"Maybe we should wait for them to come back out. You still got that gun in here?" Naomi opened the glove box.

"I thought you hated guns."

"I do, but I sure would like to scare him."

"My little girl is going native. Just another good old gal."

Naomi continued to dig through the papers in the glove box.

"I don't carry it on me." A good thing, thought Emily.

Naomi stopped pawing through the jumble and slammed the door shut. She looked at her mother expectantly.

"It's home in my nightstand. And, no. We are not going there to get it so you can scare the pants off some redneck barbecuer."

"Okay. I'll find some way to get back at him for copping a feel. Maybe Lewis can help me."

"I'm sure you can think of something on your own." Emily hated the idea of her daughter in league with the detective. If anyone was going to help Naomi, it would be her. Emily.

They continued down the road in silence. Emily decided to take her daughter's mind off Elmer's obnoxious move on her.

"The good news is, we've got a name."

"What?"

"We have the name of another woman Everett Pratt was bothering."

"Or a woman he was bothered by." Naomi chuckled. "What are we waiting for? You're not working tonight, so let's have a talk with Amy Bushnell and see if we can figure out why she had such bad taste in men."

<hr />

Toby parked his rusted truck beneath a dying sabal palm in a pull-off just after the turn east toward Stuart. He rolled down the driver's side window and spit into the dirt next to his tire. It was late afternoon, and if a person didn't know he was parked there, they wouldn't be able to see him from either direction. But he could see any car approaching and taking the turn off the highway.

He squinted at his watch. The person he arranged to meet was about fifteen minutes late. He'd wait another few minutes and then... Then what, he asked himself? He'd planted that barbecue rod in his cousin's truck thinking he could extract money from the owner of the truck he found it in, but what if the guy wouldn't give in to his blackmail plan? Could Toby go to Detective Lewis and tell his ex-partner he lied? That would blow Toby's chance to be considered for a lighter sentence. *No. He would not tell Lewis the truth*. He'd be out the money his scheme would have made him. It had been worth a try. He'd think of another plan. He shrugged his rounded shoulders and spit again.

"That's my shoe, you jerk." A man stood at the side of his truck.

"Heh. I didn't hear you drive up." Toby shifted around on the truck's cracked plastic seat, frightened he hadn't kept alert for the visitor's arrival.

"I walked. You think I'm stupid?"

Toby had hoped the man was stupid, had hoped he would come alone as Toby asked. Toby shook off his discomfort the meeting was not going as planned. The guy showed, at least. That had to mean he was scared.

Toby heard the sound of a car approaching. It turned from the highway onto the county road, then made a sharp left and drove into the pull-off. Toby's heart began to pound. *What now?*

"That's my ride. I came to tell you to back off. For the second time. I didn't kill Everett Pratt."

Toby ignored him. "You were told to come alone."

"Why would I put myself in that kind of danger? I'm sure you're packin' so I thought I'd even the odds." He nodded to the driver of the car who slid down in the seat and waited. "Insurance."

"The barbecue rod was found in your truck."

"Someone must have planted it there just like you then planted it in Bill's truck."

"I've got something to show you that may make you sing another song." Toby reached into the bag on the seat and extracted a jar of barbecue sauce.

"I'm sure if these bottles find their way to the medical examiner's office he'll find one of them exactly matches the sauce on Everett Pratt's body."

"The medical examiner's office already did that, and none of the barbecuers' sauces matched, dummy. Why would mine match now?"

"Cuz you changed the recipe as soon as you realized you'd left a clue on the body, before the cops took samples. The date on this one is from the day before the murder. The samples were taken several days after that. You held back the supplies you made before the murder and provided the cops with your altered recipe, then sold the supplies to the public. I bought me one." Toby shoved the bottle in the man's face. "You got your insurance. I got mine."

The man laughed.

"This ain't funny. You know what I want. And this time no trouble. Not like the last time we met."

Toby shifted around in the seat, feeling the old aches from his beating at their last meeting.

"Let's walk. I feel too exposed, too near the road." The man signaled to his partner in the car to let him know where he was going.

"Fine, but I keep my gun on me in case you decide you'd like another piece of me."

Toby's contact nodded, and the two men walked into the brush and trees at the side of a cow pasture.

"How much?" asked the man.

"Five hundred now and then there will be other installments."

"I should just throttle the hell out of you right here." The man's voice was filled with rage, and Toby could almost hear his teeth grinding in fury. "Or just call the cops on you."

"I wouldn't do that." Toby decided to bluff. "You'd be talking to my friends. Your word against that of a retired detective." Did he know Toby had been indicted for a number of crimes, that he was awaiting sentencing, and had been thrown off the force? Toby held his breath.

Toby watched the man's shoulders slump. "That's your card in the hole, and I guess it beats mine." He reached into his pocket.

What appeared to be the shadow of a dead palm frond hanging off the tree moved and materialized into another man. Oh, crap, said Toby to himself. *It was Mr. Smith.*

⬥

Emily pulled to the curb in front of Amy Bushnell's house located in the Oak Park area, one of the best locations in the community. Oak Park was an older subdivision where the residents took pride in the appearance of their houses. Yards were mowed often, plantings pruned and weeded, paint fresh and driveways free of dirt and debris. So different from the fish camp, thought Emily.

She decided not to call first, thinking she'd take Mrs. Bushnell by surprise and see what that might yield. She and Naomi rang the bell and waited.

"Yes?" The woman who opened the door was younger than Emily, probably only in her mid-forties, but she wore her hair in a style reminiscent of the mid-sixties. Helmet hair, thought Emily, teased and sprayed so that it looked more like a lacquered bubble than natural growth.

"Hi. My name is Emily Rhodes, and this is my daughter Naomi. Mrs. Pratt thought you might be able to help us." Emily smiled her best preschool teacher smile, wide and reassuring.

"Mrs. Pratt?" Mrs. Bushnell grabbed the front of her blouse near her throat and gulped. "Maybe you should come in to talk about this."

She showed them into her living room and offered them a seat on the couch.

"You can't think I might be involved in Mr. Pratt's death. How could Mrs. Pratt believe that?" Her voice was now both defensive and filled with fear.

Emily decided not to beat around the bush.

"Mrs. Pratt doesn't think that of you. She knows her husband was a predator, and she thought perhaps Everett tried to get familiar with you. If he did, you might be able to tell us something about him that might help us find his killer." Emily kept her fingers crossed behind her back, hoping Mrs. Bushnell would not ask what right she had to question her.

"Mr. Pratt and I became friends. We met at my church."

"Didn't you know he was married?"

"I thought he was at first because he and his wife attended church together, but then he began to attend alone. He told me they were getting a divorce."

And you believed him, you poor, misled, lonely woman, thought Emily.

As if she had read Emily's sentiments, she added, "My husband died several years ago.

"So then you and Mr. Pratt became more than friends."

Amy Bushnell slumped into the chair across from the couch. "Yes. For a while. I thought he loved me. He said he did. He even gave me an engagement ring."

Emily and Naomi exchanged glances.

"I ended the relationship several months ago."

"Because you found out he was lying. He wasn't divorced after all. Right?" Emily reached over and patted the woman's hand.

"No. That's not it."

Emily and Naomi waited in anticipation.

Mrs. Bushnell seemed agitated, almost angry, but clearly reluctant to talk about what happened.

"Unless it's relevant to his murder, I will not reveal anything about your break-up with Everett."

"Everett made a pass at my daughter. I threw him out of the house." She arose. "And now I think it's time you left."

⸎

Emily was silent in the car.

"A lot of men take up with younger women when they discover age catching up on them. All of the women he had relationships with were in their forties. Maybe that didn't do it for him any longer and he wanted something even younger." Naomi spoke in disgust.

Emily nodded in agreement. "The old letch. Then she acted as if she was the party responsible. As if she wasn't desirable enough or something. Why do women blame themselves for these things?"

"I still can't figure what Mrs. Bushnell saw in him." Naomi said. "But then I'm not such a good judge of men myself."

"She was lonely, and she thought he was a good Christian man. That's counts for a lot around here."

"Especially if you're a woman of a certain age. Anything over twenty-five, I guess." Naomi sat back in the seat, arms across her chest.

Emily gritted her teeth and nodded. "Yep. Over twenty-five."

"Oh, Mom, I didn't mean to say there aren't plenty of good men out there, ones who like a mature woman."

"You mean an 'old woman.'"

"No. I mean someone like you. I mean, you. There are men who find you attractive."

"Oh, lucky me. A crazy, unpredictable bass fisherman who likes fish better than women and a cop who thinks I don't have a brain in my head."

Naomi sneaked a peek at her mother and smiled. "No. I meant Hap."

They both broke out in laughter.

"Hap thinks my hair is the wrong color, not blue enough, and he finds me too young for his taste. Probably too conventional too. I'm not into wearing a red teddy while he wields a six shooter, and yells, 'giddyap.'"

"Like I suggested before. Try an online dating service. I might subscribe to one myself. It sounds a lot safer finding out about a guy in cyberspace than in person."

They rode in silence for several miles.

"Are you going to tell Lewis about Amy Bushnell?"

"Why should I? There's nothing there."

"But, Mom, he doesn't know about her, does he?"

Emily pondered that for a moment. Naomi was right. She could let him know she found another of Everett's women and not tell him the full story. That would show him.

As if reading her mind, Naomi tapped her mother's shoulder and waggled her finger at her. "That's rotten. This is a murder investigation. He needs to know everything if he's to track down the killer. Maybe Mrs. Bushnell's daughter decided to whack him."

"I was just thinking, that's all."

Emily's cell rang. It was Lewis. *Was he reading her mind, too? And at a distance?*

"Where are you now?" he asked.

"Heading back home from town. Why?"

"I found something you might be interested in."

"What?"

"It's a surprise, but I bet you've never seen anything like this."

"I hate surprises."

"Okay then. I found the Pratts' still. Meet me at the intersection of 441 north and 68."

"Great." Emily flipped her phone shut.

"What was that all about?"

"Lewis says he found the location of the Pratts' still and wanted to surprise me with it. I already know about that old still. There's nothing there. It hasn't been used in years."

"You didn't tell him that?"

"Well, he recruited Rodney St. Simonton to spy on us. Daisy told me Rodney didn't do the job as Lewis wanted though. Good old Rodney. He only told Lewis what he already knew. That we went to the trailer that night and roamed around in the woods looking for the still, but he didn't tell him we found it."

"I guess Rodney knew he'd better not cross Daisy."

"Better to cross a cop than Miss Daisy DuBignon St. Simonton. The first might land you in jail, but the latter will guarantee silence so cold it could reverse global warming."

CHAPTER 16

E mily parked her car in the shade of a live oak to wait for Lewis.

Not two minutes later, the big police cruiser pulled up behind her. "We'll take my car since I know where I'm going." Lewis swung the passenger side door open for Emily and reached around to unlock the back so Naomi could get in.

He seemed to be delighted to show them around as if he was high on information he thought Emily did not have. Emily struggled not to show the pleased smile threatening to curl her lips. I know where we're going, too, thought Emily, but I've got to hide it from Lewis. She plastered a look of intense interest on her face and tried to appear as if she valued every word out of his mouth.

"We spotted this late last night and took a closer peek at it this morning. We can't stay long, and we'll have to be careful the Pratts don't know we've located their operation."

"Why did you think I'd be interested?"

"Come on, Emily. You know you're dying to crack this case. Besides, I made you an unofficial deputy when I gave you that assignment to talk to

Everett's girlfriends. By the way, did you find out anything I already don't know?"

"You mean from the women at the fish camp? Nope."

"Mom." Naomi reached up and punched her mother in the shoulder.

"Okay, fine then. We did find another woman who dated Everett."

"Date him? How do you date someone who's married?" he asked.

"I'm sure I wouldn't know." Emily pursed her lips as if she'd bitten into a lemon.

"I'm not married. You know that." The vein in Lewis' forehead began to bulge.

"And we're not dating anyway." Emily stared off into the passing fields replacing the sour citrus look with one more serene.

Lewis let go of the wheel and threw his arms in the air. "I know that."

"Watch the road and don't yell at me."

"Hey!" Naomi shouted from the backseat. "Could the two of you try to behave like adults for once? I thought we were here to take a look at some evidence."

"I didn't mean to upset you," Emily said.

"You didn't." Lewis said.

"I meant Naomi."

Lewis opened his mouth, then clamped it shut. "I am merely being emphatic," he said through clenched teeth.

"So where is this place?" She could tell her calm tone of voice and the smile on her face were driving Lewis crazy, and that was exactly what she intended. She continued to look out the windows at the scenes she had observed when she and Daisy searched for the Pratt still. At the turnoff to the walking and biking trail she and Daisy had taken, Lewis didn't slow. Emily reached out and grabbed Lewis' arm.

"What?" There was surprise in his voice, but something else on his face.

"Nothing."

Maybe he knew another way into the place. They continued north another five miles. Emily began to wonder what was going on.

"What are you trying to pull here?" There was irritation in her voice.

"Huh?"

"We should have turned back there some miles. The Pratts' still is that way." Now Emily was shouting and pointing off toward the west.

"Now what would you know about their still?"

Emily swallowed. *Trapped.* "Uh, everyone around here knows where they have their still. Common knowledge."

"Common gossip. That still hasn't been operational for years." Lewis fixed Emily with his bird of prey look. Then he broke into laughter. "I guess my sources about the still are more accurate than yours."

Emily looked shocked, then understanding dawned. "You knew! You knew Daisy and I found that old still. I'm such a fool. Rodney told you everything we did that day. Wait until I tell Daisy he lied to her."

"Now don't go getting you ponytail all snarled. Of course he told me you went to the abandoned still. He was worried about both of you and knew you needed protection. You were almost right. The Pratts do have a working still, but it's well hidden. And when we found it, we also found several containers of rat poison, not that we wouldn't expect that around a place where they stored corn, but..."

"You think Melanie Pratt tried to poison her husband. Oh damn. I thought she was innocent."

"I think someone in the family tried to poison him, but I can't prove a thing. Yet."

Emily could forgive Lewis the fun he had at her expense. He was doing his job. And Rodney was protecting his wife. Of course, she had no intention of ever forgetting what Lewis did to her. Using her friends as spies and leading her on. She'd just let it go for now and as long as it took for him to think she was over it. Then...

Lewis was saying something to her. "What?"

"So do you want to see the still?"

"Big deal. We saw the other one."

"But this one is bigger, huge, really huge, and its location, well, the location is everything."

His enthusiasm piqued her interest.

She turned around to look at Naomi. "Got anything pressing?"

Her daughter shook her head.

"Then let's see this fascinating location."

Lewis turned onto a dirt road.

"This can't be Pratt property. It's too far away from their place. Unless they own this parcel too." Emily looked at the passing scenery with interest. A mix of Cyprus trees, banyans, sabal pines, live oaks and scrub palmetto covered the area. The jungle made of the vegetation almost reminded her of the dense forests up north and looked just as impenetrable.

"The Pratts do own the property, just not the Everett Pratts. The county records indicate this section belongs to another Pratt." Lewis slowed and pulled to the side of the road.

"You mean Lorelei Pratt?"

"Well, sort of. It's still in her husband's name, but technically it's hers."

"Miss Prim and Proper is making moonshine?" Emily found the idea shocking, but also satisfying. Emily found the woman somewhat annoying, but kept her mouth shut to Hap who seemed to like her just fine.

"I doubt she knows about it. C'mon." Lewis got out of the car and started down the dusty road. He hadn't gone but a few steps when he turned and walked into the trees at the road's edge.

"We'll never get through here." Naomi paused and watched Lewis duck under the limb of a live oak and disappear.

"Where are you?" called Emily.

"Just walk toward the big oak and duck around the limb that almost touches the ground." His voice came from the other side of the tree and was nearly swallowed up by the density of the branches between him and the women.

Emily shrugged and did as he said. Once she got on the other side, she saw Lewis standing at the beginning of a trail that had been cut through the brush.

"C'mon, Naomi," she yelled.

"A path," said Naomi, "and concealed so well, you'd never see it from the road even if you were walking and looking for a way in."

"From now on, both of you need to stay behind me. It's dark in here, and I don't want you stepping where you shouldn't."

"Like on a gator or a snake?" Emily shuddered and looked down at her feet.

"That too. Try to move quietly." Lewis smiled and signaled them to follow him.

It was almost as dark as night among the trees.

Lewis glanced skyward. "It's getting late in the day. I guess I should have brought a flashlight."

Naomi followed her mother close enough that she bumped into her several times.

"Ground's spongy here for a while, so watch those Cyprus knees. They stick up and can trip you." Lewis trod carefully around the knobby protrusions at the base of the trees. Spanish moss trailed off the limbs giving the area a creepy, otherworldly feeling. The banyan trees with their exposed roots and bottoms split into numerous trunks only added to the ghostly feeling of the place.

"I know you're scared Naomi, but you're fogging up my shirt collar," Emily said. "Could you step back a pace or so?" She reached up to brush away the tickle on her neck and touched something with more substance than Naomi's breath.

"Help! Get that off me. It's some kind of an animal with prickly fur." She flicked at it again with her hand and caught a fist full of beard-like hair.

Lewis turned and pulled her toward him. "It's just Spanish moss."

"Oh. I hate Spanish moss. It's making me itchy just like when you got fleas." Emily scratched at her neck. Lewis bent to do the same to his ankle.

"Mom, take a look at this one." In front of them stood a banyan that made the others look like mere children in size. Most impressive was the "trunk" coming off one side. It stood over four feet in height, and along with the others, which looked like the fingers of a giant's hands arched over the ground, it made a grey tent-like structure.

"What lives in there?" Emily bent her head close to the opening between the fingers or knees and tried to peer in.

"I wouldn't do that." Lewis pulled her back. "It's a great place for spiders and bugs and, well, it's not someplace you'd want to explore, especially without a light."

"Where's Naomi?" asked Emily.

A cry penetrated the woods.

"I told you both to stay behind me. Don't the Rhodes women know how to follow orders?"

This was no time to argue with him. Emily plunged ahead toward the source of the yell. She hadn't gone ten steps when the ground went out from beneath her feet. If Lewis hadn't grabbed her by her shirt, she would have plunged into an inky chasm and joined her daughter at its bottom.

"Naomi. Are you hurt?" Lewis shouted into the depths of the hole.

There was no reply.

"What is this? A cave of some sort? Can we climb down there?"

Emily tried to peer down into its depths, but roots and vegetation obscured her view. "We've got to get her out of there."

"It's a sinkhole. You must have heard about them here in Florida. They've been known to swallow up entire backyards."

"How deep is it? We should go for help."

Lewis called Naomi's name again. "The fall probably knocked her out."

Emily wanted to believe Lewis' words, but the concern in his voice made her frantic to find her daughter. "I'm going down there."

"We'll both go. I'll climb down first, then help you. The sides are rock covered with crumbling dirt and vines. Watch your footing as you go." Lewis began to lower himself using his feet and hands to crab walk down the sides.

The shadows were so deep she could barely see the top of his head when he got to the bottom. He reached back and helped her down the steep sides.

There was no sign of Naomi.

"This is so neat." The voice came from the far side of the hole.

"Naomi?" Emily ran toward the voice, stumbling over the rocky floor. Suddenly a bright light blinded her.

"I found a flashlight," Naomi said.

"Could you shine it someplace other than in my face?"

Her daughter lowered the light, turned and directed the beam toward the far wall.

"Where does this go?" The light revealed a tunnel. Naomi moved down it.

Emily followed. The tunnel widened until it formed a large room. In the center of the room stood a still, another still, much larger than the abandoned one Emily had found. Its copper sides gleamed in the light, and there were indications of recent use. This was a working still. There were sacks of corn stacked in the far corner. Several propane tanks stood to one side of the huge boiler. The area smelled sour.

"Are you hurt, honey?" asked Emily.

"Just some scrapes and bruises, I guess, but look at this."

Lewis followed them down the tunnel and into the still room, but remained quiet as the women explored the sinkhole.

Emily turned to him. "Is this your surprise?"

Lewis stood with his arms crossed in front of his chest. "Why do I think I can keep two steps ahead of you women? I wanted to show you this by taking you around to the other way in. Instead you find your own entrance. I told you to stay behind me."

He dropped his severe pose. "You sure you're not hurt?"

"I'm good." Naomi continued her exploration of the still.

"The propane is to fuel the fire, right?" asked Emily.

Lewis nodded.

"But isn't it dangerous to do that down here? There's no ventilation."

Lewis chuckled. "They figured that one out too."

He walked over to the back wall and pulled out a long pole with a board nailed across the top to form a T.

"That looks like the kind of device I saw my daddy use to hold up dry wall when he was redoing a ceiling," Emily observed.

Lewis pointed overhead. It was crisscrossed with sturdy wooden beams. The area between the beams was made of branches, some with leaves and pine needles still attached, others bare. Weeds and other brush appeared woven into the limbs. Lewis raised the pole above his head and pushed upward. He maneuvered one section of the ceiling off the supporting timbers and to one side, opening the ceiling to the sky.

"Move that platform of bush and branches and you've got a kind of skylight above." He continued to perform his task of raising and moving a series of platforms until the entire ceiling was open to the sky.

"Great camouflage. Why didn't they do the same to the part of the sinkhole Naomi fell into?"

"It was covered with brush naturally. And it's small. Why bother? But these others? They're larger. They needed to make this kind of partitioned canopy to cover up the hole."

"This is their real still, the one they use now. And you found rat poison here? The kind used to kill Everett?" asked Emily.

"The lab is testing it, but it looks like a match."

"Great." Emily smiled. She was genuinely happy for Lewis. Of course, she was a little jealous she hadn't stumbled on this first, but still, happy.

She noted Lewis' face didn't show the kind of satisfaction she would have expected for a detective who solved the case.

"Maybe not so great. The lab told me they'd probably only be able to tell if the poison in Everett's body was the same as the kind found here, but there's little chance they can say the poison came from this particular batch. And even if they could, which Pratt do I arrest for attempted murder?"

Now Emily felt genuinely sorry for him. And, of course, there was that glimmer of hope that she might still stumble onto the answer. After all, he had bet her a bottle of shower gel that he would find the poisoner before she would. There were bubbles at stake in winning this bet, and perhaps someone to soap her back.

"We'd better get out of here in case the Pratts show up. I don't want to let them know we found this. Yet." He carefully replaced the camouflaged ceiling and gestured toward the back of the area to a slope that angled upward and then leveled off. A door stood at the end of that area. Lewis pushed on it, and it opened to a clearing. Once out the door they turned around. From the outside it looked as if the door was to a small storage shed, not to the still sinkhole.

"Clever," said Emily. She noted the door was held shut by two U-shaped handles through which a section of wood could be slid. Lewis slipped the wooden bolt through the U-brackets to hold the door closed.

"Yeah, it looks like an old shed in the middle of the woods. Hard to find, unless you were looking for it." Lewis sounded proud of his discovery.

"So that's a sinkhole," said Emily. "We always read about them in the papers up north, but the stories indicated they're some kind of mysterious phenomenon like crop circles."

"Nothing mysterious about them. This entire state is made up of sand and porous limestone. Erosion produces cavities in the ground. Some fill with water. In years when drought occurs, the holes reveal themselves. The rest of the time they look like ponds or gator holes, or are covered with brush or several feet of dirt."

"The Pratts took a chance then. Their entire operation could be flooded if we got a lot of rain. Or a hurricane."

"I forgot to leave the flashlight." Naomi held it up.

"I'll run it back." Before Lewis could grab the light, a twig crackled, then another. Footsteps. Lewis stopped and drew his pistol from under his jacket.

The sounds got closer.

"I'm going to see what's going on. You gals stay here and be quiet." Lewis moved ahead toward the sounds and was soon lost in the shadows.

Emily and Naomi crouched down, huddled together near the base of a Cyprus tree.

"Ouch!"

Emily glanced at her daughter. "Quiet."

"I'm sorry, but I'm kneeling on one of these Cyprus knobs. They're all over the place."

Suddenly the air erupted in the sounds of gunfire.

"Let's get out of here." Emily grabbed her daughter's hand and ran. After winding in and out of trees and through swampy areas, over knobs that threatened to trip them, they slowed up.

"If we keep running, we're going to twist our ankles or break a foot." Naomi stopped to listen.

"Or we'll lose our way." Emily looked around her and wondered where they were. Which direction was the road? Off to the west the sun began to dip behind a hammock of trees. The last thing she wanted to do was spend the night in this place. If the gators don't get us, she thought, the moonshiners will.

❦

Lewis positioned himself at the base of a live oak. Its wide trunk gave him adequate cover from whoever was shooting. He could hold out here until it got dark then make his way back to the car. He figured it had to be the Pratts checking their still. Maybe they got wind of something going on with the authorities. It was hard to keep anything quiet when it came to 'shine, especially if those who bought it found out the Feds or police were onto their source. Moonshine in the south, thought Lewis, was a tradition, and one you tampered with knowing there would be consequences.

His only concern was the two women he'd taken here. He mentally whacked himself on the head. *What a dumb ass.* He just had to show off to Emily, show her what a great detective he was, how he tracked down the real still. Now he'd put both of them in real danger. They could run into the men who shot at him or they could lose themselves in these swamps and woods. Either way, the outcome wasn't pretty.

He listened. He heard no voices or the sound of anyone moving around. If the Pratts thought he was a Fed onto the still, he figured they were hightailing it back home, putting distance between themselves and evidence of moonshining.

The woods were silent. It was time to move, time to find the gals and hope they were all right. As he struggled to get to his feet, he admitted to himself there was another problem. He felt blood run down his arm from a gunshot wound. It was too dark to see how bad it was, but his entire right side felt like it was on fire, and wetness soaked through his shirt and his jacket. He slid the gun into his shoulder holster, groaned with the pain of the movement and held the useless arm with his left hand.

He felt the barrel of a gun press into the back of his neck. "Throw your pistol on the ground and get up. Do it real slow."

⚜

She could hear footsteps through the dried brush.

"You hear them?" she asked her daughter.

Naomi nodded. "We have to hide."

"Where?"

"I've still got the flashlight, but I don't dare use it or it'll give away our position. If we can find our way back to where I fell into that sinkhole, we can hide in there."

"Don't be silly. If it's the Pratts, that's the place they'll want to look, to check on their still."

"They'll search the main part of the hole, not in that passageway. It's almost dark now. They won't see us if we hunker down near the opening."

Emily looked skyward. "Unless they decide to make 'shine and open up all those hatches. If there's a full moon tonight, they'd be sure to see us."

"I don't think they're here to distill. I think they're checking on things. It's our only chance."

As they attempted to backtrack to the sinkhole, Emily could hear voices coming closer. "Hurry."

She turned to look behind her. Naomi was gone.

She knew she shouldn't yell for her daughter or she'd give away her position to their pursuers. The voices got louder. They couldn't be far behind. She needed a place to hide, but the trees surrounding her didn't look any different from those she'd seen in other parts of the area. Where was the sinkhole? She worried she might fall into it the way Naomi did, so she got down on her hands and knees and began to crawl forward, reaching out, hoping she'd touch nothing but air—the entrance to her hiding place. Maybe Naomi was already there.

Her hands continued to feel terra firma, mostly terra, and mostly damp, filled with leaves, dirt, moss. Something moved beneath her right palm.

Enough of this. She leaped up and heard a voice from behind, close, very close.

"I see someone."

It sounded like a man. The voice was followed by a sound Emily dreaded, that of a hammer being pulled back, the sound of a gun being cocked. *Oh, hell!* She ran for the cover of the trees up ahead, giant monsters whose fingers dug into the ground around their trunks. Whoever was pursuing her would search that area, too, she thought. A small cry of despair escaped from her lips.

She felt something like a slap alongside her face followed by the sound of a shot.

I'm dead unless I find someplace to crawl into and hide myself.

She had an idea, a horrible idea. She ran toward the gathering of grey trees ahead, the gnarled roots of both cypress and banyans and mantles of trailing moss a macabre sight in the shadowy darkness of the woods. She took a deep breath and plunged into their midst searching, searching, until she disappeared.

CHAPTER 17

"Now get to your feet, slowly, and turn around."

Lewis thought his legs might go out from under him, but he managed to struggle from his crouch. He tried to keep the pain of his wound from showing in his expression. *No sense in letting the enemy know you're vulnerable.*

"Lewis. You. You let them get away?" Donald Green stood before him holding not a gun but the butt of a fishing rod pointed at him.

"Kind of far from the lake, aren't you?" Lewis nodded toward Donald's hand, then staggered a bit.

"You're hit. You'd better sit down and let me look at that."

"Make up your mind. You just told me to get up."

Lewis heard Donald express his concern with his usual growl as Lewis slid down the trunk of the tree and leaned back onto it.

"What are you doing here, Green?"

"I saw you head north out of town with the gals in your car, so I thought I'd sorta tag along and see what you were doing."

"Playing hooky from the bar. Emily said you weren't fond of the work."

Another growl escaped Green's throat. "She said that about me, did she?"

"Naw. I'm just feeling a little testy right now so I made that up. When I'm a hundred percent again, I'll tell you what she really said."

Donald leaned over and moved the lapel of Lewis' jacket to one side, unbuttoned his shirt and looked at the wound. "Light's not good, but it doesn't look like the bullet hit an artery. You have lost some blood."

"Hurts like hell." Lewis leaned back against the tree trunk and let out a moan.

"Where did you leave Emily and Naomi?"

Lewis ducked his head so Donald couldn't see his expression of embarrassment. "They're hiding out."

"Where?'

Lewis raised his eyes. "I don't know. Find them, would you?"

"You're some detective. Everyone in these parts knows the Pratts cook barbecue and make moonshine. And most folks know where they make moonshine. Here. And you didn't have the sense to keep Emily and her daughter away from the still?"

Lewis looked Donald in the eye. "I know. I was an idiot."

"You were showing off for Emily, making her think you were on top of this case when all you had was the location of a still the Feds have stayed away from for months. Rumor is they're waiting for the Pratts to start distilling, and then they'll arrest them. Now you've blown their cover."

"How do you know all this?"

"Cuz I listen real good instead of sounding off like some pompous ass. Even your old partner Toby knows enough to keep his mouth shut and listen."

The unfavorable comparison between Toby and himself made Lewis want to jump up and punch Donald, but Lewis knew he was right. He could have checked with one of his friends in Alcohol, Tobacco and Firearms before he marched in on the still, but he didn't. He played the Lone Ranger, and he knew Captain Worley would have his head for it. He'd be lucky if he wasn't riding a bicycle on parking meter patrol next week.

"Go find them," he said to Donald. "Take this. You'll need it." He held his pistol out to Donald.

Donald shook his head. "I'm good." He strode off into the woods and was soon hidden by the jungle of trees. Lewis couldn't even hear his footsteps as he walked through the underbrush.

Lewis leaned his head back against the trunk. *I've made a mess of things. I only hope I haven't gotten Emily or her daughter killed.*

He reloaded his gun in case the Pratts came back this way.

⊛

When Naomi turned to give her mom a hand down the slope leading into the sinkhole, she found Emily wasn't behind her. She didn't dare yell for fear the Pratts or whoever the guys were with the guns would hear and know where to look for her. Now her dilemma was whether to stay hidden where she was, snug in the unused end of the hole or try to climb the steep sides and search for her mother. She looked up and saw the last rays of the sun over the lip of the depression. She'd never be able to find her mother now. She wrung her hands and began to chew on her nails. She hoped her mother found herself a good hidey hole too. Lewis would find them soon, she hoped, and if not tonight, then tomorrow. Naomi looked toward the sky again. It was hard to make out the perimeter of the hole now. Everything was bleeding into darkness.

※

Emily had indeed found herself an almost impenetrable hiding place, impenetrable to anyone over five feet tall carrying more than one hundred pounds of flesh on them. Before she entered the tent created by the Cyprus knees and the banyan roots, she took a long stick, pushed it into the largest space and poked it around hoping whatever might be in the bowels of the trunk would come out and find another home. Or was riled up enough to take defensive action. She'd find out soon enough. She took a deep breath and crawled in on her hands and knees, then wiggled back against the inside. She pulled her knees up into the circle of her arms, her entire body within the tree's roots. No one would find her here, assuming she could stay put long enough to wait out those looking for her.

She heard voices and footsteps coming nearer. She had squeezed her eyes shut not wanting to discover what the inside of her hiding place looked like, fearful she'd see some living creature peering back at her, a spider, or, horrors, a snake. Now she opened her eyes and caught sight of a pair of legs, jeans-clad, walking past. She scooted farther back into the tree.

"I can't see a damn thing out here," she heard someone say. The voice wasn't that of anyone she'd count as a friend, but she thought it sounded familiar. Maybe Jasper Pratt or his scummy friend. She waited, holding her breath, then let it out in a whoosh.

The dim light faded to purple darkness and silence rained down on her hiding place, broken only by the distant sound of a frog croaking. She waited for what seemed like an hour before she squirmed out of the protection of her hole. *Now I've got to find Naomi.* Dirt, leaves, dried moss and other prickly stuff covered her clothes and skin and tangled in her hair. She brushed it all off with her hands as best she could. Something tickled her in the small of her back. She reached back with her hand under her blouse expecting to dislodge a spider or bug. *Nothing there.* But she still felt crawly all over. *Which way back to the sinkhole and the still?* And did she dare go that way or would she encounter the men chasing them? *So damn quiet out here*. The crawling feeling intensified, this time moving upward along her spine and under her bra.

A hand landed on her shoulder and squeezed. Before she could cry out, another covered her mouth.

"Shhh. It's me, Emily," Donald Green whispered into her ear. "Where's Naomi?"

Donald's sudden appearance frightened Emily mute. She struggled for words and finally croaked a shaky, "I don't know."

⚜

The two men Toby met ran for their truck and sped off down the highway toward the coast.

"You ruined my deal," Toby cried as Mr. Smith strode toward him.

"I don't like you making deals on the side, Toby." Barry, Naomi's ex, appeared at Smith's side. "I told you. He thinks he's smarter than everyone else, but he gets himself in too deep, gets distracted by his dealings and makes a mess of everything."

If Barry thought his words would bring Smith's wrath down on Toby, he failed to understand Smith.

"And still you hired him. You're more of an idiot than he is. He's your responsibility. You take care of him, one way or the other. I don't need any glitches in what we're doing. You're not paying me enough money to tolerate this kind of incompetence." Smith paused for a moment, then walked close to the other man. Barry was taller, heavier than Smith, but Toby knew Smith was the dangerous one. He'd rather take a beating from Barry than to be put into Smith's hands for punishment.

"Look," Barry's voice was light, conciliatory. "I'm sure Toby will be happy to drop this little, uh, endeavor and concentrate on his work for you. Me. His work for me."

Smith's head snapped around, and he pierced Barry with a steely glare. "Shut up. I didn't tell you to speak." Smith walked closer to Toby until Toby could smell his breath, a warm rush of garlic- and wine-laden air.

Toby gulped. "Sure thing. I can forget this. It's not important anyway."

Smith reached out and grabbed Toby's arm. Oh no, thought Toby, not this again. The pain made his vision go black. "But it was important enough to get you the attention of those men, and they may decide to go to the cops. Then you're no good to me."

"No, no. They won't tell the cops. They're the ones who killed that barbecue guy, and I'm the only one who knows it. I was trying to lift a little cash off them to keep quiet about it."

Smith continued to grip Toby's arm, but his hold let up a little, enough that Toby thought his arm might not be broken.

"I don't like things messy," Smith hissed. His grip again tightened on Toby's arm. "I should kill you."

Barry came to Toby's defense. "We need him. Who else can fit in with these cowboys around here?"

Smith's hold seemed to tighten even more. A moan slipped from between Toby's lips.

Smith gave a final twist to the arm and shoved Toby backwards. "Then, if I can't kill the little toad, I'll need more money from you to complete my mission."

"I'll double what I'm paying you, but I need time to get the money. The original amount now and the rest when we deliver the two women to my contacts in North Africa."

"And Detective Lewis," Toby squeaked as he rubbed his arm.

"What?" said Smith.

"I thought since we were doing the women, we could throw in the detective too. Toby liked the idea," said Barry.

"Why should I care what Toby likes? No detective on my boat. Too many things can go wrong."

"Sorry, Toby."

Toby ducked his head to hide the scowl on his face from Mr. Smith. Smith reached out and laid his hand on Toby's arm again. Toby flinched.

"The detective is all yours, Toby. After we get the women, that is." Smith's lips made some kind of twitching movement at the corners. A smile of some sort, thought Toby, and prayed fervently he'd never see it again.

As Toby drove back into town, he thought about the evening's events. If Smith and the husband thought he'd give up his plan to blackmail Pratt's killers, they had to be fools. Toby just needed to make certain he wasn't being followed when he set up the next meeting with his pigeons. That was a delicious feeling to wrap his mind around. And then there was Detective Lewis, now his to handle in whatever way he wanted. Toby contemplated the myriad ways he might kill Lewis.

It's getting dark, thought Toby. He flipped on his high beams and noticed lights in his mirror. When he made the turn toward town, the vehicle followed. As he sailed past his old place of employment, police headquarters, he gave the place the finger and chuckled. *Ain't never going back there again*. Retirement suited him, or would suit him as soon as he got his money from the blackmail and the job for that gal's ex-husband. And, oh yeah, when he got the charges dropped against him. Toby stuck a new chaw of tobacco in his mouth and turned the radio to the local country station. *Yep, life was just fine*. He glanced in the rearview mirror. No lights were back there now. Toby pressed his foot harder on the accelerator as he made his way toward his cabin on the Kissimmee and sang out of tune with one of his favorite songs about liking women who were trashy. *Yes sir, he did indeed like gals that way*. Toby was about as happy as he'd ever been.

❖

"I think Naomi intended to hide in the far end of the sinkhole that houses the Pratts' still." Emily was almost running to keep up with Donald. "Do you know where the still is? Can you find it in the dark?"

Donald muttered something under his breath and Emily quickened her steps to stay at his side.

"What did you say?"

Donald stopped and turned to her. "I said for you to keep your mouth shut so you don't alert whoever's out there, but no, you have to keep blabbering on. Damn Yankee women. You can't shush them once they think they have something important to say."

"Sorry."

"'Course I can find it."

"Well, you're headed the wrong way, Mr. Green." Naomi's voice came from behind them. "It's back there. I just crawled up the sides of that thing."

They turned and Naomi pointed through the trees in the direction they'd come.

"They left anyway. I heard their truck," said Naomi.

Emily and Naomi grabbed each other and hugged. Donald rolled his eyes in embarrassment at the emotional nature of their greeting and stomped his feet in impatience.

"Let's get moving. We've got to get Lewis."

"What's Donald doing here?" asked Naomi.

"I have no idea, but he always turns up when there's trouble of some kind, like at fires or fishing for dead bodies."

Donald stopped short. "Okay, I'm only going to say this once more. Shut up, both of you."

"But there's no reason to be quiet now. The Pratts or whoever it was have left."

"I know that, but now you're annoying me with all your chatter. And we should hurry."

"Why?" insisted Emily.

"Because your boyfriend has been shot."

"Who?" asked Emily.

"You know. Lewis."

"He's not my boyfriend," Emily spat back at him, then her lips clamped closed for a second. "What do you mean, 'shot'?"

"Well, you take this thing called a gun and you aim at someone, pull the trigger, and..."

"Donald." Emily said his name in a tone of voice that said she would counter no more snarly comments from him nor sarcasm about Lewis.

"Come with me. He needs a doctor."

"And you just left him and started wandering around here?" asked Emily. Anger at Donald was helping her overcome her shock and her concern about Lewis. He just couldn't die, she thought, not when we haven't made it past being shower buddies yet.

"He insisted I find you gals first. And, of course, I agreed with him."

"Yeah, I saw how thrilled you were to see me," Emily snapped. The sound of a siren split the night air.

"I guess he got tired of waiting for me to find you all and called for help on his cell," Donald said.

"You couldn't do that for him? Before you left him to die there alone?" Emily silently vowed she'd find a way to fire Donald. She could barely stand being near him. *What a selfish...*

He led them through the tangled underbrush and around trees and vines toward the road. An ambulance and a police car sat on the shoulder with their lights pulsating, creating odd red images like demons dancing through the gnarled branches of the live oaks.

The E.M.T.s were about to place Lewis into the ambulance. Emily ran ahead and grabbed the gurney.

"Are you okay?"

"Are you worried?"

"Of course, I'm worried. You could have been killed."

"Well here I am, still kicking. Does that make you happy?"

Emily looked down into his face, white with pain. "I'm happy you're not likely to die."

"Because? Say it Emily, please. Only the E.M.T.s can hear us. Donald and Naomi are back there." He nodded with his head toward the two figures bringing up the rear.

"I'm happy because, well, because I, well, I kind of like you. Some."

But Emily's confession came too late. Lewis didn't hear it. He had already passed out from the pain.

"You jerk. You can't even stay awake for some love talk." She mentally kicked herself for her selfishness. "Is he still alive? Or did I shock him into unconsciousness?"

One of the E.M.T.s looked at her. "That's love talk? Wow, no wonder he passed out. Too much passion for one night."

If the guy hadn't been carrying one side of Lewis' stretcher, she would have tripped him for his sarcastic tongue. Instead she caught up with him and grabbed his arm.

"I was trying to spare him an overload of feelings. I guess I blew it. He could have experienced cardiac arrest."

The E.M.T. shook his head. "He'll be fine. Now would you let go of my arm so we can get him to the hospital?"

Emily looked down at her hand, which gripped the E.M.T.s arm like a vice. "Sorry."

The ambulance pulled out, leaving Lewis' police cruiser and Donald's truck at the side of the road. The officers from the other car had entered the woods to investigate where Lewis had been shot.

"Better leave his car. Someone from the department will come get it. You gals can ride with me," Donald said.

"I don't want to ride with you, Donald. You ran off and left Lewis to die. If anything happens to him, I'll..." Emily didn't know what she'd do, but it was something, maybe put a dent in his big ole truck or scratch the paint on his fine bass boat. Something.

Donald gave her one of his exasperated looks and got into his truck.

"Mom, it's our only ride back to town." Naomi got into the passenger's side and slid to the middle to make room for her mother.

Emily crossed her arms over her chest and stood unmoving.

"Fine," said Donald. He started the engine and shifted into gear.

"Mom." Naomi's voice mimicked the exasperation in Donald's tone.

Emily turned away from the truck and marched down the road. Donald rolled down his window. "Last chance."

Emily ignored him.

"Mooooooom, please."

Emily continued walking.

Donald sped off, leaving nothing but darkness in his wake.

Emily continued down the road. When the truck pulled out of sight, she turned and reversed her direction to follow its taillights disappearing in the distance. *What a jerk I am. I was going the wrong way.*

This is creepy, she thought. *It has to be at least two miles back to the main road and then ten into town.* The night sounds around her began to register in her consciousness. *What was that? Maybe a wild pig?* She stopped to listen. A small canal paralleled the road, and she envisioned it filled with alligators, all of them hungry, all of them in vile moods. Something moved under her foot. She jumped to one side. *Had she stepped on gravel that rolled under her sole or was that a snake?* She picked up her pace. A low rumbling sound caught her attention. *Donald must be coming back.* She stopped to listen more closely. It was thunder.

⚜

Several rained-soaked miles down the main highway, a car came up behind her. She turned to wave it down, an act she'd tried several times before, but the vehicles simply cruised by without slowing. Her hair flopped in her face and her clothes hung on her like soppy, tattered rags. *I must look like a homeless person. No wonder I can't get a ride.*

To her surprise, this time the car stopped for her.

Someone was in the passenger's seat, so Emily pulled open the back door. The dome light came on, and Emily recognized the driver. Everett Pratt's last lady love, the one he found at church, Amy Bushnell.

"I couldn't see well, but I thought that was you. What are you doing out here all alone?"

Emily tried to squeeze the water from her hair before she hopped in. "I, uh, my car broke down."

"I didn't see a car back there," said Mrs. Bushnell.

"It was on one of the county roads off to the west, about two miles back."

"And you walked all this way?"

"No one would stop for me." Emily sat back, then quickly leaned forward. "I'm going to get your seats soaking wet."

"Don't worry about it. They're leather. They can take it." The passenger turned around to look at Emily.

"This is my daughter, Rachel. Say hello to Ms. Rhodes."

Emily's mouth dropped open. The daughter was blonde and blue-eyed, a beautiful twelve-year-old. This had to be the younger sister of the daughter Mrs. Bushnell told Emily Everett had put the moves on.

"Hi."

The girl smiled. "Hi."

"I didn't know you had two daughters, Mrs. Bushnell."

"What made you think that? Rachel is my only child."

CHAPTER 18

Mrs. Bushnell chatted about the weather, the economy and her job at the newly opened candy shop downtown. "I hope it works out. Stores tend to go under quickly around here. What do you think? Will it last?"

Emily's mind wandered back to the interview with Amy Bushnell and her confession that Everett Pratt had made a pass at her daughter. *This daughter, this girl, this child*? *What a horrid man. No wonder someone killed him.* She sneaked a peak at Mrs. Bushnell's face. Could she have killed Everett? She certainly had motive, but Emily couldn't see this delicate woman wielding a barbecue poker. Poison? That was another matter. Emily wondered why Mrs. Bushnell had not contacted the authorities and reported Pratt. It was a question she wanted to ask her but not with the daughter in the car.

"Ms. Rhodes? Are you all right? You seem to be someplace else."

"Oh, sorry. I'm fine. I was just worried about a friend of mine who's in the hospital. I need to go visit him. Could you drop me there?"

"Oh, certainly. I'd be happy to." Mrs. Bushnell glanced at Emily out of the corner of her eye, and

Emily knew the woman was reading her mind. But Mrs. Bushnell said nothing.

When they pulled up in front of the hospital, the rain let up a bit. "Well, so much for a continuation of that drought," said Mrs. Bushnell. Emily caught the nervousness in her voice and in the laugh that followed.

"Thanks for the lift. And, Mrs. Bushnell..."

"I know. We need to talk. I'll call you. Soon. Very soon." She drove off, leaving Emily standing at the curb. Emily made a mental note to herself not to wait for that call, but to get in touch with her as soon as she was certain Lewis was okay. And after she'd given Donald a piece of her mind.

Naomi sat in a deserted waiting room. Donald was not with her. "Mom! We were worried. Donald is looking for you right now. We drove back to pick you up, but you were gone."

Emily hugged her daughter. "I'm just fine, maybe a little wet. So you convinced Donald to come back for me. How long did that take you?"

Naomi looked as if she wanted to deny she was the one who talked Donald into changing his mind about Emily, but Emily held up her hand and shook her head.

"Okay, we were almost here when I told him that if anything happened to you he'd have to answer to Lewis. He turned around to find you, but we guessed someone had given you a ride, so we scooted back here using a shortcut Donald knew."

"Never mind Donald. How's Lewis? Have you heard anything yet?"

"Nothing other than he's in surgery."

Emily and Naomi sank down onto the uncomfortable chairs in the waiting room. The hours ticked by until the morning light penetrated the hospital windows. Emily kept checking at the desk. Still no word. Finally at nine o'clock, Emily again approached the nurse on duty. She shook her head, and Emily headed back to her chair. A few minutes later the phone on the desk rang. The nurse answered it, listened intently, then beckoned to Emily.

"He's out of surgery and doing well. Only relatives are allowed to visit, but you look like his sister and niece to me, so go on up to his room, number 212. There's already someone there now, so you can't stay long."

Emily was curious who could be there already. She stopped in the doorway, then entered. Lewis turned his head.

"We're so happy you're alive," she said in a whisper. She *was* happy he was alive, so happy she wanted to cry, but that would have made two women weeping over him. The other woman, seated near his bed, her face stained with tears was Lewis' ex-wife. She held his hand with one of hers, with the other, she wiped the tears from her eyes.

She turned an angry, tear-stained face toward Emily. "What are you doing here? You almost got him killed. Couldn't you have the decency to stay away?"

This wasn't the moment to take on the woman, thought Emily. For once her better nature won out. She gave Lewis a tremulous smile.

"Naomi and I just wanted to say hello and see that you were recovering. We'll talk some other time." Emily turned to go.

"You come back here. I've got some things to say to you." The woman tore herself from his side and followed Emily out the door. In the hallway she grabbed Emily's arm.

Although Adrienne was far taller than she, Emily's work in the bar hauling cases of beer and booze developed the muscles in her arms, shoulders and back. She pried the hand off her arm, then took her by the elbow with her other hand in the woman's hair, and pulled her down the hall, away from Lewis' room.

In a low voice Emily said, "Now is not the time for you to throw one of your fits. Your ex-husband almost died. If you want to be here, be here for him and leave me out of it or I'll pull every auburn hair from your head and kick you off your stilettos. Got me?"

Adrienne opened her mouth to speak, but Emily gave a yank to the hair to emphasize how serious she was.

"Better do as Mom says," said Naomi. "She's like a bobcat when she gets riled."

Emily gave Adrienne's hair another tug, then shoved her back down the hall. "Get in there and do your grieving wife thing or whatever you think you

were doing. It almost looked like the genuine arti-
cle to me. Maybe you can fool him too."

Captain Worley walked off the elevator and approached them. "Is there anything I can do to
help?" he asked.

"Arrest her for assault," said ex-wifey.

Worley looked hesitant for a moment, then
smiled at Emily, ignoring Adrienne's words. "How's
he doing?"

"He's fine. Go on in. I know he'll be pleased to
see you."

"I told you to arrest her."

Worley again ignored the outburst. I guess he's
got her number, thought Emily.

Finally Worley turned to the ex-Mrs. Lewis. "If
you're going to be this excitable, I don't think you
should be in there with him."

"What? Why you second-rate cop. I'll have your
badge for this."

"And if you can't control yourself, I'll have to
remove you from the hospital."

Adrienne gave him a look filled with rage, then
spun on her heel and stalked down the hallway to
the elevator.

"I'll be back." She punched the button, and when
the car failed to appear, she began to pummel it
with both hands. Worley and the two women
watched. Finally the doors opened and the wife got
in, catching her heel on the lip of the car. The heel
broke off with a snap, lodging itself in the door
mechanism. The door hit the heel and opened

again, then continued to open and close, open and close, until the doctor who exited the elevator when Adrienne got in, reached down and handed the broken heel to her. The doors slid shut and Worley, Emily and Naomi gave out a collective sigh of relief.

"I thought they were divorced," said Worley.

"He is. She isn't," said Emily.

"You want to go in with me?" he asked.

"No, I think he's had enough women for the night. Tell him I'll be back before I leave for work this afternoon."

"I wonder who called his ex?" asked Naomi as they took the stairs down to the main floor.

"They probably searched his wallet for next of kin, and her name was still there."

"She seemed real upset. Or was that an act?" asked Naomi.

"Who knows? What I hear tell of her she's a drama queen. I just wonder what she wants out of him."

Emily sounded sanguine about Adrienne's presence in Lewis' room, but her insides churned with anger and concern at the woman's appearance and what Lewis might make of it when he was back to himself once more. Would he welcome the prodigal ex-wife's return or want to throw her out on her ear?

The hospital's doors closed with a muffled whoosh leaving them in a world smelling as clean as if it had been washed of all its dirt, emotional as well as physical. Emily drew in a breath of the laundered air.

"We need a ride home," said Naomi.

Emily took her phone out of her pocket and contacted Vicki who drove up a few minutes later.

"What'll it be, ladies?" Vicki said once Emily and Naomi were in the car.

"Take us to my car first. Then a cup of strong coffee, and do you have any Key Lime pie at your place?"

"Yep. Just baked one yesterday." Vicki gave a sniff, then another. "I'm glad to get you the pie, but maybe someone should consider a shower first. You both smell like you spent the night in the swamp."

"We did," said Naomi.

"Shower." The word came out of Emily's mouth with a shaky moan. She thought back to the night on Jekyll Island, and how she pulled Lewis into the shower with her. She burst into tears.

"Why is she crying about a shower?" asked Vicki.

Naomi wrapped her arms around her mother. "Lewis will be fine," she said, correctly guessing Emily's concern.

"Sure," said Vicki, "There's nothing in the world Key Lime pie can't make better."

⚜

Lewis opened his eyes when Worley entered the room. He tried for a look of strength, but every atom in his body ached.

"Where's Emily? She was here a minute ago."

Worley smiled. "So was your wife."

"Ex-wife. It wasn't the gunshot that put me in this state. It was waking up to Adrienne hanging over my bed. My own fault. I forgot to take her number out of my records as emergency contact."

"Emily talked her out of staying."

Lewis watched the flicker of a smile appear on Worley's lips, then disappear to be replaced by his usual stern look.

"Did she now? And she and Naomi are...?"

"Just fine, as is Donald. What the hell were you doing at the Pratts' still with that motley posse?" This time there was no smile on Worley's face. Lewis was expecting this, and he knew he deserved any reprimand Worley might throw at him. He'd acted like a rank amateur.

"Never mind. We'll talk about that later. Right now, I have other news," said Worley.

The floor nurse entered the room. "He's had too many visitors already. Now shoo. Anything you have to say can wait until he's rested."

Lewis held up his hand. "Wait. What news?"

Worley hesitated a moment, then said, "We dropped the murder charges against Bill Harper and released him. Damn that Toby." He clapped his hat on his head and left.

❦

Vicki said it, Emily thought. Key Lime pie will make everything better. She forked the creamy dessert into her mouth. *Mmmmm.*

"I made two," said Vicki. "I've got plenty. Why not drop a piece off to Lewis on your way to work this evening?"

Emily and Naomi were stuffing themselves on coffee and the pie in Vicki's kitchen. Her husband was off playing golf, and the house was quiet. Emily was about to reply to Vicki's offer when the rumble of a loud truck pulling into her drive next door cut off her words.

Emily looked out the side window. "Oh great. It's Donald."

"Donald! I haven't seen that old curmudgeon for weeks." Vicki sprang to the window. "Hey, you. Over here. I got pie."

Donald presented himself at her door, bass cap in his hand, wiping his feet on the mat. Vicki let him in, turning to give Emily a look that said, "This one's a keeper, so neat and polite." So crabby and cantankerous, Emily thought. Of course, Vicki liked Lewis too, thought he was equally mannerly and tidy in his ways. *And always so damn right.*

"Someone at the hospital had to tell me you got a ride." Donald's tone said he was displeased she hadn't called him.

"Someone in an ambulance had to cart Lewis off to the hospital because his friend left him to go charging around in the woods last night," she spit back.

"At his insistence," said Donald.

Vicki gestured toward a kitchen chair, and when he sat, she placed a steaming cup of coffee at his hand.

He looked up and winked at her. "Some women are appreciative of a man's efforts to rescue little gals that go wandering off in the dark."

Emily threw her fork onto her plate and pushed away from the table. "I am not sitting here after the night I've had and listen to a ratty fisherman bad mouth me. I'm going home." She slammed out the door.

"Pie?" she heard Vicki offer Donald.

Soon Naomi followed her into the house. "Get some sleep, Mom. Donald offered to come into work early today, so you can rest the remainder of the afternoon."

"He did what?"

"He's worried about you. He said you seemed more strung out than usual."

"I am not strung out. Ever. I should go over there and give him…" She heard the truck start up and pull out of the drive.

"Too late. Why not give him the benefit of the doubt. He was doing what he and Lewis thought was the best thing to do."

"Lewis could have died."

"Lewis knew he wasn't going to die, and so did Donald. They were both worried about us. Lewis felt responsible for getting us into that situation. In fact, Donald stopped by his room to see how Lewis was doing. He ran into Worley, who told him it was a good thing Lewis was lying in a hospital bed shot up because he wasn't going to be doing detective duties anyway. Worley put him on paid leave. He was showing off for us, Mom, taking us up there to see the still. It got him in more trouble than he bargained for."

"I'll bet Donald was thrilled to hear of Lewis' leave."

"I think Donald was angry at Lewis, but he's the closest thing Lewis has to a guy friend. That doesn't mean he was happy he was shot or put on leave."

"Donald is never happy."

"He is sometimes, usually when you're around."

"Only because he has an easy target for his barbs."

"You're anything but easy, Mom."

Emily fell into the couch and dropped her head into her hands. "I thought he might die."

"Lewis? Naw. He's too tough for that." Naomi joined her mother and put her arms around her. "Sleep. You need it. Now."

"You too, honey."

The two women helped each other down the hallway and flopped into Emily's king-sized bed. Soon Emily could hear the soft, even breathing of her daughter. As exhausted as she was, she had a difficult time getting to sleep. She could still envision the blood covering Lewis' shirt and jacket and see the pain in his eyes.

⬧

The following night Toby drove north on Route 441 out of town careful to avoid any cop cars. He was anxious to finish his own clever plan and get on with the kidnapping of the women for Smith and

Barry. After he wrapped up his business, he wanted to get out of the county, perhaps the state, and find him a hidey hole until he could think of how to finagle a way out of his prison sentence. He'd heard his cousin Bill was free, and that wasn't good. Something had gone wrong. What it was, Toby couldn't imagine. But once he got the money out of his scheme, he'd drop a dime on the guys he'd blackmailed. *That would fix things. Somehow. Those guys were the killers, right?* They should pay—both Toby and the state, he thought.

Toby knew Smith and Barry wouldn't be following him tonight, yet he kept looking into his rear-view mirror and nervously biting the inside of his mouth as he drove toward the old rodeo grounds. Mr. Smith and Naomi's husband decided the best time to grab the two women would be the first night of the barbecue competition at the festival grounds, which would be crowded with people. Smith and Barry could blend in with the influx of people from the coast and other places coming to the cook-off. Toby was certain their victims would attend; he learned through his contacts that both of them were scheduled to work at one of the beer booths.

Tonight was the perfect time for Toby to settle his business with his blackmail victims or "retirement consultants" as Toby preferred to think of them. He smiled to himself as he thought of the money he could put under his mattress to replace the pension he'd lost when the police department fired him.

That was mostly the doing of his partner and his partner's girlfriend, the Yankee gal. *Well, they'd get their up and comin's soon.*

Smith's bilge pump had lost pressure, so he and Barry took it up to Port St. Lucie for a repair, and while they were there, they decided to take in a "gentlemen's club" in the area. Of course, they did not invite Toby along. Toby had never been to a club like that, and he was eager to go, but Smith ordered him to keep an eye on things.

"It's not your style," Smith said to Toby. Toby knew he'd been insulted somehow, but couldn't figure out how his style being different from theirs was degrading to him. He shrugged his droopy shoulders as he drove along, chawing on his tobacco and contemplating with extreme pleasure how the night would turn out for him. Making a quick buck was his style, that he knew.

He'd told the men to meet him with the money at the rear entrance to the grounds, but Toby wasn't taking any chances. He arrived a half-hour early and scouted out the entire place to see if anyone was waiting to take him down. The old rodeo was deserted. He parked behind one of the buildings, hidden from the road, but where he could keep his eye on the rear gate. Any minute now, he thought to himself as he checked his watch.

Suddenly, the doors of the building next to the one where he was parked swung open. A police car pulled out and behind Toby's truck. He slammed the truck in gear and started toward the exit, but another police cruiser pulled in from the street and blocked his way out. He jerked the wheel to the left and headed toward the pens where the livestock were held. One of the gates was open and Toby sped through it, down the dirt-packed arena and out the other end, smashing his truck through the far fence. Boards flew in all directions, hitting the windshield of his truck and smashing the glass. Good thing the fence is old or I'd a done more damage, he thought.

He stepped on the accelerator for more speed and saw only another rickety fence standing in his way of freedom. He plowed through that also, skidded as he attempted to maneuver the truck onto the paved road, corrected for the drift of the back end and screeched onto the concrete. When he checked in the rearview mirror, the police cars had backed out of the grounds or taken the road that led through the place in order to pursue him. *Ha! The sissies. Didn't want to chance scratching their cars or themselves by going through the fences.* Toby switched off his lights and headed north out of town. The only thing that gave away his presence was the banging of his left front fender attached now by only several screws, and threatening to drop off every time he hit a bump. He'd need some duct tape.

Somebody ratted him out, probably the guys he was blackmailing. *Aw, heck.* He'd lost money on that one, but he still had the kidnapping plan. But now he was left with the problem of where to hide until he picked up the women and took them to Smith for transport. The cops were certain to be waiting for him at his cabin. He stuck a fresh chaw in his mouth. He'd have to go underground for a while. He knew just the place.

CHAPTER 19

Emily had waited for Mrs. Bushnell to call the next day, but she didn't. When Emily attempted to get in touch with her, the phone rang until the answering machine kicked in. This wasn't something she wanted to leave on a machine. On her way to work Emily stopped by the Bushnell house and rang the bell. No one answered, and when she peeked in the garage door, the car was gone. Had Mrs. Bushnell skipped town because she lost her nerve and decided not to talk to Emily?

Emily stopped by the hospital to see Lewis, and checked the Bushnell house on her way to and from work. It continued to be deserted. She hadn't told Lewis of her conversation with Mrs. Bushnell. He seemed to be weak and recovering from his wound slowly. Besides, she said to herself, what could he do? He was bedridden, and when he got out of the hospital, he would still be on leave.

She ran into Captain Worley several times when he too visited Lewis. He told her they had executed another search warrant on the Pratts' trailer looking for weapons that might match the one used to wound Lewis. The search turned up nothing. Besides, he told Emily, Jasper and Elmer had alibis for that night—Melanie and Jasper's wife said they were both at the trailer sucking on beers. Not that he believed the women, he said. Neither did Emily. She was as convinced as Worley that Jasper and Elmer were responsible for shooting Lewis. Why were these women so eager to protect men who didn't deserve their loyalty? Maybe it was in their genes, she thought. She had uppity genes, making it hard for her to stand by any man who was a killer.

At work, she tried to avoid conversation with Donald. The out-of-sorts look on his face said he was happy with the silence. But who could tell with Donald? He always seemed to have that sour look whether he'd just won a fishing tournament or lost a ball on the ninth.

Emily sat uneasily on her information about Amy Bushnell's daughter until the first night of the barbecue contest. She could have taken the story to the cops, but it wasn't her story to tell. It was Amy Bushnell's. If Lewis was still active he would have known what to do. Now Emily had to figure that out for herself. If she couldn't find Mrs. Bushnell, perhaps she should pay a visit to Melanie Pratt. Everett's wife must have known about his interest in young girls. A horrible thought crossed her mind. Would he have tried something with his own granddaughter? She appeared to be about twelve when Emily saw her that one time at their house. This was something she couldn't let go any longer. She needed to talk with Melanie tonight either at the festival in the Pratt booth or later at the trailer.

She and Naomi pulled beers until after eleven. They'd shared a ride to the festival, held at the new rodeo grounds. Should Emily tell Naomi what she knew and ask her to come along to talk with Mrs. Pratt or should she figure out some way to unload Naomi? She knew this was something for her to do alone. Melanie and her daughter-in-law would be uncomfortable when Emily confronted them, and they certainly wouldn't want an audience. What could she say to Naomi?

At that moment, Donald sauntered by the beer booth, acting as if he didn't see her and Naomi.

"Donald." She wiggled her finger at him to come over.

"Erg," he said, but walked over to her.

"We need to talk. This is silly our working together and not saying a word to one another."

"You could offer me an apology and thank me for saving you the other night."

Saving *her*? Emily would have preferred slinging a pint of beer at him rather than say she was sorry for anything, but she kept those feelings to herself...for once.

"Sure. Fine, but let's discuss what happened first. I'll meet you at the far side of the rodeo arena in half an hour."

"Why there?"

"Didn't you park your truck over there? I thought I saw you pull in earlier tonight."

"Why not talk right now?"

"Donald, I'm working now."

"Okay. Half an hour."

"You can give me a ride home, so Naomi can take my car."

Donald's face did something twitchy, which Emily chose to interpret as a smile. Maybe Naomi was right. Maybe he liked Emily.

"Don't hold me up. I got a bass tournament tomorrow morning early. I don't want to be late."

Naw, thought Emily. He didn't like her. He only liked creatures that breathed with gills.

After he left, she and Naomi closed up the booth. Once they'd made certain all the kegs were stored securely in the beer cooler truck, she handed the car keys to her daughter.

"Take the car on home. I've got to meet a second with Donald. He insisted. He'll give me a lift."

Naomi's face darkened for a moment. "Gee, I told some of my friends from our park, I'd go along with them to the Burnt Biscuit after I got off. They drove all the way out here to pick me up."

Emily took back her keys and revised her plans. "Okay. I'd just as soon not have Donald drive me home anyway."

This was even better, thought Emily. Earlier Emily determined that Melanie Pratt wasn't in the Pratts' booth. She must have stayed home tonight, thought Emily. She could scoot off to the Pratts' and talk with Melanie while the guys, Jasper and that greasy Elmer dude were busy at the booth.

After Naomi left with her friends, Emily strolled down the line of closed booths. She could hear the sounds of clean-up going on within some of them. Others were dark, their occupants snugged up in the trailers parked nearby. The Pratts' booth was shuttered. Alongside it stood a tiny trailer, light spilling from a single window. Emily paused a moment and heard an argument going on inside. She listened for several minutes. No female voices. She heard only Jasper and Elmer. Great. Maybe the boys were staying in the trailer for the night. The lights went out, so she waited hidden within the shadows of the booth. No one came out. They must have retired for the night, she thought. That made sense to her. To-morrow was the big contest, and they'd need to get up at four to begin their cooking.

She smiled to herself. Things were working out better than she imagined. She'd have the Pratt women all to herself tonight. She wouldn't need Donald as back-up at the Pratts' after all. Only the three generations of women would be there. No creepy Pratt male with his equally creepy sidekick.

For no more than five seconds she chided herself for standing up Donald, then tossed off any guilt over leaving him hanging for the night. Her car was parked in the far lot, the other side of the grounds from where Donald had left his truck. It was better he didn't know what she was up to, she reasoned. He'd say it was too risky. She knew better.

As she approached the car, she looked up at the stars blanketing the night sky. The moon shone bright overhead, silvery, with only a lacy wisp of a cloud draped across it like a senorita with a veil. *Beautiful.*

Her car stood alone with the exception of an old pickup truck parked to the far side of it. Something about the truck looked familiar. Just another old ranch truck, she told herself, then stopped in her tracks. *It couldn't be.* As she pivoted to run back to the rodeo grounds, a hand encircled her arm and pulled her around the front of her car. When the smell of the man assaulted her nostrils, she recognized the truck.

It belonged to Toby.

⚜

Smith watched from a distance as Toby tossed Emily into his truck.

"Think he can handle her?" asked Barry.

"He outweighs her by a hundred pounds. How hard can it be to grab one tiny woman? Even for Toby." Smith looked around the parking area. No one else seemed to be there, but he didn't want to expose himself in case a security guard came through. Let Toby take the risk of being caught in the act.

"Let's go. We rendezvous in a half-hour." Barry sounded nervous.

Smith began to worry he'd get cold feet about selling his wife into white slavery.

"You're not having second thoughts about this, are you?" Because if he was, then Smith would demand more money. And then get rid of Barry along with the two women. Smith never intended having passengers on his boat all the way across the Atlantic. *Too much trouble.* Barry was too stupid to think that one through, thought Smith. He sighed, loud enough that Barry heard him.

"You're not tired of this already, are you?"

Smith delivered one of his black looks. "I am never tired, just thinking. Your friend Toby had better forget about adding the detective to the passenger list. I warned him about that."

"He's frosty with that. Don't worry. He'll do as he's told. The guy has no imagination or initiative of his own."

Smith thought about how "frosty" he could make Toby, like a side of beef in a meat locker.

The two men walked back to their SUV hidden in the woods near the entrance to the rodeo grounds. The figure in the backseat was making ineffectual yelling sounds through her gag and pounding her feet against the back door.

"Shut her up or I will." Smith wondered how he'd gotten himself into this. Money, of course. Was there enough money in the world to put up with these rubes, he wondered.

They drove past another SUV also concealed deep within the trees. This one held the tied-up bodies of Naomi's friends.

"No picking up cowboys on the dance floor tonight," yelled Barry out the window as they passed.

"Shut up," said Smith, "or I'll shut all of you up." *Not enough money in the world.*

⁂

Clang, clang, clang. Emily's hands were bound behind her, but Toby had thankfully not gagged her.

"What the hell is that racket?" Emily could barely see where they were going because of the smashed windshield. She hoped Toby's side had a clearer view of the road or they could end up in a ditch.

"It's my fender. Not that it's any of your business. Now shut your trap or you'll never see your daughter alive again."

The racket abruptly stopped as the fender dropped off and landed in the parking area. Toby shrugged and pressed harder on the accelerator. The truck fishtailed onto the highway and away from the rodeo grounds.

Out the side window, she could see the road leading to the hiking trail fly past. Just like the ride she took with Lewis the night he got shot. *No, not like that at all. This one would surely lead to her death or to Naomi's or...* She didn't want to think about what lay ahead.

This was déjà vu, she thought. Toby turned left and headed down the same road that skirted the location of the Pratts' operating still.

He pulled over about a half-mile from where Lewis had parked his cruiser when he showed Emily and Naomi the still. He slammed on his brakes, and the truck rattled to a stop. He pulled her from the passenger's seat and dragged her into the woods.

"Where are you taking me?" Her heart thudded in her chest as he walked her through the trees along a well-worn path. Wherever they were heading, Emily needed an escape plan.

"Never mind. Shut up. You talk too damn much." Toby gave her a shove that almost brought her to her knees.

She struggled for balance. "Where's my daughter?"

"I told you to shut up. If you don't I'm gonna have to knock you out and then drag you. That won't be pleasant."

For you, Emily thought. She couldn't imagine Toby moving a dead weight along the path. She didn't think he wanted to do that much work.

"Are you taking me to her?"

Toby grabbed her arm and pulled her to a stop. He stomped up and down in a kind of lunatic frenzy. "Why won't you just shut up? Shut up, shut, up, shut up."

Geez, the guy is coming unhinged. Maybe that's good, if I can rattle him enough that he makes a mistake.

The moon in a cloudless sky wrapped the landscape in an eerie glow. She could see almost as well as if the sun was out except the world was reflected to her in shades of grey, black and white. As they walked, the terrain began to look familiar. They had to be nearing the Pratts' sinkhole still. Did Toby know this, she wondered. He seemed to be certain of where he was going, but she wondered why he would choose the still as a rendezvous point with whoever he was meeting. It couldn't be the Pratts, thought Emily. *Could it?*

Out of the corner of her eye Emily caught a fleeting movement, a large shape running across the path, other smaller shadows hovering at the side of the trail ahead of them, then several dashing in front of them. One figure hesitated, tried to run in front of Toby, then turned to return to the shelter of the dense vegetation.

"What the hell?" said Toby.

The large shape turned sharply, its back illuminated as it crashed through the brush and back onto the path. A wild pig, a sow. Toby and Emily stood between her and one of her piglets.

⁓❖⁓

The car pulled up next to Donald's truck. At first he didn't recognize the man behind the wheel until the driver's windows were next to each other.

"Detective. What are you doing here? I thought you were still in the hospital."

"I just got out tonight and thought I'd cruise on up here to see what was going on."

"Word is you've been suspended. So I guess you're just a civilian being nosy then."

"I'm looking for Emily."

"So am I."

"Really?"

"We had a date of sorts."

Donald could see a smile slowly cross Lewis' features. "It looks like she stood you up."

"Give her time. She's just closing the beer booth."

"You're deluding yourself, Donald. I already checked there, and the booth is shut up tight."

"Something's wrong then."

This time Donald watched Lewis throw back his head and laugh. "Just because she got a better offer doesn't mean anything's wrong. I could understand why she'd turn down your invitation."

"I didn't invite her. She invited me."

The detective gave no immediate reply to this. He looked away from Donald across the moon-washed field.

"I think we should look for her car." The concern in Lewis' voice surprised Donald. Lewis actually believed something was not right.

"It won't be around. Naomi would have driven it home."

"Hop in. We'll take a look anyway."

The two men drove across the parking area and around the back of the rodeo arena. The livestock so energetic and lively earlier seemed to settle down in their pens. A few low calls from the steers and a momentary bellow from a bull were the only sounds from the animals housed within the enclosures.

The headlight caught a lone security guard in front of them. He signaled for them to stop, and shined a mag light into the car's interior. He recognized Lewis.

"Howdy, Detective. I heard about the shooting. It's good to see you up and around again. What can I do for you?"

"You see a little blonde-haired woman wandering around here?"

"Nope." He shook his head and looked down at his feet. Then, as if discovering something in the dirt, he looked up at Lewis. "Wait now. I did see someone looked like that earlier. She was in a truck with someone heading off the grounds. The guy was a short, fat dude. He hardly seemed her type."

"Toby." Lewis and Green said the name together.

"Where was this?" asked Lewis.

The security guard pointed to the parking area on the other side of the rodeo arena. "I can't be certain it was the gal you're looking for. I only got a glimpse, but it was over there. To your far right."

"Thanks." Lewis punched the accelerator and headed to where the guard pointed. The headlights picked up Emily's red sedan as they raced across the parking lot.

"I can't see Emily voluntarily getting into a vehicle with Toby Sands." Lewis stomped on the brakes and threw open the car door. Donald jumped out of the passenger's side. Lewis followed. Donald looked back and saw Lewis wince as he emerged from the car. Sure he was out of the hospital, Donald thought, but still in a lot of pain. Lewis caught up to Donald and grabbed his arm to pull him back.

"Let's not muck up what might be a crime scene. I'll take a good look around the area to see what's here."

Donald shrugged. "Go play cop, but I can see there's nobody here."

"There could be something in the dirt—tire tracks, boot marks, Emily's footprints. Let me take care of this."

"You're no longer on the force, detective. Shouldn't you call the police to investigate?" Donald's tone was sarcastic.

"And Emily may be in real danger. You want me to put in a call to the department and wait for a real detective? Time may be important here."

Well, he had him there, Donald thought. He gestured for the detective do whatever it was he had in mind.

Lewis walked around the area, shining his flashlight onto the ground. There was one set of boot tracks, deep and small. Fat Toby, he thought. Then he could see another set of prints, smaller than the first. He thought of Emily's tiny feet at the condo after she shed her wet sneakers. If Toby did anything to her, thought Lewis, he would... He could see in the dirt where there was something of a scuffle, the booted person behind the other. The tiny feet disappeared, and the boot prints led to the vehicle parked beside Emily's. *Toby carried her to the truck, shoved her in, and drove off.* Lewis shined his light following the dirt tracks. The light bounced off something ahead. He walked up to it. *Interesting.* Part of a fender from an old truck. From Toby's old truck.

"What did you see?" asked Donald.

"Toby took her. No doubt of that. But where did he go?"

"To his old cabin."

"Every cop in this county is looking for Toby, and the first place they'd look would be that cabin. Toby's trying to stay out of sight, so he'd take her somewhere else, someplace well hidden, off the beaten path."

"We need someone who knows Toby's haunts. Who?"

Lewis' shoulder throbbed, and he felt his shirt wet with sweat under his jacket. He must be running a fever. Think, he told himself, think.

"Girlfriend maybe?"

Donald scrunched up his face with distaste. "Are you mad?"

Only the pain in his shoulder kept Lewis from laughing at that one. Then he had it. "Cousin Bill."

"Oh, like the guy Toby turned in for murder would hide him."

"No, of course not, but Bill might be willing to talk to me. He would know Toby's habits and favorite places."

"I'll drive."

"Why?"

"Look." Donald nodded at Lewis' chest.

Blood had seeped through from his wound onto his white shirt, which now looked like it was tie-dyed.

CHAPTER 20

"On one condition." Lewis begrudgingly allowed Donald behind the wheel. "You're not dropping me off at the hospital."

"I didn't say a thing."

"But I can read your mind."

Donald nodded. It looked to Lewis as if it was a gesture of agreement, but, despite his words to the contrary, Lewis never could read Donald's intentions.

Donald jammed the accelerator to the floor, and they headed for the exit from the rodeo grounds.

"Stop a minute," said Lewis. "I caught the reflection of moonlight off a car in those trees. Somebody's parked in there."

"Now we're rousting teenagers making out?" Donald gave one of his characteristic throaty growls of disdain, but he slowed and turned the car toward the wooded area.

"I'll have a look." Lewis prepared to open his door and get out.

"No. You stay put. Here." Donald handed him a large neckerchief.

"Bleeding on your shirt is one thing, but ruining the upholstery?"

Lewis gave a little snicker. Donald's priorities were clear. Lewis knew if he was bleeding all over Donald's truck, he'd be riding in its bed.

Some clouds obscured the moon, and Lewis couldn't see what Donald was doing in the stranded vehicle. Soon he emerged from the woods with two young women.

"Naomi's been taken too," Donald said.

"Toby got her? What's the guy's game?" This didn't sound like a Toby scheme, thought Lewis. Too big for him to handle on his own. He had help, but who?

The young women were unhurt, but scared. Donald seated them in the car.

"Now is it time for real cops?" he asked Lewis.

Lewis extracted his cell from his coat pocket and handed it to Donald who punched in the number Lewis told him to. He turned his attention to the frightened women.

"What happened?"

"A big SUV, black, pulled in front of us as we were leaving the rodeo. Two men jumped out, both with guns," said the blonde woman.

Lewis started to reach for his notebook, but, of course, he no longer had it. "Describe the men."

"One was real lean, didn't say a word. The other…"

The second woman, small like Emily, interrupted. "The other was Naomi's ex-husband."

With a crash, the parts of Toby's scheme came together in Lewis' head. He groaned and looked at Donald who ended his call and stared back at him.

Donald's jaw line tightened, and his cheek began its angry twitch. Lewis had seen the reaction many times, times right before the man exploded in rage. This time he kept his reaction under icy control. "We should have taken care of that hunk of mud when we had the chance. Scaring him wasn't enough."

They had tried to frighten Naomi's husband several months ago by threatening to pay him a visit if he ever bothered her again. Obviously, it wasn't enough of a scare, thought Lewis. This time they'd get it right. If they had the chance.

The sow made straight for Toby. With a swipe of her long tusks she hit him mid-calf. Only the protection of his boots kept her from severing an artery. The charge brought Toby to his knees.

"Get up. We've got to get out of here." With her hands tied behind her, it was difficult for Emily to run, especially when the moon slipped behind a cloud and shuttered the path ahead of her in darkness. She preferred to have her hands in front of her to protect her face or out to the sides for balance.

Despite the awkwardness, she knew she had to get away from the pig at least until mom found her prodigal young one. Emily struggled down the path, trying hard not to fall. She heard crashing in the underbrush behind her. *Toby? Mother pig? Baby oinker?* She couldn't take the time to look.

The moon slid from behind the cloud. The light made the woods as light as day. She knew where she was. The sinkhole housing the still had to be just ahead. If she jumped into the hole without her hands to cushion her fall, would she break her leg or her neck? She had no choice. *Jump. Now.*

She miscalculated a bit and caught the far lip of the hole with one knee, but the fall took her into the hole and to safety. She lay there a moment on her back, wiggling body parts to make sure everything worked.

Noise at the opening of the sinkhole caught her attention. She could see shadowy movements just beyond the top. The sow squealed and grunted. Somebody yelled. That must be Toby, she thought. Something fell on her, something not big enough to be a human, but it was as smelly as Toby, perhaps more so, and it was wiggly. *Oh no, the piglet.*

The fall seemed to daze the little thing for a moment, and Emily hoped it would remain quiet. If mama knew where her kid was, she'd never leave the area. And Emily would never leave this prison.

"Toby. Where are you? Are you okay?" Why was she asking that? She didn't care. In fact, it would be nice if Toby fell into the hole and broke his neck or got trampled and slashed by pig mother love. But then, of course, how would she get out of here?

It appeared her shouting aroused the piglet who began to yell in piggy language. Its cries were answered by the mother whose head appeared at the top of the hole. Emily looked with fear at the formidable tusks on the hog. She was glad for a moment that she was down here and not up there with mama.

"Toby. Where the hell are you? You've got to get me out of here." Was he dead? Did he run off?

The vocal exchanges between mother and baby continued unabated and reverberated throughout the otherwise still night. Emily longed to put her hands over her ears. It was gut-wrenching to hear the little piglet's cries of distress. *Was he hurt? I guess not. He's yelling lustily and running around like he's just fine.*

She couldn't stand the noise. There was nothing for her to do but find her way back into the sinkhole to the still and hope she could figure out how to get the door back there open. Without her hands, that seemed impossible, but remaining here and listening to the anguished exchanges were not helping her situation. She began to wander back toward the still. With the branches and other brush creating the ceiling for the sinkhole, the light became dimmer as she moved farther from the rabbit's hole she'd fallen down. Soon she had to walk with extreme caution, fearing she would smash her face into the walls, or if she went far enough, run right into the still itself. The thought of metal making abrupt contact with her nose made her take one step at a time, pausing after each one before she moved her foot out to test the ground ahead of her.

The piglet's screams grew louder.

What the hell is going on?

She felt the animal dash by her leg.

"No, no, little one. You go back. Don't follow me. I'm not your mama."

Emily wondered how long it would take mama to decide to take the risk and jump into the sinkhole back there. And then Emily would become her target, an easy one as she stumbled around in the darkness.

~⁂~

This is not good, thought Toby, as he ran from the sinkhole trying to put distance between himself and the angry pig. Soon the cries of mother and piglet grew more distant. He'd circle around and move back to his truck hidden in the bushes at the side of the road. There he could wait for the arrival of the other package and his buddies in crime. He was pretty certain Emily would never be able to get out of that sinkhole by herself. It was too steep to climb without help, and especially without the use of her hands, and the door at the other end was locked. He'd made certain of that earlier today. I'm a crafty one, he thought. *Yup, I know every hidey hole in these parts including the Pratts' still.* That gave Toby another of what he considered his brilliant ideas. He could blackmail the Pratts by threatening to give away the location of their still. Toby congratulated himself for being able to plot while on the run. As for Emily down in that hole? He'd just tell Mr. Smith and Barry he threw her in there to keep her out of the way. There was no need to say anything about the pig and her falling into the hole. What a brilliant idea, Toby thought, and he did a high five from one side of his brain to the other.

He revised his earlier, negative assessment of the situation. Everything was working out just fine. He checked his watch. Time to make the call, the one he knew Lewis would welcome, the one where Toby offered to let Lewis save Emily from the bad guys. Toby reached in his pocket for a fresh chaw. *Empty*. He must have dropped the packet when he was doing battle with the pig. No matter. He'd soon have all the money in the world he'd need to replenish his supply, and this time he'd buy the good stuff. He punched in the number.

"You've got ten minutes to get out to the Pratts' still or your little girlfriend will be dead. I went along with these guys because they threatened me, but I can't hold them off forever. They'll be here soon with your gal's daughter. Come alone."

—❦—

Lewis signed off after Toby's message. His arm ached, and the bleeding wouldn't stop, but he knew he had this one chance to find Emily and her daughter. Lewis leaned against his car while Donald and the police talked to the young women who had been with Naomi. He pushed himself away from the car and moved toward the driver's side, then opened the door, and slid in.

Donald turned his head when he saw the overhead light come on. "What are you doing, you idiot?"

Donald ran toward the car, but Lewis had it in gear and gunned it toward the road, leaving Donald behind. He heard Donald yell for one of the cops to give him a ride to his truck. Lewis checked his rearview mirror. Donald flailed his arms around, but the cop kept shaking his head. Procedure, thought Lewis. They'd want to finish taking the young women's stories before they attended to someone losing his ride. Lewis smiled and pressed the handkerchief harder against his wound. It would be awhile before he had to worry about a bass fisherman following him.

The car headed north on the highway taking the route he'd used the night he tried to show up Emily and Naomi. He regretted taking them to the still. But damn Emily. She had a way of getting under his skin, thinking her intuition could get her farther than his detecting skills. Your fault you got shot, he said to himself. He just had to show her where the real still was, make her look stupid that she'd nosed around a moonshine location not used for years.

In his rearview mirror Lewis saw headlights come up on him fast. Soon they penetrated his car. Damn fool is going to ram me, he thought. He gave the car more gas to pull away, but his pursuer kept up with him. Then the flashers came on.

"Pull over," said a voice from the loud speaker in the cop car behind him.

Lewis groaned, but knew his vehicle could never outrun a cruiser. He watched in his mirror as a familiar figure emerged from the car. It was Captain Worley.

"Lewis, what the hell are you doing flying down this road at over eighty miles an hour?"

"Sir. What are you doing on patrol?"

"I'm short-handed because one of my detectives was stupid enough to get himself shot, and now he's on leave."

"I know this looks bad for me, but I got a message from Toby..."

Before Lewis could finish what he was saying, a car pulled up behind Worley's cruiser.

"Now what?" asked Worley.

Donald stepped out of the driver's side of the car.

"He'll tell you all about it. Toby's behind this entire thing." As Lewis spoke he considered his words. Worley had to know Toby wasn't capable of being behind anything.

"Stanton. Honey."

The individual speaking in those sugared tones might be hidden behind the pulsating lights of the cruiser and the headlights of the other vehicle, but Lewis recognized their owner without seeing her.

"Adrienne. What the hell are you doing here? And better yet, Donald, why is she with you?"

The expression on Donald's face was one of concern mixed with self-satisfaction. "She drove into the parking lot at the rodeo grounds right after you left. I don't know how she found you there, but I think she must have followed you from the hospital out to the rodeo grounds. I had already put a call into the police about you. Worley arrived about that same time. We could see your tail lights heading north, so we all followed."

Lewis stepped out of his car. His legs felt as shaky as Jell-O squares.

"Are you okay, darlin'? Adrienne wrapped her arms around him. All at once it felt good to have someone support him. He must have lost more blood than he knew. The world began to grow darker, his vision yellowed at the edges and pulled in on him. He sank to the ground.

Toby leaned back relieved he'd delivered his message and certain that Lewis was on his way to the still. He hadn't yet caught his breath from his run to the truck. He looked down at his hand, still on his cell. It was shaking. It might be from the anticipation of confronting Lewis with the odds in Toby's favor for once. He rejected the other possibility that it was going to take some time to recover from his flight. All the way through the woods, he ran faster than he ever thought he could, not stopping or hesitating to look behind him, terrified that any minute he would feel the pain of a sharp tusk in his calf. He had no idea what happened to the Rhodes woman, nor did he care. For all he knew, she lay bleeding to death at the bottom of the sinkhole. All he focused on now was the next victim in his scheme, the partner he blamed for all his misfortune. He was certain the trembling came from the excitement of taking Lewis down. Finally.

There was the issue of timing, he admitted to himself. If Lewis didn't put in an appearance soon, Toby's partners would show up, and Toby would have to give up his revenge on Lewis. Or, worse yet, they would show, and then Lewis would appear. A messy situation, but one Toby was certain he could handle. Somehow.

He saw lights on the road behind him, a large car approaching slowly. He knew Lewis would be driving his own vehicle since he was on leave. This car had to be the detective's. As the headlamps got closer and brighter, Toby could discern the make. He groaned and slumped down in his seat. Right now a disappearing trip down a sinkhole sounded good. It was Smith's SUV. Time to execute Plan B.

Toby always had a Plan B. And C. Maybe D, if necessary.

The SUV stopped behind the truck, and Smith emerged from the driver's side.

"What the hell are you doing out here on the road? A blind man could find your truck. You're supposed to be in there with your prey, hiding out near the still, you told me."

"It's not my fault." Toby got out of the truck and approached Smith. "We got ambushed by a pig. It ran off, but I had to think fast to save her for you, so I pushed her down the sinkhole. Yep, I knew you'd want her alive, not mangled by some fatback on the hoof."

"You let a pig run you off?" asked Barry. His face was black with anger and disbelief. And animal rage. Toby's mind quivered. He began to under-stand why the daughter found this man so frighten-ing.

"Where's your cargo?" asked Toby. The question was barely out of his mouth when he knew he'd made a mistake, asking it, asking anything.

Barry nodded toward the SUV. "Back there, safe and sound for now."

Smith gave him a dark look, then turned his at-tention to Toby. "Perhaps you'd like to show us your pig." He moved to Toby's side and placed his hand on his shoulder.

Oh, no, not again, thought Toby. Sweat poured from his pores like someone had dumped water over him. Something warm ran down his leg. He waited for the crushing pain of Smith's grasp on him. But it never came. Instead, Smith gestured toward the woods like a gentleman sweeping his lady into the ballroom, civilized, genteel, graceful of hand. Deadly to Toby.

"Yes sir." Toby began down the path with Smith and Barry following. After several steps he turned. "Maybe you don't know about the wild pigs around here. They've got tusks over four inches long, long-er on the boars."

"Interesting. Don't you find that interesting?" Smith asked Barry.

"It's just a damn pig," Barry replied dismissively.

"Oh, you have no idea how mean they can be. This one had piglets. She was riled."

"Keep walking, Toby," said Smith. Again that tone of voice, even, smooth, almost sensual, and beneath it, Toby knew, was black ice.

The night was eerily still. The moon was out, and a breeze blew the clouds away from its face. They nestled in the sky to the east, gathered above the trees that lined the field.

"Here we are." Toby paused at the edge of the sinkhole.

Barry peered into the darkness below. "Can't see crap down there."

Smith joined the two of them as they tried to penetrate the dim chamber.

A screaming wail split the night air, and a sinister shape charged out of the brush.

Smith grabbed the husband and shoved him in front of him using him as shield against the oncoming animal. Barry struggled against Smith's steel grasp. Toby took one step backwards and fell into the hole.

※

"Where am I?" Lewis came to, aware his head rested in someone's lap. Certainly not Donald's or Worley's, he knew.

"We're going to take you to the hospital, sweetie. You should never have left. It's a good thing I was keeping an eye on you and followed you to the rodeo grounds."

Oh, crap. It was his ex-wife, what's-her-name. His focus was on Emily's safety. He cared little for the comforting arms of Adrienne who always disappeared when things got tough and reappeared when he got a raise, a promotion, more money. He was on leave, and he might be demoted back to foot patrol, so he couldn't figure what she had in mind this time.

"I don't know what your scheme is, Adrienne, but I know you've got one. Right now, however, I've got more important things to consider. I'll talk to you later."

Shaking her arms off him, he got to his feet and shoved open the door of the car.

"The ambulance will be here soon," said Donald. "You get back in there with your wife until it arrives."

"First, she is my ex-wife. Second, Donald, there is the matter of Emily's safety. You do want to help her, don't you? And you can't without my cooperation because only I know where she went."

"Tell me."

Lewis stood toe-to-toe with Donald. I can't let Emily die, thought Lewis, even if I have to give her up to this bonehead bass fisherman.

"You going to help me or let her die?"

"You might as well go along with what he wants. I know this guy. If he says he's going to do something, he will." Worley's face wore an expression of surrender.

Donald walked over to where Adrienne stood in front of the police cruiser listening to the conversation between the men.

"You wanna get out of the way?" Donald's voice was polite, but firm in its request.

Adrienne pressed herself against the front bumper. "I'm not going to let my husband..."

"Ex-husband, I believe." Donald's voice took on a sterner note.

"As I said, I'm not going to let Lewis chase after that floozy. You'll have to run me down first. Kill me with my own car. Go ahead."

Oh, boy. I hope she moves, thought Lewis, or...

Donald snatched her away from the bumper, lifted her off her feet and tossed her to Worley. "Hold this for a while, would you?"

Worley tried to catch her, or at least Lewis thought he did, but the captain dropped her. She landed with a thump into the sand at the edge of the road. A look of pleasure crossed Worley's face for a half-second, but it disappeared when Worley reached out his hand to her. "Sorry about that, ma'am."

She slapped his hand away and burst into tears.

"Let's go." Lewis and the three men headed for the police cruiser. "What about me?" wailed Adrienne.

"Better get into the car, darlin'. Hear that?"

She quieted herself and listened. "I don't..."

"Male gator looking for a mate," said Donald.

Lewis heard her yelp then begin a keening wail. When he looked back, he could see she'd gotten into her car.

"I hope she doesn't follow us." said Lewis.

Worley held up his fingers from which dangled Adrienne's car keys.

CHAPTER 21

The piglet continued to let out squeals and run after Emily. She made it to the still, up the slope to the shed, but the exit door was bolted shut from the outside. Her only escape was to climb onto the still and use the T-bar to lift a ceiling section off the sinkhole. Then she could climb onto the roof and out of the sinkhole. Except she had no idea how she could do all that with her hands tied behind her back. A faint returning squeal came from the end of the sinkhole she'd just traversed. Mama wanted her kid, thought Emily. If the mother decided to jump in to rescue the little ham, Emily was in danger. Neither the pigs nor Emily could get out. Emily would be trapped in an enclosed space with an enraged mother who was better armed than Emily. How long could she last dodging those tusks? Long enough for the kid to age and grow tusks of his own? She couldn't wait for that.

"Hey, you, lady."

The utterance came out of the darkness only feet from where Emily stood. She couldn't see him, yet she knew it was Toby by the wheedling sound in his voice.

"What are you doing here? The last time I saw you, you were running for safety."

"I fell down here. Just like you did. Can't get the door open?"

"No, I just like it here so much I thought I'd hang around for a while. Undo my hands and maybe we can figure out how to get it open."

"Heh, heh. No deal." Toby hesitated, then continued, "I'm sure my pals will be showing up any minute now to get me out of here."

Emily picked up a note of uncertainly in Toby's voice.

"Heh, heh yourself. If your pals were coming to get you out, they'd be here by now. Maybe they don't know about this end of the sinkhole? You forget to tell them?"

Toby was silent.

From the sound of the piglet screaming for his mother, Emily could tell it continued to run around the still, brushing past their legs. Then the howls would recede as it dashed back down the tunnel and returned to squeal once more.

"Hey, you still there, little man? Untie my hands, and we'll get out of this together."

"Yeah, then what?"

Emily could tell Toby was reviewing his options. If his buddies didn't show and he helped Emily out, then what? He probably figured Emily would turn him in, and that's exactly what she planned. She had no intention of telling him that.

"I think your guys have deserted you, and you're a wanted man. All the cops in the county will be looking for you. You need me. I'm your ticket to reduced jail time. I can testify you helped me." She let Toby think this over for a moment.

"What's your plan?"

Emily wasn't about to share her idea for escape with him, or he'd do it without her help.

"Untie me, Toby and I'll back your story to the cops."

A commotion at the far end of the sinkhole caught Emily's attention. The piglet's cries faded once more as it fled down the tunnel. Soon its squealing was joined by a lower and louder grunt. It was as Emily feared. Mama finally took the plunge and jumped into the sinkhole. Soon she'd head this way looking for escape. Emily's time had run out.

"Quick, Toby. Untie me now. The sow's coming, and she won't be happy to find us here with her young'un."

Emily could feel his hesitation.

"Now!" she yelled.

He fumbled with her ropes in the dark. The cries of the two pigs seeking a route out of their prison got louder. Mama may have found her lost one, but now she was separated from the rest of her litter and eager to get back to them.

Emily flexed her wrists, reached out her hand and located the still. She used the pipes coming off it for handholds and climbed to the top.

"Where are you?"

"Up here. Can you find the back wall? Go over to it. There's a wooden T-bar leaning against it. It's for lifting the ceiling off this hole. Hand it to me."

Emily listened as the pigs continued to rustle and run around the far end of the tunnel. Could the baby tell mom there was another end, one with humans in it?

"I get it now. I can just push this up and remove the ceiling, Toby said."

"No you can't. You're too short down there. I can do it from here. Hand it to me."

"I'm coming up there too."

"There's no time. I'll move the ceiling, then you can crawl up."

Emily heard movement from below, a grunt followed by some swearing. "I told you. You're too short."

The pigs' cries got louder.

"Oh, God, they're coming. I'm going to get eaten by a pig. Eaten alive."

"Hand me the damn T-bar or I'm coming down there and kick you in your boys."

The T-bar hit her hand. Emily grabbed it and maneuvered it toward the ceiling. Grunting noises came from below. She couldn't tell if it was Toby trying to get on top of the still or the pigs had come into the still room. She pushed and felt the ceiling move. The bar was heavy for her to handle, and it was awkward moving a section aside, but inch by inch she slid the covering off and moonlight shone into the room below.

"I can't get up there."

She dropped the bar and balanced herself on top of the still. She stood on her tiptoes and reached above her head until her hands touched one of the heavy roof beams. By walking herself across the top of the still using the beam for balance, she could just reach the floor-to-ceiling support pole. It was made of a hand-hewed tree, rough enough that she could use the cut-away nubs of branches to pull herself up.

"Help me," she heard Toby say from below.

She couldn't look down or she'd lose her nerve and her balance as she shimmied up the pole. "I'll go out and open the door."

"Don't leave me here with these pigs." Toby screamed something else, but Emily couldn't make it out. Now at the top, she hopped across the roof beams and ran toward the shed.

Emily slid the wood through the brackets and opened the door.

Toby fell out onto the ground. Emily slammed the door before the pigs could follow.

"She got my shoe." Toby was sobbing.

Emily reconsidered her save. It should have been the pigs, she thought.

"Quit your bawling. You're safe now."

She watched his face in the moonlight as the realization of how close he'd come to being taken out by a wild pig swept across it.

Emily stood with her hand still on the wood, prepared to slide it back through the handles to secure the door. She felt a nudge and knew the sow was leaning her weight against it. As she was about to slide the wood home, her eye caught movement at the edge of the clearing.

Two men, one she recognized as Naomi's husband, the other unfamiliar to her walked out of the woods. She knew now what Toby's game was, and fear paralyzed her.

"What have you done with my daughter?" she asked.

The stranger smiled, and Emily thought she was looking into the eyes of a reptile.

"She's safe for now."

Emily stepped in front of the door, her hand on the wood. "What's in there?" asked Barry.

"A still," she replied.

"A still. I've never seen one. Move away from the door. I want to take a look."

Toby stepped forward. "There's a p..."

Before Toby could finish what he was saying, Emily smiled and flung open the door swinging it so that she stood behind it.

The sow and piglet rushed out. Disoriented by losing its mama, the piglet ran straight into the husband's legs. He stumbled and fell as he raised his gun to fire. The shot went high, and the piglet retreated to the cover of the woods. But the sow wasn't finished with the humans who had separated her from her offspring. She turned sharply and rushed him. Before he could redirect his weapon, her tusks caught him in the thigh. He yelled and grabbed his leg.

As suddenly as the attack began, it was over. The sow dashed for cover. Emily could hear her and the piglet running through the grass and brush.

"Emily," came a voice through the thicket. Lewis, supported on one side by Worley and the other by Donald, struggled into the clearing. Naomi brought up the rear. Emily rushed to embrace her.

"What happened to you?" she asked.

"My creepy husband and that other man threw me into the back of their car and drove me out here, then left me in the back seat while they ran off into the woods. I was struggling to get my ropes free when Donald, Lewis and Captain Worley drove up." She glanced at her ex lying still on the ground. "I think he could use a hospital." She murmured the words in a matter-of-fact manner, no emotion in her voice. Worley used his cell to call for an ambulance and looked at Barry's wound. He stepped back and shook his head.

Toby looked at the gathering crowd of those who were not his friends, groaned and sank down onto a mound of dirt.

The shadow that was the man with Barry slipped back into the woods and disappeared.

Emily turned to Lewis. "Are you okay?"

"I'm fine, but what about you?"

Before she could speak, Toby jumped up from his seat on the dirt mound and let out a yelp of pain. Soon he was dancing around the clearing slapping his body and yelling.

"Ants. Fire ants." He ran off into the underbrush. They heard him for a while, then everything got quiet for a minute.

"The pigs are out there, Toby." Emily chuckled.

Several seconds passed, and Toby's yells got louder once more as he rushed back into the clearing.

"Pigs. Wild pigs." Toby ran past them and through the open door. Emily slammed it shut and slid the wood through the brackets. Through the door they could hear rustling and sobbing.

"That should keep him for a while." Emily slapped her hands together as if she were dusting them off.

❖

"I explained to Adrienne that you would be placed on foot patrol, demoted and receive a reduction in pay. She decided to return to Georgia and her friends and family." Worley walked out the hospital door beside Lewis who sat in a wheelchair pushed by Emily.

"That was a gross exaggeration, wasn't it, Captain?" Emily helped Lewis into Stan her sedan.

"We'll see." Worley clapped his hat onto his head and gave them a salute goodbye.

"I'll probably need a lot of care," said Lewis.

"We can all help with that." Emily pulled the car out of the lot.

"Where are you taking me?"

She ignored his question. Emily had pigs on her mind this morning after last night's pursuit by them.

"You know I've been thinking about that mother pig. She was not going to let that baby go even if it meant risking her own life by jumping into the sinkhole. Humans are kind of like that too. They will do almost anything to protect their children."

Last night while the medical staff examined his shoulder, Emily told Lewis about Amy Bushnell's daughter.

As Emily drove out of the parking lot, Lewis took up the matter of Mrs. Bushnell.

"So you think Amy Bushnell..."

"I do not. She threw Everett Pratt out of her life, something his wife could not do. Mrs. Bushnell took care of her daughter that way. What could Melanie do?"

"You think Melanie Pratt was protecting her daughter-in-law? She's a grown woman."

"Did you forget that Melanie has a granddaughter?" Emily's hands gripped the wheel tight enough she could almost hear the plastic crack beneath them.

She saw Lewis' jaw twitch when she said this and knew he was feeling an anger that matched her own.

"Let's pay them a visit."

"You're on leave. You have no authority to question them."

Although she tried to hide her intentions from him, she knew he caught the implication in her statement.

"Try to remember you have no authority to question them either." He crossed his arms over his chest and wore a pleased look.

She pulled up in front of Lewis' small house. A truck sat in the driveway, Donald Green's truck.

"You're leaving me in care of Donald?" Lewis' look of happiness was replaced with one of anger and disbelief.

"He's not going to hurt you. I have to work this afternoon, Clara does too. Naomi's leaving this evening to go back to her parents in West Palm, and Vicki's playing bridge. Who else can I get?"

"I don't need anyone."

"Ha."

Lewis maneuvered himself out of the car and walked toward the house. Without a word of hello, he passed Donald, leaning against his truck. Donald shrugged, spit out the toothpick he'd been twirling around in his mouth and followed Lewis. The two men entered the house without acknowledging one another's presence.

That's done, thought Emily. She felt a little guilty lying to Lewis, but only a little. It wasn't a matter any longer of who could solve this murder. She knew only she could because she had the right credentials. She was a woman and a mother.

As Emily hoped, Jasper's truck wasn't in the driveway. She assumed he was off with his friend reconnoitering a new still location or perhaps doing some barbecue business thing. The granddaughter would be in school. Emily had Melanie and her daughter-in-law to herself.

Emily pieced together most of the story. Everett Pratt liked young girls, liked them younger as he got older. She knew that from his interest in Amy Bushnell's daughter. Either his wife or his daughter-in-law Stacy poisoned him to prevent him from abusing the child in his own home, his own flesh and blood. Which one did it?

Both the women answered the door when Emily knocked. It was as if they knew she would come.

They offered her sweet tea and she took it, anything to help dissolve the lump in her throat threatening to keep her from asking them the awful questions she knew she had to ask. She settled herself in an arm chair across from the women who sat on the edge of the couch as if poised to deny or flee. The old window air conditioner stirred the stale air in the room.

She decided to do away with any niceties.

"One of you knew Everett would rape Riana. It was only a matter of time and place. You wanted to prevent that from happening so you decided to kill him with rat poison."

Emily looked into each woman's eyes. If they weren't the window to the soul, Emily at least hoped they would give her insight into the conscience.

"You're like a dog with a bone buried in the yard. You'll just keep at us until you dig up the truth, won't you? I fed him poison." Melanie's look did not waver. "I'm not sorry I did that. He stole my daddy's barbecue recipe from me, he took my self-respect with his chasing all those women, then he tried to take my little girl. I wasn't going to let him do that."

Stacy reached out and grasped her mother-in-law's hand. "You might as well tell her the rest, too."

"That's for you to tell."

The daughter-in-law took a deep breath. "Everett came to me a number of months ago and let me know what he had in mind for my daughter. He said he'd leave her alone if I had sex with him. So I did. And once I had, he told me if I didn't continue, he'd tell Jasper I was screwing his daddy, that I came on to him, that I was the one who seduced him."

"She told me what was going on, but I already suspected that," Melanie added.

The two women moved closer on the couch, their hands entwined together. There were no tears, their words held no despair. They spoke the simple and awful truth about what happened.

Melanie continued the story. "I told her not to worry. I let her in on the poisoning, told her it would soon be over, told her to be patient. Then came the night before the barbecue contest, and he still wasn't dead."

Emily waited, knowing the story would all come out if she let them talk. It was cathartic, a cleansing of their consciences, and Emily knew it. It would be wrong to interrupt now.

Stacy looked up from her hands. "Everett said he was tired of me. That he was going after my daughter when he got home. I knew I had to take action that night."

There, Emily thought. She said it. It was finished.

Emily finally spoke. "You killed him with the barbecue poker."

So intently had she been listening to the story she did not hear anyone approach the house. The door slammed open, and Jasper stepped in.

"Don't say another word. You keep your mouths shut."

In two strides he crossed the room and jerked Emily out of the chair. "I'll take care of her, so no one will know."

Emily wiggled in his arms like an opossum in a trap. If she could open her mouth, she might be able to persuade him to let her live.

"Jasper, your daddy was a bad man. That's no secret any longer. And the authorities know he was a child sexual predator."

Jasper gave the women a dark look.

"No, no," Emily continued quickly, "not because your mother and wife told the cops. Someone else did, another woman whose daughter he tried to molest."

He loosened his hold on her somewhat.

"I know you are trying to protect your family, but if you do something to me, then your daughter won't have anybody. The cops know I'm here, and they'll come looking for me. Then you'll have to make up more lies." Well, that was a lie too, thought Emily. Lewis might guess she'd come here, but he didn't know it for certain.

"You want me to let you tell the cops my mama and my wife killed Daddy?"

"It's a hard choice, Mr. Pratt, but it's best for your child. You don't want to go to jail too, do you?"

"Oh, he surely does not." Melanie Pratt's voice surprised Emily. It was tinged with anger and sarcasm. "No, my no. He's just like his daddy. He uses women."

Melanie turned her eyes on Stacy. "And you're no better than him if you let him use you the way Everett did me. You already covered up for him by tossing that barbecue poker in someone else's truck. Now you're gonna take the wrap for him too?"

"Mama." Jasper's tone was threatening.

"You did it. I know you did." Melanie stood up and confronted her son.

Her daughter-in law remained on the couch, eyes cast downward, then she slid forward on her seat and looked up at her husband. "I told you what he was doing to me and was going to do to our daughter. I don't know what I expected you to do, maybe go to the cops, but you chose another way, didn't you?"

Jasper made a sound of disgust in his throat. "Yeah, it was the same way you and Mama chose to handle the situation, but I was more successful. Women. Useless creatures."

"You killed him because he was messing with your property. You didn't kill him to protect us, did you?"

Emily realized Stacy spoke the truth.

Jasper towered over his wife, his arm raised as if to hit her, to make her take back the words she'd branded him with, but he never delivered the blow. Instead, he let his arm drop.

"I'm outta here." He reached out his hand to turn the door knob when the door was shoved open, and Jasper flew backward across the floor. His head hit a cupboard handle with a thwack, and he slid unconscious down onto the floor.

Donald stood in the open doorway, the butt end of a fishing rod in his hand. "You ladies need any help?"

CHAPTER 22

Police cars lined the Pratts' driveway, flashers working overtime as E.M.T.s attended to Jasper's head, and the authorities sorted out who needed to be arrested for what crime.

Donald and Emily stood at the edge of the property and watched the Pratt family members being taken into custody.

Emily turned to face Donald. "Did Lewis send you?"

Donald hesitated before replying. Emily knew he did not want to admit he might have been sent in by Lewis.

"Yep."

"I asked you to keep an eye on him, and, for the second time in less than a week, you abandoned him." Emily tapped her foot in frustration as she stood chin to chest with Donald.

"Sorry, but he said you were going to get yourself into trouble."

"He should know by now that I get myself out of trouble as easily."

"Jasper..."

"Jasper. Phooey. He was making a break for it. He was no danger to me."

Donald's cell rang. He listened for a few minutes, then handed it to Emily.

"He wants to talk to you."

Emily filled Lewis in on the confessions by Melanie, Stacy and Jasper.

"I found out something you might like to know, Emily. Toby was identified by Arnold Patton and Jeff Knowles, two barbecue contestants, as the guy who tried to blackmail them. They came to the police station the other night and reported him. Toby thought they killed Pratt because he found the barbecue poker in their truck bed."

"Stacy said she tossed it there to get it off their property, but I don't think she intended to frame someone else." *Or did she?* Emily couldn't be certain.

"The D.A. will sort that one out later. We wondered at the time why Arnold and Jeff were so forthright about Toby's blackmail. We figured they were innocent of the murder. Listen to this. Toby bought some of Arnold and Jeff's barbecue sauce right after the murder thinking it was his ace-in-the-hole. He could give it to the cops to use as a match to the sauce covering Pratt. Toby rightly assumed the murderer would change the sauce recipe so no match could be made, and that's just what Jasper did. Toby thought if he bought some of Patton and Knowles' sauce dated the night of the murder or around that time, he could threaten them with it so they'd continue to pay him blackmail. Maybe the murderer would have, but these guys gave him a beating, and then when he wouldn't back off, they turned him in."

"You know, sometimes I think Toby is cleverer than we give him credit for, in a skewed way, I mean. He has a million ideas, but then all his schemes fall through. Like the one with Naomi's husband and that other guy. What were they going to do with us?"

"No idea. Toby won't talk much other than to say he's responsible for saving you from them."

Emily laughed. "That's good old Toby." There was silence for a minute.

"I guess you heard that Naomi's ex-husband didn't make it. He bled to death from the pig's slashing him with her tusks," Emily said.

"She's okay?" Lewis sounded concerned.

"She's shocked, but she'll be fine."

"The authorities haven't identified the other guy, the one you and Naomi saw with her ex. Toby says his name was Mr. Smith. Not much of a lead."

Emily remembered the man's cold eyes and shivered. She hoped she'd never see him again.

※

Naomi left for West Palm and her new job the next day. "Not that I don't love being with you here, Mom, but rural Florida is too wild for me right now. I need manicured lawns, not scrub palmetto and fields with cattle and cowboys, sinkholes that gobble up people, stills and wild pigs, and gators on the fairways and in every stream, pond and canal around here."

"Gators crawl into the swimming pools down there, too, you know." She hugged Naomi. She understood perfectly what she was saying. She needed to get away from the cast of characters who peopled the killings, kidnappings and blackmail in Emily's neighborhood. The scary wildlife were only symbols of the awful events of the past month. Emily might be her biological mother, but Naomi was running back to the comforting arms of her adoptive parents, the only family she knew growing up. Emily appreciated her needs and trusted she'd be back.

Emily had her own departure to make. April was approaching May. It was time for her to go back north to her apartment there. Or give it up and settle full-time here. She was torn making a decision. She had just enough money from her retirement, her inheritance and her job at the country club to keep both her apartment up north and her little park model down here. If any emergency presented itself, she was in financial trouble. She wasn't ready to decide now. Maybe it would be clearer to her when she was back north this summer and away from all the hubbub here.

She hadn't seen Donald except at the bar. Neither of them spoke of the murder. Emily was still angry Donald would so easily abandon Lewis to save her butt. She'd have to forgive him sometime, and soon, or the silence between them could turn to cement and become permanent. He'd never admit he was wrong, she thought. She'd have to be the bigger man and approach him. Maybe she'd let him take her out fishing before she left. She'd gotten fond of sitting on the lake in a boat with her line in the water. Maybe she was losing some of her "Yankee."

Toby was in county lock-up, to be tried on charges too numerous for her to think about all at once. All she knew was he would be serving time in prison for the foreseeable future.

Riana, the Pratt granddaughter would have been placed with family services, but Lorelei Pratt offered to take her. Lorelei rented a small cottage close to the Blue Heron Retirement Center, and Hap visited them daily. He said Riana was withdrawn at first, but Emily was certain if anyone could pull her out of her shell, Hap could.

Lorelei was not so generous when it came to Milo, the bassett hound. "On no account will I have that bag of fleas in my house."

She remained unswayed despite the begging of Riana. Hap had just the solution, one Emily would never have thought of. The dog went to live with Donald.

"Donald?" she asked Hap when she heard the news.

"He likes dogs. You didn't know that?"

"I thought he only liked fish." Emily admitted to herself she didn't know Donald as well as she thought. But who did?

"Does he know the dog has fleas?" If Emily thought an infestation of bugs was a deal breaker, she was wrong. Donald took the old hound off for a flea bath, bought him a spiffy, blue-plaid collar and got him a doggy cap to shade his eyes when they went out on the boat.

Lewis was still on leave, but he told her Worley was considering a more lenient punishment than foot patrol until retirement. Lewis confided he thought Worley felt sorry for him because of his crazy ex-wife. Emily thought perhaps the good word she'd put in to Worley behind Lewis' back might have made the captain go easier on him. Worley seemed to like her. He said she had spunk.

Much recovered, Lewis invited her over for drinks. She thought back on their evening in the condo on Jekyll Island and felt her heart hammering in her chest. She was excited.

She curled her hair and let it fall in a cascade down her back, put on a pair of dangly earrings, her best red dress and got into her car. She got back out again, went into her house, took off her earrings and red dress and pulled her hair into a pony tail. She slipped into her jeans and a tee-shirt and left the house. No sense in telegraphing her lust so loudly.

Down the road a half-mile, she turned around. Before she used her gate card to get into her park, she backed up and parked in the lot. *I'm being silly. He doesn't care what I wear. It's just a drink at his place.*

Well, yes, the voice in her head said, but remember what happened the last time the two of you got together alone. You pulled him into the shower with you. He's probably expecting something like that to happen again.

If he does, she argued back, then he'll have to initiate it. She glanced around the parking lot to make certain no one saw her talking to herself.

She flipped down the visor to look at herself in the mirror. She was clean, her clothes were pressed, her make-up looked great, and she had a twinkle in her eye. She was presentable. He'd have to take that and that alone.

Lewis opened the door dressed in jeans and a tee-shirt, a very snug fitting tee. Despite the bulky bandage on his shoulder, the shirt showed off his chest and muscular arms. Emily was used to seeing him in a shirt and jacket, and she had only a dim memory of what he looked like soaking wet in the shower with all his clothes clinging to his body, plus she was tired of using her imagination to create him naked. The hot tee-shirt helped fill in the empty spaces where her mind drew a blank. But not enough. She could use more.

She didn't know what to say so she led with "Hello," followed by, "Look. We're dressed alike." *Dumb, Emily. Dumb.*

He held out his hand and pulled her into the house. "You smell good."

"Thanks. I took a shower. I mean, I washed, cleaned up, bathed. Uh, you smell good, too."

"I did the same."

Emily again envisioned him in the shower on Jekyll Island.

"Wine?"

He gestured toward the couch where wine, cheese, crackers and a lighted candle awaited them. They sat next to one another.

"How are you feeling?" She nodded toward his shoulder.

He poured them each a glass of wine. "Great. I'm healing nicely according to my doctor. I just won't be lassoing any cows for a while."

Pity, thought Emily. *I wonder if he's allowed to lasso women, little ones like me who wouldn't struggle too much.*

"To murder." He clinked his glass against hers and looked into her eyes, then leaned in, his lips only inches away. She could feel his warm breath on her cheek. She moved closer to him. Nothing was going to ruin this moment, she thought, and closed her eyes, eager for his mouth on hers.

"Stanton."

"Emily."

The doorbell rang. "Expecting someone else?"

He looked aggravated at the interruption. "I'll get it and tell them to get out of here. Back in a jiff."

She sat back and took a sip of her wine.

He opened the door. His ex-wife stood on his porch. "Stanton."

"Adrienne."

"Aren't you going to ask me in? I want to explain myself. Why I behaved as I did the other night. I shouldn't have run off."

Oh yes you should have, thought Emily. She gave Adrienne a gay little finger wave from the couch.

He looked back into the room toward Emily and swallowed. "Uh."

Emily got off the couch and walked to the door. "Let me help you with this."

She slammed the door in Adrienne's face, then took Lewis' hand in hers and led him back to the couch.

Adrienne's voice came through the door. "Fine, then. You're busy now. We can talk later."

He got up and walked across the room.

Here goes my night, thought Emily. She watched in despair as he opened the door.

"We have nothing to talk about." It was said with Lewis' firm, no-nonsense cop voice. "Nothing."

He closed the door and turned to Emily. She heard Adrienne's steps retreat down the sidewalk and a car start.

"Where were we?" he asked.

"We were on the couch playing checkers."

"Shall we?" He gestured toward the sofa. They resumed their positions.

"Emily."

"Stanton."

They leaned toward one another, and Emily again closed her eyes.

Kiss me. Now.

The doorbell rang.

Emily popped up off the couch, ran to the door and swung it open. "Go away."

"Emily?"

It wasn't Adrienne. It was Donald.

"I wanted to drop by to see how Lewis was. Then I saw your car, and I was going to drive on, but I thought, what the hell, this is a good time for all of us to talk."

"No it isn't."

He ignored her. "I know Lewis needs his rest, but..."

"You're right, and I was just about to get him off to bed when you rang."

"I can wait, and after he's tucked in, the two of us can go somewhere for a nightcap."

"Donald, are you just playing with me? I've got the only nightcap I need right here." She lifted her glass of wine to emphasize her intentions.

"Coffee then?"

"Tell you what. I'll let you take me bass fishing tomorrow morning bright and early. We can talk then. Goodnight. See you in the morning."

She tried to close the door, but Donald leaned against it, keeping it open several inches.

"You can bring Lewis along. I doubt he can do much with that arm of his, but maybe we could cut him up for bait." His voice came through the door followed by a deep chuckle. "Don't keep him up too late. We leave the boat ramp at five, just before sunrise."

Oh, yeah, he got it, Emily thought, but offering him a fishing opportunity was about as tempting to him as offering sex to another man, or that was how Emily read it. Of course, she'd never suggested sex to Donald.

She peeked through the opening in the door and watched Donald retreat to his truck. "That's taken care of. I can't think of anybody else who's rude enough to bother us now."

He patted the couch next to him. "Sit, please." She resumed her seat.

"Are you really going to meet him for fishing tomorrow?" asked Lewis.

"Of course. He's my friend, and he likes to fish. So do I." Then she gave Lewis a severe look. "He's your friend too, you know. He did what you asked even though he wanted to take care of you when you were hurt."

Lewis looked as if he might try to deny this, but instead he said, "I guess if I'm to have a guy friend, Donald's the closest I've come."

Lewis got up from the couch. "Porch light." He flipped it off and hit the switch on the wall, turning off all the lights in the living room. The candle flickered invitingly.

"Before we go any farther, I'd just like to say what a good detective I think you are. Salute." He raised his glass to her.

"Thanks for saying that, but you know I didn't get it quite right. I thought Melanie's daughter-in-law bashed him over the head. Jasper wasn't even on my list of suspects."

"Why not?"

"He was too obvious."

"Well, you came close enough to force his hand."

"You'd have gotten it sooner or later if you hadn't been put on leave."

He shook his head. "You did something I could never do."

"What's that?"

"You thought with your heart, not your head. In this case, it was the right approach. Thank you, Emily." He pulled a package from behind him. "This is for you."

"What is it?"

"Go ahead. Unwrap it."

She saw a twinkle in his eyes, and it was very sexy. She tore off the paper.

"A bottle of shower gel?"

"Our little wager. Remember? I bet you I would find the poisoner before you did. But you won. This is pay-up time."

Oh, yes it is.

She turned the bottle around in her hand. *Bubbles?* She smiled.

It was exactly what she wanted.

"And this time, Emily?"

"Uhm?" She kicked off her shoes and looked around the room. Which way to the bathroom, she wondered.

"Let me remove my clothes before you pull me into the shower."

"Better start dropping your drawers now then."

THE END

ABOUT THE AUTHOR

Lesley retired from her life as a professor of psychology and reclaimed her country roots by moving to a small cottage in the Butternut River Valley in upstate New York. In the winter she migrates to old Florida—cowboys, scrub palmetto and open fields of grazing cattle, a place where spurs still jingle in the post office. Back north, she devotes her afternoons to writing, and when the sun sets, relaxing on the bank of her trout stream, sipping tea or a local microbrew. In her words, "I come to the 'Big Lake' to write, hang out in cowboy bars and immerse myself in the Florida that used to be. No beaches, no bikinis, no sand. Just cows, horses and gators."

www.lesleyadiehl.com